I0817811

BREAKVALE

A Novel

DUSTIN
HOWARD

Breakvale is a work of fiction. Names, characters, places, and events in this novel are products of the author's imagination. Any resemblance to actual people, places, or events is entirely coincidental.

Copyright © 2020 by Dustin Howard

All rights reserved
Reproduction in part or in whole of any work contained within is strictly prohibited without permission from the author.

Published in print and digital e-book
by Moderator Press Publishing.

ISBN 978-1-7368507-0-1
LCCN 2020924876

Cover Design by Megan Aguas
Cover Photograph by Ingmar Nolte

To all my friends and family.

— DH

Welcome to Breakvale...

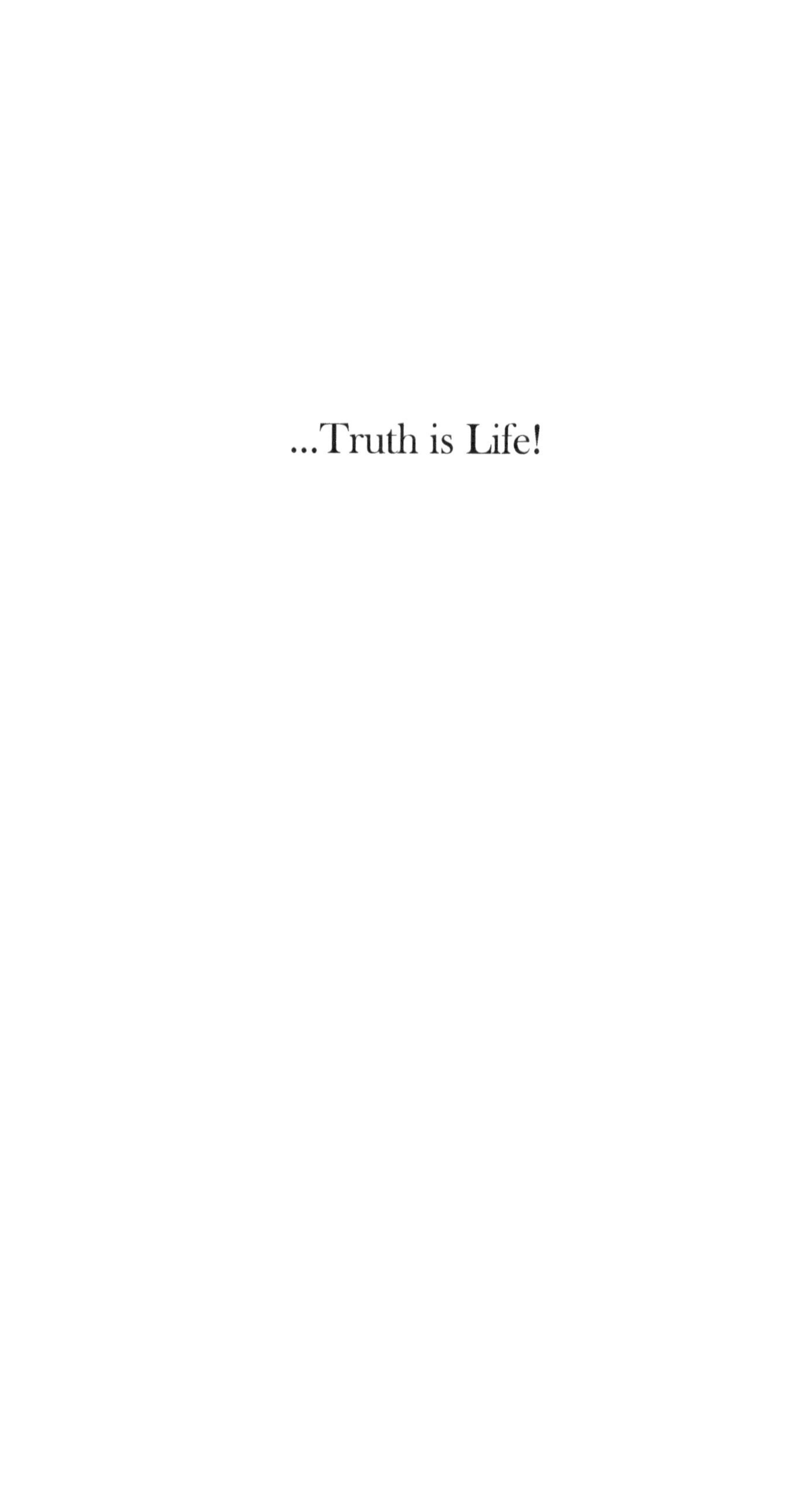

...Truth is Life!

BREAKVALE

Prologue

"Brothers and Sisters," he proclaimed, his voice calm and even. "Take hands and recite our prayer with me."

He paused a moment before beginning, then was joined quickly in unison by the others. "We pray to thee, Dark Lord of the Hidden Realm, reveal to us your ancient wisdom and bestow upon us your wretched guise, that we may beset upon this world Your unhallowed and malevolent legions, and bring to their reckoning all those who would seek to rebuke your infernal glory. We thank thee, Lord, for thy unholy blessings, and harken to your heralds of Eternal Damnation, when we may revel with You upon this earth until the End of All Things. We pray for this in your name. Amen."

Standing around a large stone dais, seven figures, hooded and cloaked, each picked up a ceremonial dagger laid out before them and raised the blades above their veiled faces.

Positioned at the head of the dais, their leader reached down to remove the gag plunged into the mouth of a woman who lay restrained against the cold stone slab. Her eyes had been sewn shut to prevent her from bearing witness to her own sacrifice. The woman screamed for help and struggled against her bondage but could do nothing to escape.

"We offer to you the soul of this woman, an unwilling sacrifice, as a tribute to you, Lord," the leader proclaimed.

“Brothers and Sisters, we will now release this soul in His honor.”

Three figures standing on each side of the dais simultaneously plunged their daggers into the woman’s chest, careful to keep their aim between her ribs. They sank their blades deep on the first strike as the woman on the dais tried to cry out in short, breathless agony. They withdrew their blades in unison, then began to stab the woman frantically and violently, this time aiming for any part of her body they had yet to maim. They coated themselves in her ruby-rich blood, allowing it to spurt and spew across their cloaked bodies.

Their leader did not join in the savage revelry, but stood domineeringly over the woman, quietly reciting something unintelligible. As the woman perished without a final breath, he was certain the Master would be pleased with this offering.

1

"Welcome to Breakvale," read the sign that zipped by on the rural highway into town, "Where Truth is Life." He had been on the road for six and half hours now, and Grayson Ender had finally reached his destination: a small town in the middle of nowhere West Virginia. The town was settled in a small valley, and as he rounded the final corner of that final stretch of road, he could see from a height the entirety of Breakvale, stretched out below him and occupying the shallow valley in every direction. It was seven o'clock in the mid-August evening, and the whole of Breakvale looked awash in hues of orange, red, and yellow as the sun began to sag behind the hilltops. The scene was almost picturesque, he thought, except for the sight of the power plant looming on the horizon, with its dingy gray stacks wheezing clouds of vapor into the air, standing imposingly over the rest of Breakvale.

Grayson descended rapidly down into the valley and into town, taking the only thoroughfare through the heart of Breakvale. He couldn't help but feel a sense of charm and wonder at the antiquity of the main street. The road was flanked on both sides by old brick buildings with modern shopfronts. Many of the buildings must be a century old, he thought, and he wondered if any might have existed during the Civil War. There were few people out, which on a Wednesday evening was not all that surprising; most of the people in a town like this would be in church, Grayson figured. Near the end of the main street, he passed what looked like a bar. A few patrons loitered outside, standing next to their motorcycles, clad in riding gear. They watched with inquisitive eyes as Grayson approached in his Wrangler but gave a friendly wave and a brisk nod as he passed. It was reassuring, he mused, to know that the bikers in Breakvale were friendly.

The GPS on his phone indicated the turns to take from the main street to bring him to his destination—a small row of townhomes, clustered together with a few other rows to form a tiny community, a complex with the innocuous name of The Sparrows. It seemed a boring, droll name for a housing community, meant to sound inviting and wholesome, perhaps, or maybe classy but affordable. The living arrangements were already made, and the accommodation was provided for him by the school. Despite their muddled brown exterior, the inside of the townhomes looked fresh and modern in the pictures that were sent to him. It wasn't his first choice, but then he didn't have a choice. As he pulled his Jeep into his designated parking spot under the cover of an awning, he shifted into park and shut the engine off. He paused for a moment to breathe deeply and exhale. *It's only for a few years*, he reminded himself. *It's not for forever.*

The porch light of the townhome in front of him flickered on and the door popped open to reveal a lanky fellow in jeans and a flannel button-up hustling excitedly to greet him. Despite having only spoken to the property manager on the phone, Grayson could tell by his energetic approach that this was the man he'd spoken to previously.

"You must be Grayson!" the man exclaimed, taking his hand and shaking it firmly.

"I am!" he said, attempting to match the man's enthusiasm. "Ed, right?"

"Ed Spurlock, at your service! You have a pleasant trip?

"The drive wasn't horrible. There's some pretty country out this way," Grayson said.

"You ain't wrong about that fella. Ain't a more beautiful place in the whole great state uh West Virginia than right here in Breakvale," Ed boasted. "But you must be tired. Why don't you come on in here with me and we'll getcha' settled in. You got any bags?"

Grayson motioned to the back end of his Wrangler. Together they carried his suitcases into the house. Looking around, he was relieved to see that the home matched the expectations set by the pictures.

"As you can see it's all fully furnished, as promised. We aim to please here at The Sparrows. Won't find a nicer place to live for a young fella like you just startin' out here," Ed said, clapping Grayson on the shoulder. He leaned in and spoke in an ornery whisper. "Now you got a lady gonna be joinin' you soon?"

Grayson chuckled. "No. It's just me."

"Ah, well, there's plenty of fine young women round here that are gonna want to be makin' your acquaintance, I know it. Just remember that if you're gonna be movin' one in, she's gotta sign the lease," he said, ribbing Grayson with his elbow before letting out a hearty laugh.

Grayson smiled. "I'll be sure to do that."

"Sorry if things are a little dusty. The place's been sittin' empty for a bit now. Not many new folks movin' to Breakvale. We tried to clean it up alright though," said Ed.

He led Grayson further into the house, stopping in the kitchen to gesture at a small box sitting on the countertop. It appeared to be filled with common necessities, including soap and toilet paper.

"A gift from the school," said Ed. "Jean's always so thoughtful. Always sendin' a welcome basket full of stuff for new teachers."

Grayson recognized Jean as Dr. Jean Thomas, the superintendent of Breakvale's schools and the woman who hired him. He glanced at the note scrawled on a tag hanging from the box.

Written in cursive penmanship, it read:

Welcome to Breakvale. Truth Is Life.

-Jean

"Now tell me again what you teach," said Ed.

"English," Grayson replied as he rifled through the basket of goodies.

Ed just nodded and glanced around awkwardly for a moment. "Well," he said in that manner which all people say when looking to end a conversation. "I reckon you're probably tired. Walkthrough papers are on the table with the house keys. Just turn it in by the end of the week."

"I can do that," said Grayson.

"I suppose I'll be on my way then," he said, stepping toward the door. "If you need anything now, you don't be shy. We take care of our own here in Breakvale."

"That's very kind of you. I appreciate it," Grayson said. He extended his hand for a handshake, which Ed eagerly accepted.

"Truth is Life, friend. You have a good night now," he said and stepped out the door, pulling it shut behind him. The phrase rang weirdly in Grayson's brain. Strange, he thought, for both Ed and Jean to use the town motto as a sign-off and as a token of good wishes.

Grayson looked around the rest of the house. As he took in all the home's modern decor, he truly felt a sense of gratitude to the school district for paying for the first year's lease on such a nice place, particularly since it came fully furnished. He couldn't help but be cautiously optimistic that maybe, maybe, the next four years wouldn't be so bad. After all, he told himself, he could still travel to Charleston on the weekends to see friends and have a social life. It was better that way, having his work separated so far from his personal life, especially in rural West Virginia.

Wandering into the bedroom, he was relieved to see the bed was already made up. He went to retrieve one of his suitcases from the living room and set it up on the dresser. Grayson pulled his cellphone charger out of a suitcase pocket and looked for an outlet on either side of the bed. Stooping low, he had to push the bed slightly to the left to uncover the outlet. He noticed a small, round hole in the drywall above and to the left of the outlet. Someone must have moved the bed to cover the hole, he figured, and made a mental note to include it on the walkthrough report.

Grayson shuffled into the adjoining bathroom to brush his teeth. The scruffy face in the mirror looked almost foreign to him. He would absolutely have to shave before work tomorrow.

Exhausted, stripped down to his underwear, and anticipating an alarm that would sound too early in the morning, Grayson rolled back the covers of his new bed and climbed in. The sheets were cold and felt foreign to him, but he closed his eyes and tried to let the room and everything around him go dark until he finally faded into a comfortable sleep.

***

Grayson woke up the next morning drenched in a cold sweat. Despite the coolness of the room, he felt radiant with heat, and he had to slow his breath to relieve the rapid palpitations of his heart. His first night in Breakvale had been marked by a nightmare, followed by the first case of sleep paralysis that he had experienced in more than a year. It must have been the stress of the move, he told himself, as he tried to gain control of his conscious mind and shake the fog from his brain.

He couldn't remember the nightmare, but the sleep paralysis was always the same: his eyes would open, and he could see the ceiling above him. He could move his eyes slightly to look around, but his limbs were immobile, as if they were strapped down so tightly he could barely flex his muscles. He couldn't move, but that wasn't even the worst of it—it felt as though he was completely awake. His brain was fully aware of the paralysis, but he couldn't force himself to wake up. All he could do was lie there and struggle, and the longer he struggled, the more he began to fear that maybe he really was paralyzed. After what could have been minutes or hours, he would be released somehow, and able to wake up fully. To Grayson, the most terrifying part of the whole experience was never truly knowing the difference between dream and reality. He stood up defiantly from the bed, shaking each limb to confirm his autonomy, and shuffled off into the bathroom to get himself ready for the day.

Clean-shaven, clad in a navy blazer and khakis, and out the door by 5:45 a.m., Grayson pulled up in his Jeep to his other home-away-from-home for the next four years: Breakvale High School. He was due to meet the principal, Dale Daggett, for a tour of the facility before the first day of classes was set to begin.

Entering the main office, he was greeted by a cheerful woman in a yellow dress sitting behind a long desk. She sprang up.

"You must be Grayson," she beamed. She was a tall woman, perhaps six feet tall by Grayson's estimate, with long, curly brown hair and half-rimmed glasses. Her disposition seemed brighter than her dress, and she radiated a motherly presence.

"I am," he said.

"My name's Linda. Linda Carver. I'm the secretary here. It's so nice to meet you," she said with a pleasant country twang. She reached across the desk with a gesture to shake hands, which Grayson accepted.

"Likewise," he said.

"Dale's been expecting you. If you want to go on down that little hall," she indicated a small hallway behind him. "His office is on the right. Good luck today!"

"Thank you," Grayson nodded.

He proceeded down the little hallway, passing a large conference room on the left before coming upon the principal's door. It was only slightly ajar, and he knocked thrice gently. A moment passed, then the door swung open wide. Standing in the doorway was a short man, squat and slightly balding, sporting a thick mustache. To Grayson, the man looked like a heavier-set J.K. Simmons, and he had to stifle his impulse to laugh. Though he looked grumpy, as soon as he opened his mouth to speak, Dale Daggett's expression softened.

"Mr. Ender, how do you do?" he said. "Dale Daggett. It's a pleasure to have you."

"Thank you, sir. I'm happy to be here."

"Please, we don't have a lot of time so let's show you around and get you settled in. The students will begin arriving in about half an hour," he said, holding his arm out, palm open, indicating to Grayson that he should step out of the doorway.

Principal Daggett took Grayson around the small campus, showing him the grounds, the various classrooms, and the gymnasium. He was particularly proud of the "state of the art" computer lab that the school installed over the summer. He spoke highly of the school preparing students for the "modern-day workforce." The computer lab didn't appear to be anything special, and certainly wasn't anything he would sing high praises about. Charleston may have been small compared to other metro areas, but at least there "state-of-the-art" meant computers with the latest operating systems and not machines that were already technologically outdated. Compared to the rest of the town's antique appearance, however, Principal Daggett could be forgiven for his misplaced excitement.

Being led down a hallway opposite the entrance to the computer lab, Principal Daggett stopped at room number 4. He withdrew a small set of keys from his pocket and used one to unlock the door, which he held open for Grayson. It was a decently sized classroom, capable of accommodating thirty students, though it contained only twenty-three desks. The room was old, like the rest of the building, which was built perhaps in the Thirties or Forties. The walls were half-trimmed with pine wainscoting, above which the rest of the walls were painted a pale green. There was a large black chalkboard fixed to the wall at the front of the class, in front of which stood a large, antique wooden desk.

"These are yours," said Principal Daggett, handing Grayson the keys. "And this is your classroom. Please feel free to arrange however you want."

Grayson took a breath, unsure of what to say about the classroom. He could smell the old varnish on the wainscoting, and he let it tickle his nose for a moment. No doubt the classroom was hideous; but it also had a certain charm, much like the rest of Breakvale.

"It's excellent. Thank you," Grayson said. He walked over to the desk and dropped his bag on the old oak top. On the desk was a plaque bearing his name, and he stared at it in surprise.

"We've been expecting you, Mr. Ender. We're very glad to have ya here and wanted you to feel welcome right away," Principal Daggett said in observation of Grayson's surprise. "Now, I went ahead and prepared a class roster for all six periods you'll be teaching."

He indicated a manila envelope sitting on the far-right corner of the desk. Grayson picked it up, unwound the red string clasp, and withdrew the rosters. His largest class was eighteen students, which would feel tiny compared to the thirty or so he had grown accustomed to teaching in Charleston.

"I appreciate all of the planning you've done," Grayson said.

"Think nothin' of it. We're happy to have you on board. The departure of your predecessor was untimely and unfortunate, so we're overjoyed to have you on such short notice. If there's anything I can do to make the transition easier for ya, just say so," said Principal Daggett. He clapped his hands once and then started for the door. He turned back before closing it. "Truth is Life, Mr. Ender. Good luck today."

Grayson couldn't help but be struck at hearing the town motto repeated at him once again as if it were a customary sign-off for when people say goodbye. It was weird, certainly, but he could think of instances in other languages where the repetition of a common phrase was considered polite or even expected.

Perhaps it was a quirk of the town, he thought—there were bound to be a few in a little place like Breakvale.

Seven o'clock came quickly. He had enough time to push the heavy oak desk into the corner adjacent to the blackboard and out of the direct line of sight. There were still many old books stacked in the bookcases that lined the wall along the back of the classroom. Several were sets of textbooks, some printed thirty years ago or more. He cringed at the thought of the outdated lessons and theories they probably contained. If he were lucky, he thought, some of them might have short stories or poems that would be worthwhile. He decided he would investigate their merits over the coming days.

Scanning the rows of books, he noticed a few that looked nearly brand new. He plucked one off the shelf. It was a book of modern poetry. On the inside of the cover, handwritten across the top in blue ink, was a message declaring ownership:

This book belongs to Emily Hunt

He pulled a few more books off the shelf to check the inside covers. All were scrawled with the same message. It occurred to him that he knew nothing of his predecessor. He wondered if this was the English teacher whom he had replaced and if it was, why would she have left her books.

The warning bell rang ten minutes later, indicating class was due to start soon, and drew Grayson out of his contemplation. He shelved the book in his hand and took a position at the front of the classroom, standing propped up against his desk. Slowly at first, then more hastily, all the students shuffled in. He took a quick, self-assured breath as the final bell rang and the last student darted through the door and flung himself into a seat.

"Good morning!" Grayson said jovially. A few students muttered good mornings, but he was not satisfied with this response. "I said, good morning!" he repeated, this time louder.

More students chimed in, though a few rolled their eyes at his lame attempt to procure an excited reaction. Grayson was undeterred. He picked up the class roster for the first period and began the roll call without introducing himself. He took notice of two students sitting toward the back near the windows. By the process of rollcall, he noted that their names were Drew McIntosh and Alexis Carter and determined by their continued handholding and whispering that they must be a couple. This was potentially problematic, as he always discouraged dating students from sitting next to each other.

"I am Mr. Ender, your new English teacher. Here's a little bit about me," he said, beginning to pace the front of the class. "I am twenty-eight years old. I graduated from the University of West Virginia with a bachelor's degree in English education. I have many favorite authors, some of whom I will get to share with you this year. When I'm not teaching, I spend my free time writing, reading, watching movies, or going on hikes. That's all about me. Now I want to hear about you. We're going to go around the room, and I want you to introduce yourself to me in this same way."

For the next half hour, the students introduced themselves, some sheepishly, others obnoxiously. Despite the familiar classroom scene, Grayson felt a kind of tension from the students that he couldn't blame on start-of-term anxiety alone. Throughout the class, he caught his students exchanging concerned glances. Some kept their gaze fixed on their desks, looking up only briefly during their introduction. The rest of the period passed without much interest or incident, though; and when the bell rang, the students stood up and shuffled out. The girl that Grayson earlier identified as Alexis stood near the door with her boyfriend for a moment, then doubled back and approached Grayson at his desk.

"Mr. Ender?" she said meekly.

"Alexis, right? What can I do for you?"

She stepped closer to his desk and leaned in. "Ms. Hunt…she told me that if she ever left, that I should tell whoever replaces her to look in the middle drawer, under the sticker, when no one is around."

The warning bell chimed twice.

"Sorry, I have to go. I don't want to be late for next period."

Alexis gave Grayson an apologetic look and walked hurriedly out the door. Well, that was strange, he thought. He reached around his desk to pull the middle drawer open, but it didn't budge. He tried again more forcefully but couldn't open it. He bent down to look at the drawer and saw a small keyhole. Grayson pulled the keys from his pocket and attempted to find one that matched the desk drawer lock. There were five keys on his key ring, and each key was incompatible with the lock. Maybe Principal Daggett will have the key, he told himself, and made a mental note to ask him about it at the end of the day.

For the next six periods, the question of what was locked inside the desk drawer burned in the back of Grayson's mind. He told himself he would wait to see if a key was available or try to pry the drawer open as a last resort. It seemed very strange to him that a teacher would ask a student to deliver a message to her replacement, particularly after that teacher quit the school. Then again, he thought, there were a lot of things about Breakvale so far that felt two steps left of normal.

When the final dismissal bell chimed and the last student exited the classroom, he heard a knock at the door. To his surprise, Principal Daggett stood there in the doorway grinning at him.

"How'd your first day go? Students weren't too mean to ya I hope," he said.

"No, not at all. They were all excellent," Grayson replied in earnest.

"That's good, that's good," Principal Daggett replied.

"Say, I'm trying to open the middle drawer here, but it seems I don't have the key for it?" Grayson said, furrowing his brows. "I need someplace to put my pens. Do you have the key by chance?"

Principal Daggett walked up and leaned in over the desk. "No, afraid not," he said. He reached over and slid the top left drawer open. "Looks like ya got other working drawers though."

"Of course, thank you," Grayson said coolly. "I'm sure one of those will do."

Principal Daggett stood back and smiled. "Glad you had a good first day. We're very happy to have you here at Breakvale High," he said, walking toward the door. "Remember, you just tell me if ya need anything. See ya tomorrow."

Grayson sat at his desk for a moment in silence. Unable to get the drawer open, he packed up his bag to go home. He decided that either he would need to look up a how-to video on picking a lock or go buy a crowbar.

2

At home that evening, Grayson sat at his kitchen table reviewing lesson plans. On the one occasion that they had spoken on the phone before his arrival, Principal Daggett insisted that for the first year, whatever he had been teaching in Charleston would be more than adequate to satisfy the curriculum at Breakvale High. As this meant he could simply reuse all the lesson plans he had already created, he was happy to agree to the arrangement; still, he felt the lesson plans needed reviewing, and on a Thursday evening in a town that shut down with the sunset, he had little else to do anyway.

Half listening to some paranormal adventure show on the Travel Channel as he worked, Grayson felt his phone vibrate on the table. He was excited to see the name of an old friend from back home splashed across the screen. He answered the call with a stupid, childish grin.

"Hey, Seth!"

On the other end was his closest friend and confidante, Seth McCormick. The pair had been friends since elementary school, having both grown up on the same street. Despite a somewhat turbulent past, Seth remained the most consistent thing in his life.

"I thought you weren't due back from Turkey until next week?" said Grayson.

"Yeah, well there was some turmoil near where we were staying, and we decided to play it safe and just flew back early. I'm stuck at JFK waiting for the connecting flight back home," Seth explained.

"I can't believe I missed you by a couple of days!" Grayson bemoaned. "When you get settled in, I'll come back to Charleston for the weekend."

"How's everything going there? Where the hell are you again?"

"Some little place called Breakvale. It's like almost seven hours from home, but I can make the drive in a day. Things are…odd here. I can't quite put my finger on it. The people are friendly. But like. Weirdly friendly."

"That's how it is in those small, backwoods sorta places though. Everyone is 'yessir, no ma'am, howdya' do?' types. Country bumpkins. Politeness is basic currency to them."

"Yeah, I suppose," Grayson paused. "It's really good to hear your voice."

"Yours too, man. I have so many stories to tell you when I see you. And Aaron took so many pictures."

"How is Aaron?"

"Aaron is Aaron. Things are good. This trip was what we needed to get us out of our rut. Honestly, you know I was ready to strangle him. But we really had a chance to talk and clear our heads. Being away from home, having a change of scenery, it gave us a fresh perspective, ya know?"

"I'm glad to hear it, Seth."

"Thanks. Yeah, I know hicktown isn't really what you had in mind, but you're doing that community a service. No way would they be able to get a teacher like you if it weren't for their incentives on your student loans. Four years to be debt free…it'll be worth it, man."

"I suppose so. Still, it's gonna be a boring four years over here. You have to come visit me!"

"You know I will dude!"

"Hey, so I gotta tell you about this student that talked to me today—"

There was a knock at the door.

"—hang on. Someone is at my door?"

Glancing out the peephole, he saw two men standing at his doorstep, one of them holding a fruit basket.

"Seth. You're not gonna believe this," Grayson whispered. "There are two dudes at my door. One's carrying a fruit basket. I'm gonna have to call you back."

"What, dude that's crazy. Hey, actually, I need to go find my gate. Can I call you later?"

"Sure thing, we can chat later."

They exchanged quick goodbyes, and Grayson ended the call. He took a deep breath, unlocked the door, and opened it.

The two men instantly smiled at the sight of Grayson in the doorway. Their smiles were toothy and uncomfortable to look at. One was much older than the other one carrying the fruit basket. They were both dressed in pressed button-down shirts and khakis.

"Mr. Ender," stated the older one.

"That's me," Grayson acknowledged.

"My name is John Arthur. I'm the pastor at the First Baptist Church of Breakvale. This is my associate pastor, Ross McCrory. May we come in and visit for a moment?"

Ross McCrory held up the fruit basket and offered it to Grayson, who now felt he was hardly able to refuse.

"As long as you're not vampires," Grayson quipped.

Ross snickered quietly, but John Arthur said nothing. Acquiescing, he swung the door open wide, gestured for them to enter his home, and accepted the fruit basket from Ross as he stepped past him. Their eyes met for an instant before he glanced down and away from Grayson's gaze.

Grayson studied the pair as they crossed the living room. Pastor Arthur was older, perhaps in his fifties or sixties, of average height and lean build. His balding head was swaddled by wispy silver hairs around the sides and back. Grayson cracked a smile at the realization that this man bore a striking resemblance to the farmer in the *American Gothic* oil painting. His counterpart, however, was different. He was smaller in frame and stature, with an almost meek or timid disposition. Grayson figured he had to be near in age to him, or perhaps Ross was a little younger. He was clean-shaven and wore his dusty blonde hair combed neatly to one side.

Grayson closed the door and followed behind them. He sat the basket on the kitchen table nearby and turned to the pair standing awkwardly in the living room.

"Thank you for the basket. Please, sit," he invited, offering the couch. "What brings you here to visit?"

John Arthur straightened his collar. "Well, young man, you may not know that the First Baptist Church of Breakvale is the only church here in our little community. It was the first building ever built here. In the early days of Breakvale, it was used as a schoolhouse to educate and reform the native Indian children so they could become productive members of civilized society. After that practice was unfortunately abandoned, the building was sold to my great-great-grandfather, who converted it to a house of worship for those seeking the true word of God. Since that time our church has continued to serve the Lord and the needs of this community."

"I see," Grayson muttered. He was already irritated by the pastor and knew exactly how this conversation was going to play out. "Native American children didn't need civilizing, Mr. Arthur. In fact, their cultures were superior to their colonizers in many ways."

Pastor Arthur simply cleared his throat. "Yes, well. You see, the great people of Breakvale have never needed another place to worship. We have always served the community with pride and respect for the Lord. As such, I feel it is my responsibility to welcome all new members of this community personally. 'Who shall go out before them and come in before them, who shall lead them out and bring them in, that the congregation of the Lord may not be as sheep that have no shepherd.'"

"Numbers, chapter twenty-seven, verse seventeen," Ross interjected quietly.

"Yes, very good, Ross," said Pastor Arthur. "It is my job to ensure that the sheep are not without their shepherd."

"Let's cut to the chase, shall we? You'd like me to join the congregation on Sundays, Pastor?" Grayson predicted.

"Naturally. Almost everyone in Breakvale attends on Sundays or Wednesdays. It would be encouraging for the youth to see their newest teacher worshiping the Lord in His house," Pastor Arthur pressed.

"Respectfully, Pastor, I intend to spend most of my weekends back in Charleston, and my evenings are generally reserved for grading papers or creating lesson plans, or working on my own passion projects," he informed. Pastor Arthur opened his mouth to offer a rebuttal, but Grayson continued, "What's more, and I mean this with full offense, if you think any culture deserves to be forcefully assimilated, I shudder to think about what you preach, and I don't want anything to do with it."

Pastor Arthur looked indignant for a brief moment but twisted his face back into a cordial smile. "I believe we've had a misunderstanding, Mr. Ender. The schoolhouse did a great service to the children. They gave them an education and a means of survival at a time when they would otherwise have starved or died of disease. I don't condone forced assimilation, as you say. But I do condone saving lives."

"*Yeah*, I'm really not sure that's any better," Grayson admonished. "Look, if it's necessitated where my students are concerned, maybe I'll consider stopping by. But don't hold your breath."

Pastor Arthur stood up from the couch, prompting Ross to follow suit. The pastor extended his hand, which Grayson initially wasn't going to accept, but then hastily decided to grasp it as firmly as possible to send the man a message. They locked their eyes for an instant. Grayson hadn't noticed Arthur's sharp, dagger-like stare until that moment, but as quickly as he recognized it, the sharpness vanished.

"You are welcome at any time. The doors of the church are always open. Let's go now, Ross. I'm sure Mr. Ender is very tired after his first day," Pastor Arthur opined, looking unblinkingly at Grayson. "Truth is Life, Mr. Ender. I do hope to see you in the pews."

"Thanks for stopping by and for bringing the welcome basket," Grayson said disingenuously, following them to the door. Pastor Arthur exited first and continued without stopping. Ross McCrory paused at the door, his gaze fixed downward, and stopped just short of closing the door. At the last moment, he looked up at Grayson.

"It was nice to meet you, sir," he said.

"The pleasure was mine," Grayson replied.

He slipped out quickly and closed the door firmly behind him. Grayson swiftly locked the door. He sighed in exasperation. People in this town so fucking weird, he thought.

He slipped off to his bedroom. His mind raced with the unresolved questions from the day and the sheer strangeness of everything he had so far experienced. And this was just the first day, he thought. He lay down on his bed and allowed his mind to wander toward more pleasant thoughts. Grayson replayed the conversation he had with Seth, letting himself feel a sense of comfort, something he used to feel when they lay in bed together. He remembered the softness of Seth's chest, the firmness of Seth's arms wrapped around his body, and how safe he felt in his embrace. Grayson let the memories continue to spin, reliving the most intimate and passionate moments of their relationship. He slid his hand into his underwear and, in minutes, was driven to climax.

Grayson finished on his shirt, which he immediately stripped off in frustration and tossed on the floor. Returning to his better senses, he felt a pang of disgust at having allowed himself to revisit those memories. For as much as he loved Seth, he knew that they would never share that level of intimacy again, and ultimately it left him feeling more hollow and alone than before. Reluctantly, he rolled over and went to sleep.

***

Grayson's eyes shot open. He could see the ceiling above him. He felt himself lying there on the bed in near darkness. A faint light from the adjacent bathroom illuminated most of the bedroom to his left. He tried to move his arms and legs, but they felt as heavy as stone and completely immobile. His head was propped up just enough by his pillow that he could see most of the room around him. His eyes darted back and forth, and he tried desperately to command his limbs to move and wake himself from the sleep. He looked up at the ceiling and took a deep breath, trying to calm himself.

He detected movement from his peripheral vision. His eyes darted toward the bedroom doorway. There, against a backdrop of darkness, glinted two crimson orbs. They drifted closer, but at a glacially slow pace, until he recognized them as a set of glowing red eyes. They locked his gaze and stared back at him, rendering Grayson fixated and unable to look away. The eyes drifted closer still. As they crossed into the light cast from the bathroom, a shadowy mass formed around the eyes. From it, one long, inky tendril extended into the bathroom until it pierced the light and extinguished it. Cast into darkness and rendered immobile, all Grayson could do was stare back in silent, paralytic terror as the red-eyed mass drifted closer, growing taller and more imposing, until it stood at the side of his bed, a swirling, writhing mass of opalescent darkness. It said nothing. It did nothing. It only stared directly into his eyes. It stared at him for what could have been minutes or hours. Grayson tried to scream, tried to cry, tried to make any sound at all, but his vocal cords produced no audible sounds.

The figure extended its inky black tendril again, reaching for something out of sight to the left of Grayson's head. He tried looking away again and again, but the eyes kept him locked in place, even as he heard a dreadful scratching noise, like a nail scraping deep across a piece of wood. Then it stopped. The eyes remained silently fixed above him for several moments longer and then blinked out of existence. In an instant, he was freed, and what little of the room was visible from the moonlight filtering through the window seemed to fade into complete darkness.

Grayson shot straight up out of bed at the sound of his alarm clock. It was 6:30 a.m. The sun peeked faintly through his bedroom window. He was drenched in sweat again. He took several long, deep breaths to regain control of his breathing and slow his heart rate. He didn't remember falling back asleep, but he must have. All he could think about were the eyes—the eyes! The horrible, crimson orbs that transfixed his own stare for what felt like an eternity in the darkness. Then he remembered the carving sound.

He leapt out of bed and turned to where the thing had reached its inky black tendril. To the left of his bed stood his wooden nightstand. There on the face of the bottom drawer were four deep claw marks. Grayson's heart fluttered. It was impossible that what he had witnessed last night was anything more than a dream, yet gouged in the wood of the nightstand was the physical proof that something was in his room last night.

Grayson felt inconceivably compelled to open the drawer. With a shaking hand and racing heart, he reached down and pulled the drawer open. There in the wooden bottom of the empty drawer was another set of scratch marks that extended all the way to the back. He yanked the drawer out entirely. Taped to the back of the drawer was a small metal key. Grayson turned it over in his fingers for a moment, then realized why it looked familiar. It was the missing key to his classroom desk drawer. There was no doubt about it in his mind. It looked exactly like the style of three of the other keys on the key ring. Something in his gut, though, told him this was the one. He held the key in his hand and sank down onto the bed, his mind turning somersaults trying to comprehend all the possibilities and probabilities related to his experience. He sat the key down on the bed and took a nervous walk through his home, checking for any further indication of his late-night intruder. Unable to detect any other disturbances, Grayson took the key from the bed and went about getting himself ready for work.

He arrived just on time. A few students were already seated at their desks when the warning bell rang, and Grayson walked in the door. He sat down at his desk and immediately withdrew the key from his pocket. He inserted it into the keyhole and turned. The lock clicked, and the drawer popped slightly ajar. His stomach flopped in excitement. He looked up and around to see who might be watching him before pulling the drawer open slightly. Resting underneath a few scattered writing utensils and some rubber erasers was a large, round sticker. It appeared to be an old sticker from the desk's original manufacturer. Before he could peel back the sticker, the bell rang as the rest of his students shuffled in. He took the roll and then launched into his lesson, trying his best to push the thought of the sticker from his mind.

After class, Alexis approached Grayson at his desk again. She seemed more anxious than the previous day and spoke in a hushed tone. She sat her school bag down on his desk.

"Can I ask you a question?" she said.

"Of course you can. What's on your mind?" he replied.

She paused for a moment. "Do you have secrets?"

"Sure. Everyone has secrets," he said. Though he looked at her, her eyes never left his desk.

"I mean, like, bad secrets. Things you're scared to tell?"

"Everyone has something they are scared to talk about, Alexis. It's okay to keep some things to yourself until you're ready to talk about them," Grayson advised, growing more anxious about her line of questions.

"Yeah, but what if you can't? Like, what if you have to tell them to someone, like, out loud?" she whispered.

"Alexis, I'm happy to listen to anything that's on your mind, but maybe this is something you should talk to the counselor about?" Grayson entreated.

"You're right, I'm sorry. I shouldn't have said anything," Alexis replied, grabbing her school bag in her hands.

Grayson thought twice about it, then put his hand on her bag to stop her. "Wait up now," he said. "What class do you have second period?"

"Algebra."

Grayson stood up to close and lock the classroom door.

"Second hour is my conference period," he said. "I'll write you a note to your Algebra teacher to excuse your tardiness. Tell me what's on your mind."

Alexis dithered for a while, seemingly searching for the right words. After a couple of minutes, she gave up.

"I don't know how to say it," she mumbled.

Grayson thought for a moment. "Let me ask you this. I'm brand new here. You have something on your mind you want to talk about, but I'm essentially a stranger to you. Why me? Why not one of the other teachers you know better, or the counselor?"

Alexis looked up at him for the first time. She seemed taken aback by the frankness of the question. This time she didn't hesitate.

"Because you're not from here," she explained. "And also because I looked you up on social media. You have a secret, too."

It was his turn to struggle for a reply.

"If you're referring to what I think you're referring to, that's not really a secret. There are plenty of people who know," he countered.

"Not here," she said. "Not in Breakvale. And you went to some trouble to hide it, but you weren't as thorough with your Twitter account. Breakvale isn't exactly San Francisco."

"You're not wrong about that," Grayson chuckled. "But what does that have to do with this?"

Alexis looked down again. "Because it's a small town. I can't tell anyone else because they will tell my parents. But I also can't keep it a secret. Not something like this."

"Something like what, Alexis? Why can't you keep a secret?"

"Truth is Life, Mr. Ender. No one keeps secrets in Breakvale," Alexis said gravely.

"Alexis, I don't understand," said Grayson.

"If I tell you my secret, then I have nothing to confess and I'll be safe," she said, tears beginning to well up in her eyes.

They sat together in silence for a moment. Finally, Grayson reached his hand out and gently touched her shoulder.

"Whatever it is, I won't say a word to anyone about it. I promise," he said.

Alexis burst into tears, barely managing to choke out the words. "We had sex."

Grayson sat back down in his seat and allowed Alexis to cry a little longer until she had calmed herself enough to elaborate. Instead, she began to gush.

"It was a week ago. Drew's parents were gone for the weekend and it just kind of, like, happened. I thought I was ready for it, but now I'm so confused. And like, Drew is really sweet and stuff. Like, he was really, really nice, but now I'm scared everything is going to change. And I'm, like, mad at myself. Because I'm not this girl. I'm smarter than this. I know that people have sex, and it's supposed to be normal and fun. But like, this is not fun, being confused like this. And I can't tell my parents because they will freak out. And I definitely can't tell any of my friends because they wouldn't understand and would be disappointed in me. So, I didn't know who to talk to, but you seemed really cool and I stalked your social media and, I dunno, I just..." she trailed off, ending her confession with a long, exhausted sigh.

Grayson thought for a moment. "First of all, Alexis, I appreciate the trust you put in me here. I know that this can be a very difficult thing to talk about. Obviously, this is a very sensitive subject, and as your teacher, there's a lot I can't really say. But what I can tell you is that what you're thinking and feeling is perfectly normal. Sex is a big step to take in a relationship, no matter how old you are. You have to handle it maturely and responsibly, and it sounds like you've really been thinking hard about it."

"Understatement of the century," she said, rolling her eyes and breaking a little smile.

"Have you talked to Drew about how you're feeling?" Grayson asked.

"Kind of. We've talked about it a little, and he's nice and stuff, but he doesn't really know what to say to make me feel better," she said.

"You're the only person who can make yourself feel better, Alexis. I'm happy that Drew is supportive, but ultimately it's up to you to find it within yourself how to understand your emotions and feel better about this new part of your relationship."

"I know," she said. "But like, how?"

"Give it some time. Just remember that this doesn't make you a bad person, no matter what anyone says. So don't be hard on yourself," Grayson affirmed.

Alexis withdrew some tissues from her bag and began to dab at her eyes and wipe her cheeks. "I know. I'm trying not to."

The bell rang to signal the end of second period. Grayson looked up at the clock on the wall and remarked at the time.

"Yikes," he said. "I'll put a note in at the office, so they know you were with me second period. You'd better get on to your next class, if you're feeling alright."

"Yeah, I feel okay. A little better now, thanks," Alexis sniffled, zipping up her bag.

They both stood up and walked toward the door. Alexis gave him a brief hug.

"Thanks for listening," she said.

"I'm here anytime you need," Grayson replied.

He unlocked the classroom door and held it open for her. As they stood there in the doorway, Alexis leaned in to whisper to him.

"Even though you didn't say it out loud, I know your secret too, Mr. Ender. Which I think should be enough to keep you safe. And I promise I won't tell anyone," Alexis confided, before turning away quickly and walking double-time down the hallway.

Grayson stood there for a moment, unsure of what she meant, but appreciative of the connection he seemed to have made with this student. He felt sorry for her in all honesty, though it was not such a stretch to know how she felt having to keep something like that bottled up until she was ready to burst.

The rest of the day passed without any more incidents. When the final bell rang, and the students had vacated his classroom,

Grayson locked his classroom door and turned his attention immediately to the sticker in the desk drawer. It was a large, round sticker, with a logo resembling a wax seal, and printed on rather stiff paper. He peeled the sticker back gently but didn't have to use much force to pry it up. The adhesive was weak and barely tacky. Flipping it around, he discovered a piece of paper stuck to the center. It was a note, written in blue ink:

#22. The Merchant of Venice.
Act 2. Scene 2.

Grayson stared at the words for a long time. He understood the words that were pointing him to Shakespeare's play and assumed that the note must have been written by Emily Hunt, but he couldn't work out the significance of the number twenty-two. To his knowledge, the play was not the twenty-second work by the playwright. Appropriate, he thought, that the message left behind by the former English teacher was a reference to Shakespeare. It read almost more like a clue than a message of some kind.

It was at that moment that he remembered the old textbooks on the bookcases lining the back classroom wall. Sticker in hand, he walked to the back of the classroom and inspected the shelves. There on a shelf near the bottom were several copies of The Complete Works of William Shakespeare. He plucked the first one from the shelf and turned it to the twenty-second page. It was a page from the first act of Hamlet. Perhaps it's not a page number, he thought. He flipped to the front of the book to view the table of contents. Written in the top left corner of the inside of the cover, he noticed a number sign followed by the number one. Of course, he thought, it's the number of the textbook!

He shelved the book and counted down to the twenty-second book on the shelf. It was next to last, which he pulled from the shelf and turned to check the table of contents. Locating the correct page number, he turned to Act Two, Scene Two of *The Merchant of Venice*. He flipped through the pages until he spotted some words that were underlined:

"Truth will come to light. Murder cannot be hid long—a man's son may, but in the end truth will out."

Written next to the underlined passage were the letters "E.H." He re-read the underlined passage several times, then the entire scene. Grayson thumbed through the rest of the act, but there were no other underlined passages. Something about these words alone was significant enough for Emily that she went to some trouble to occlude their discovery.

He took the book and walked back to his desk. He sat down, his head whirling from the events of the last two days. The words of the passage particularly troubled him. Grayson wondered what Emily must have been thinking about when she chose those words. Any student of literature knows that a writer chooses their words deliberately, and he was convinced that Emily would have shown the same consideration. A chill ran down Grayson's spine as details about his predecessor came floating back into his mind. Had Emily been afraid that someone might do her harm—or worse, murder her? He couldn't help but feel that Emily feared that something might happen to her and wanted to make sure that someone knew about it. Even still, he thought, how did the key to her desk end up in his nightstand? Then there was that word again—truth. Truth will come to light, truth will out, Truth is Life. He stared out the windows of his classroom, watching the wind stir the tops of the trees, and in his gut, he felt both a pang of excitement at the mystery and grave concern for the truth he might discover.

3

It was his first Saturday in Breakvale, and even though he had only been living there for three whole days, it felt like a short eternity. Grayson wanted desperately to return to Charleston for the weekend to see his friends and family, but with all that had happened in the last forty-eight hours, he knew that he might be tempted to stay and never return to Breakvale. Instead, he decided to spend the afternoon exploring the town. Perhaps, he thought, he might uncover more information about his missing predecessor. He couldn't shake the words from *The Merchant of Venice* from his mind; it was like hearing Emily's ghost, though he had no proof that anything bad had actually happened to her. For all he knew, she could be living happily in some other town far away from Breakvale. Unfortunately, his gut feeling betrayed his optimism. What he knew for certain was that he possessed a message from her that no one else likely knew about.

On his way out, Grayson stopped off at the property manager's office to turn in the form from his walkthrough inspection. He walked into the office, sounding a tired little brass bell. An older woman sat at the desk reading a newspaper, clad in a pink tracksuit that looked about three decades outdated. She looked up at him over the rim of her glasses and curled her top lip.

"Can I help you?" she asked gruffly.

"My name is Grayson Ender. I just moved into unit number four. I need to turn in my inspection checklist," he said, holding it out for her to take.

She folded the newspaper up neatly and laid it on the desk. She took the paper from his hand and walked to a file cabinet at the back of the office without saying a word. When she returned, she sat back down at the desk and picked the paper back up.

"Will that be all?" she asked, looking him unnervingly in the eyes.

"Yes, that's all," he said. He started toward the door, then thought about the desk key taped inside his nightstand. He stopped and turned around. "Actually, do you know who lived in the apartment before me?"

She stared at him for a moment. "I'm not at liberty to discuss previous occupants."

"I see," Grayson said. "Well, there is a pretty sizable hole in my wall just behind the bed. I'd like to make sure it gets repaired and that I'm not charged for it."

The woman looked back at her newspaper. "We'll send someone. Will that be all?" she asked more impatiently.

"Yes. Thank you," Grayson said. He was then struck by a peculiar urge. "Truth is Life. Have a good day, ma'am."

The woman briefly glanced back up at him. For a moment her reaction betrayed her aloof demeanor. "Truth is Life. Good day, Mr. Ender."

Grayson turned and left the office. He still had no idea why the phrase carried such meaning, but the way she responded indicated that his usage of the phrase was correct and appropriate. Still, it surprised him that *she* acted surprised to hear him say it.

Driving around town on Saturday afternoon was like taking a trip back in time. He drove down Main Street, which was bustling with locals doing their weekly shopping. Grayson passed a vintage-looking barbershop that he hadn't noticed before, adjacent to which was a salon for the women of Breakvale. Couples walked two-by-two in neat order on the sidewalks, observing the same flow of traffic that they would on the road. A small ice cream parlor on the corner of Cherry and Main Streets was busy entertaining a group of children. Further down, he passed a small portrait studio and a thrift store. Tucked around the corner was a general store, completely with a wooden statue of an Indian chief out front. Across the street were a furniture maker and butcher shop, and then a small bakery and coffee house on the corner of Main and Basin streets. Even some of the vehicles that paraded down the street were in keeping with the atmosphere; Grayson counted several sedans and pickups that could easily have been fifty years old.

As he drove through the neighborhoods, he remarked at all the homes that stood erect as monuments to "a simpler time". They were modest, one and two-story homes painted in gentle pastels and earth tones, and some were even adorned with well-manicured lawns and white picket fences. He passed the mailman who, with a bag of mail slung over his shoulder, delivered mail by foot, stopping every so often to chat with a neighbor or wave hello to passersby; he gave a friendly wave to Grayson, who happily returned the gesture. It was as though the entire town was frozen in the sixties.

Grayson made his way toward the end of town and noticed that the further from Main Street he drove, the faster the illusion dissipated. He passed more rundown, shabby homes, with broken gates and cracked windows. He passed a trailer park that seemed relegated to the edge of town like a leper colony. As he eclipsed the northernmost edge of town, he spotted a gravel road that led upward toward the mountain ridge. Access to it was chained off and adorned with a warning sign emblazoned with the word "Restricted" in bold lettering. Several other signs warned of the danger of abandoned mine shafts and discouraged trespassing. Further in the distance, he could see the old power plant, slightly elevated above Breakvale and looming like a weary, weathered palace over a fiefdom.

Grayson made his way back to town, hungry and anxious for an early dinner. He didn't recall seeing any kind of diner along the way, and a Google search turned up exactly one result: Roxanne's, the town's one and only bar—and only diner, apparently. It was situated on the eastern corner of Cherry and Main, just across the street from the ice cream parlor. He anxiously pulled into a parking spot off to the side of the building and stepped inside.

The interior of the bar was adorned in lodge-style decor, with various taxidermy animals hung from the walls on all sides. Above the bar, which ran almost the entire length of the back wall, were three flat-screen televisions, each playing a different football game. There were two pool tables to the right of the bar, and a jukebox to the left near the hallway to the restrooms. Two shuffleboard tables separated the dining tables and booths from the rest of the bar. A hustling woman in a blue apron greeted him as he walked in.

"Hi there! Just you today?" she called out at him.

"Yep."

"You want a table, booth, or seat at the bar?" she asked.

"A table is fine," he replied.

She grabbed a menu and a set of flatware and instructed Grayson to follow her. She seated him at a table on the far side of the room near the jukebox. The waitress came up behind him and was ready with her pen and pad before he had a chance to sit down.

"How ya doin' hun? You don't look familiar. You new here or passin' through?" she asked as she smacked her chewing gum.

"I'm new. Just moved here," Grayson laughed.

"Well then, welcome. My name is Kay, I'll be your waitress. Can I get ya started with something to drink? Beer? Coke? Whaddya like?"

"Water will be fine to start," he said.

"I'll give ya a minute to look over the menu. Back with your water in a sec, hun," she said before bustling away.

Kay returned with the water and took Grayson's order. She was quick to write up the ticket and whisked away to the kitchen. He sat in quiet admiration of the bar's interior. The flat screens were the newest piece of technology he had seen in Breakvale yet, and while the decor felt rustic, it wasn't tacky, in his opinion, as so many lodge-style bars tend to be in West Virginia. He amused himself by watching the few patrons in the bar conduct their business. There was a family at one of the booths struggling to get their two small children to sit still long enough to enjoy their meal. Across the room two burly bikers played a game of shuffleboard. A pair of women played a game of darts against a pair of men in the far corner beside the pool tables. In many ways, this was the closest thing to normal that he had seen yet in Breakvale, which gave him an odd sense of comfort.

His food was delivered piping hot and in record time. Kay was diligent in keeping up on his refills. He watched the way she bounced from table to table like a dancer on a ballroom floor, carrying trays of food and drinks with such grace and with such ease that it seemed she could do it with her eyes closed. At the bar, the bartender chatted with a couple of patrons. She had long dark hair pulled up into a bun, and was particularly attractive, though he felt she had a tough look about her. No doubt she was the one in charge, because every once in a while, she would yell through the window into the kitchen behind her for this order or that, or to tell the cook to turn down the music. He finished his meal and paid the check while watching the men playing shuffleboard heckle and laugh at each other.

He stood up to leave but stopped in his tracks as the bar fell silent. Everyone shifted their attention, training their eyes on something behind Grayson in an unblinkingly terror. He looked around at them, then traced the path of their gaze.

Grayson felt a tingling sensation claw its way down his spine as he turned around. He watched in mute horror as a large black mass slid down the wall and slithered along the ground toward him. The shadowy mass stopped only a few feet in front of him. Like a creature rising up from the depths of some murky pool of water, the black mass rose up off the floor. He could see the familiar deep red eyes that paralyzed him in his dream, set deep into the shadow, and watched breathlessly as the figure rose higher and higher off the ground, until it towered a full foot above his head. Its outer edges swirled with the same opalescent black tendrils he had seen in his nightmare. As its form solidified, it was no longer opaque like a shadow; instead, looking directly at it felt like staring into an absolute void, as if he could fall into the black abyss of its body and float for an eternity.

When at last the towering mass had assumed its shape, it locked eyes with him and, like in his nightmare, he was unable to look away. It reached out with one long tendril and touched

Grayson's forehead. He felt a searing coldness where the being made contact, then his vision faded away until he could only see the pair of crimson eyes boring into his own. It spoke to him in a harsh, rasping voice.

"Tell me your secrets," it hissed.

"I don't have any secrets," Grayson lied.

"You're lying," it hissed again.

In that moment, he had to make a snap decision. Cower before it or show it strength. Though he didn't understand why, he didn't quite feel threatened. "Why do you want to know my secrets?" he said.

"Tell me your secrets," it said.

"I will not," Grayson said defiantly.

The creature moved closer and swelled its form. "Tell me your secrets," it rasped.

This time he felt threatened. He tried to think of something that might appease the creature. "When I was ten, I stole a video game because I couldn't pay for it."

"Not a secret," it hissed.

This struck Grayson as odd. It was a secret, he felt, since he had never told anyone about it except his mom and dad. He racked his brain for something else.

"I'm the only one who knows that my aunt had an affair with her intern," Grayson offered.

The creature ruminated on this for a moment.

"Not your secret. Tell me your secrets," it drilled, floating backward and shrinking back down to its previous size.

Grayson couldn't think of any secret that he held deeply.

"I don't know what you want," he said.

"You're lying. Tell me your secrets," it demanded.

Locked in its gaze and unable to move his body, Grayson struggled to comprehend what the being could possibly want him to admit.

"I don't have a deeper secret," Grayson said finally. "I don't know what you want!"

The creature shrieked a high-pitched, ear-ringing shriek. Grayson heard a crash and the sound of shattering glass but couldn't see anything. It reached up with another long, massive tendril and unfurled six sharp, slender fingers from its end. The entity grabbed Grayson by the head. In an instant he experienced a searing pain inside his brain, followed by a whirlwind of memories and images that flooded his mind. He saw his ex and felt a pang of longing. He saw memories of them together, of them kissing, of sharing intimate moments, and of laughter and fun. Grayson felt overcome by a crippling loneliness, and in that time, he understood what it wanted. The creature let go of him.

"I'm still in love with him," Grayson confessed as tears welled in his eyes.

The creature made a sound like a satisfied growl. Its deep red eyes sank slowly back into the abyssal darkness of its face until they disappeared with a glint of light. Grayson closed his eyes. He could feel his arms again, then his legs. His vision fully returned in time to watch the entity's tendrils fold in on themselves, like a mess of translucent serpents slithering back inside of the black void, growing smaller and smaller until its body became a kind of round, opaque shadow again. Finally pierced by the rays of sunlight shining through the windows of the bar, it faded into nothing and disappeared. It seemed to all happen in an instant.

When Grayson was able to catch his breath, he spun around. There were broken mugs and dishes all over the floor, and a glass light fixture hanging from the ceiling near him had shattered and scattered across the bar floor. He looked wildly around at the other patrons in the bar.

"Did you all see that? Tell me you saw that," Grayson shouted, but no one answered.

No one in the bar would even look at him. They averted their gazes as though making eye contact with him would invite the entity to interrogate them next.

"Please! Someone!" Grayson wailed. He took a step forward and stepped on shards of glass and felt them crunch under his feet. "I'm not crazy! You all saw that happen! Why won't anyone say anything? Why won't you look at me?"

He waited a moment, but no one even dared to breathe. Terrified and furious, Grayson ran out of the bar's emergency exit door and into the alley. His head started spinning and he couldn't catch his breath. He leaned up against the wall, trying not to hyperventilate and pass out. After a couple of minutes of steadying his breathing, he stood up and started around the building where his Jeep was parked.

"Hey!" a voice shouted from behind him. "Hey! Stop!"

Grayson turned around. It was the bartender. She came running up to him.

"What do you want?" he snapped.

She stopped in front of him. She had a clean bar mop in her hand, which she offered to him.

"To make sure you're okay. Here, you're sweating," she said.

"You saw that right?" Grayson begged.

"Yeah, I saw it. We all saw it," she said.

"Why didn't anyone answer me?" Grayson yelled.

"Because they're all afraid. Same as you are right now," the bartender said. "Listen, I know you're freaked out now, but you're okay. It must have been satisfied by whatever you told it, or you'd be dead."

"What the fuck was that?" Grayson asked breathlessly, wiping the sweat from his face.

"You're new here. Obviously no one has told you anything or you'd know," she said. "I tell you what, my shift is over at eight. Come back then and I'll explain it all. Right now, you need to calm down. And I have a bar full of broken glass to clean up."

He nodded in agreement. "Sorry about the glass," he said. He offered the bar mop back to her.

"Keep it," she chuckled. "Go home. Shower. Calm down. You're going to be okay. Be back here at eight. Beers are on me."

Still reeling from everything that happened, all he could do was agree. "Right. Thanks. I'll be here," he said, then paused a moment. "I'm Grayson, by the way."

"I know," she said. "I'm Roxanne."

She turned and walked back into the bar. Grayson stood there for a short while, twisting the rag in his hand, then proceeded to his Jeep and back home to rest.

***

Eight o'clock rolled around quickly, and Grayson had already taken a seat at a back table to wait for Roxanne. He went home but couldn't sleep. All he could do was pace his living room, replaying the encounter over and over. He thought about calling his mom, or maybe Seth, but ultimately decided he needed more answers before trying to explain it to anyone.

Someone dropped some quarters into the jukebox and the familiar twang of Brooks & Dunn came across the speakers. It was an oddly comforting sound that reminded Grayson of home.

Within a few minutes, Roxanne approached the table with two beers and sat opposite him at the table. She pushed the mug toward him. She sported a red and black checkered flannel button-up that she hadn't been wearing before and had let her long, dark hair down so it tumbled over her shoulders.

"Here," she offered. "You're gonna need this."

Grayson accepted it with a nod and took a long drink.

"What the fuck happened today?" he said finally.

"There's a lot to say. I'm not quite sure where to start," she responded, looking down at her mug.

"From the beginning would be super," he retorted.

"So, there are things about Breakvale that aren't… normal," she began.

"No kidding."

"It's no surprise no one warned you. It's not exactly something people like to talk about," Roxanne confessed, caressing the mug with her thumbs. "That thing that attacked you earlier, it's some kind of spirit, or demon maybe. No one really knows for sure."

"Where did it come from?"

"No one knows."

"What does it want?"

"Secrets, apparently. It thrives on them. It wants to know things. Private things. Things you're ashamed of or afraid to tell. The deeper and more intimate, the more satiated it feels. And if it doesn't like your answer, it'll just keep drilling down deeper and deeper."

"That's what it did to me," said Grayson.

"Your interaction with it was a lot longer than normal," Roxanne asserted.

"What do you mean?"

"I mean most people are only in communication with it for two or three minutes. Yours was twice that long," she said. "You were really fighting it. Most people just give it what it wants right away. I've only seen it break things one other time."

"So, wait. Could you hear me or hear what it was saying to me?" he asked, giving her a puzzled look.

"No. Observers never hear anything that the Beast or its victim is saying," Roxanne revealed.

"Wait, the Beast?" Grayson asked, cocking an eyebrow.

Roxanne gave a shallow, weary chuckle. "The Beast of Breakvale. It's what everyone here calls it. It's a silly name, but people take it seriously."

They both took a long drink. There was a small pause as he processed the information.

"How long has this been going on?" Grayson asked.

"A long time. At least since the town was built. Maybe longer, who knows. The records only go back as far as the forties. The town was founded in eighteen seventy-two, but all the records from the early days of Breakvale were lost when the library and town hall burned down sometime in nineteen thirty-eight."

"And there are records of the Beast going back that far?" Grayson asked, astonished.

Roxanne shrugged. "I'm not really sure. I've never really looked into it myself. Not sure of anyone who has, honestly."

"Why does no one outside of Breakvale ever hear about it? This is legitimately paranormal stuff," said Grayson.

"No one wants to talk about it. The Beast only shows itself when it wants to. A few times people have tried to talk to newspapers or tabloids about it. One of those paranormal investigation shows even came once. But only two people were actually brave enough to talk about it, so they just came off as crazy."

"Why will no one talk about it? Why the hell do people put up with this?" Grayson scoffed.

Roxanne looked him dead in the eyes. "Because they value their lives."

"I don't follow," said Grayson.

"People don't usually leave Breakvale. They disappear. Or turn up dead," Roxanne said. "As far as anyone can tell, talking about the Beast to an outsider or refusing to tell it what it wants are both ways to end up its next victim."

Grayson went cold. "What?"

"Yeah. Those two people that talked to the paranormal investigators? They both turned up dead that year. Last year Mrs. Monaghan refused to tell it what it wanted to know. She turned up dead three days later."

Grayson tipped his mug and downed the remainder of his beer. Roxanne followed suit. She took their mugs and walked behind the bar to refill them. When she returned, she pulled out a cigarette from the pocket of her flannel button-up and offered one to him.

"No thanks, I quit," he said, waving his hand gently in refusal.

"Good for you. I've been trying to for years," she said as she lit the end of the cigarette. She took a slow, deliberate drag and blew the smoke high above her head and away from him.

"This is all just so crazy. So why do people still live here? Why hasn't everyone moved away?" Grayson asked.

"You've seen the town. Everyone knows everyone. A lot of these families have lived here for generations. It's almost the perfect little American town. It's a safe place to raise kids since there's practically no crime."

"No crime?"

"No. Think about it. You're in a town stalked by a supernatural monster that kills you for keeping secrets. You'd eventually have to confess to it or turn up dead," Roxanne pointed out, swirling her beer a little in the mug. "So why risk it? It's easier to just be honest and tell the truth all the time."

"Truth is Life," Grayson said, suddenly understanding.

Roxanne raised her mug. "Truth is Life."

"That's why everyone in this town repeats that stupid motto," Grayson moaned.

Roxanne just winked at him over her mug.

"Jesus Christ. This is too much," Grayson said. He took another gulp of his beer. "I have to admit, I don't really feel any better."

"Eventually it won't bother you as much. Everyone gets used to it after a while. For us...it's just a fact of life here in Breakvale," Roxanne shrugged.

"How long have you lived here?" Grayson asked.

"I was born and raised here. My dad owned this bar. He named it after me when I was born."

"Oh. Neat. So, you help him run it?"

"No, I run it entirely. He passed away a few years ago."

"Oh, I'm sorry," Grayson said, his face wrinkling into a sympathetic expression.

"It's okay. My mom died when I was ten, so it was just him and me. And this bar," she said with a wistful, lighthearted smile.

"You've had an encounter with the Beast, then?" he asked.

Roxanne nodded. "Just once. Which is less than others who have been here as long. For whatever reason it doesn't seem much interested in me. I have friends here that are about my age and have been visited five or six times."

He fell quiet. After a moment, he said, "Nobody's ever tried to chase it off or kill it?"

"No. At least, not that I know of," she said.

"And in a hundred years of encounters no one knows anything about what this thing is or where it came from?" Grayson asked, leaning in over his mug of beer.

"No. My great-grandfather used to say that it was a shadow being," said Roxanne. "Something he picked up from his boyhood friend here. He was a boy when the church here functioned as—"

"A school for Native American children. Yeah, I heard all about that one," Grayson groaned.

"Yeah, well, he used to say that there was something that lurked in the woods around here. Something that lived deep in the earth that they stirred up when the settlers here started mining coal.

"Creepy," he said, sipping his beer. "But not exactly an explanation for what it is."

"No. But great-grandfather was always steadfast in his belief in the shadow beings," Roxanne said, finishing off her beer. "Like I said, he was a boy when they converted the building to a day school for all the kids in Breakvale. His best friend was a Choctaw boy who was forcibly relocated here. The government did really awful stuff to assimilate those poor kids. Ripped them away from their parents. Completely barbaric."

"I know," Grayson nodded.

A silence fell over the table. Grayson finished his beer and checked the time on his phone. It was almost ten o'clock. For the first time all day, his mind felt tired.

"Roxanne, I want to thank you for all of this. This is all so fucking insane. I still don't quite know what to think. But in a weird way, I suppose I feel better knowing that this is…normal? I guess?" he said. "How fucked is that?"

Roxanne laughed and hoisted her empty mug into the air.

"Welcome to Breakvale. You're officially a part of the town, like it or not. But yeah, it's fucked," she agreed.

Grayson stood up. "I should get going. I am emotionally exhausted and need to try to sleep. Thank you for the beers."

Roxanne also stood up. "Come here," she said and embraced him. Holding him by the shoulders, she took a step backward. "You're okay to drive?"

"Yeah, I'm good, thank you though," he affirmed. "I just live over at The Sparrows. Not far."

"The Sparrows? Did you pick there, or did the school set you up there?" Roxanne asked.

"The school did. Wait, how'd you know I work for the school?" Grayson asked in surprise.

"I know everything about everyone here. Even the new people. It's a bar, people talk," Roxanne winked as she picked up the beer mugs. "Also, The Sparrows is where the school likes to put new teachers on the rare occasion we get them."

He gave Roxanne a puzzled look. "Did you know Emily Hunt, by chance?"

"Yeah, sure. She'd stop in for a drink once in a while. She was undefeated at shuffleboard. Used to drive some of these fellas in here crazy," Roxanne laughed. "I was sad when she decided to move. I really liked her."

"So, she did move then?" Grayson inquired.

"Well, I assume so," Roxanne replied. "When the school year ended, she was talking pretty seriously about moving back home.

Then, one day, she just up and left. No notice or anything. Jean comes in every now and again. Said Emily put in her notice and then abandoned her lease the next day."

"Huh. Weird. Why would she do that? I thought you said no one ever leaves Breakvale? I thought you said they—"

"Disappear. Yeah, and that's what she did. Just up and vanished. No forwarding address, nothing."

"And you don't find that suspicious?"

"More suspicious than a seven-foot shadow being hell-bent on sucking out your secrets?" Roxanne countered. "No. I think Emily had her encounter with the Beast and wanted to get as far away from here as possible."

"She had an encounter with the Beast, then?"

"You sure have a lot of questions about her," Roxanne observed. "What's the deal?"

"I'm just curious, that's all. The students are good kids. I just wonder why she'd leave a nice job like this and abandon these kids," Grayson fibbed. "What happened after her encounter with the Beast?"

"She seemed fine. About like anyone else. The Beast came to her in September, I think? But the stress of always wondering if it could happen again was too much for her, I think," Roxanne explained.

"Huh. I guess so," Grayson muttered. "Well, thanks again for everything. I'm not much of a cook, so I'll probably be in a lot for dinner."

"I'll look forward to it," Roxanne smiled. "Be safe getting home, Grayson."

She turned and walked into the kitchen with the mugs. As he wandered out of the bar and back to his Jeep, Grayson thought about Emily Hunt, the Beast, and his own place in Breakvale. He wondered whether Emily really had simply moved away in a hurry, or if maybe the Beast was somehow involved in her disappearance and, if it was, why Roxanne or anyone else didn't seem to know about it. He could feel, right down to his core, that there were more truths to be uncovered.

4

More than a month passed without incident. The Beast of Breakvale had not been sighted since its appearance at Roxanne's bar, and the occurrence felt like a distant memory. Grayson struggled with addressing what he considered to be a serious knowledge gap in his students' English education and had spent the last six weeks revising his lesson plans to accommodate and correct the deficit. He had had little time to think about anything else. In that time, however, he came to know many of his students and had grown fond of them in a way that he never expected; though he taught students before in Charleston, he marveled at the difference that a small class size made; and by the fourth week of classes his students had entrusted him with many of their more personal details. Perhaps it was the culture created by the town and its motto—maybe the kids had grown up learning how to be forthright and honest because their parents so feared the Beast of Breakvale. Maybe it was simply the hallmark of a small town. Either way, Grayson came to look at each student like they were his own little brothers or sisters, further driving his desire to equip them with the strongest subject knowledge possible.

It was mid-October, and the valley surrounding Breakvale traded its cool, green foliage for the warm amber and orange tones of autumn. Breakvale itself had made a change: the entire town was decorated in the school's colors, blue and silver, in preparation for football Homecoming. It was like nothing

Grayson had ever seen before; everywhere he looked there were streamers or flags or posters announcing and reveling in the arrival of Homecoming. The local shops all ran Homecoming specials, and the town's local bakery seemed to spend the last week churning out nothing but blue and silver cakes and pastries. The figurative jewel in the town's Homecoming crown, however, was the enormous blue banner stretched across Main Street that simply read "Go Stallions!" in large, silver block letters.

Grayson couldn't help but get swept away a little by all of the enthusiasm surrounding Homecoming and decided to do something he never had any desire to do before—he volunteered as a chaperon for the Homecoming dance. He had finally taken a trip back home to Charleston—he'd been too busy on the weekends with grading and lesson plans to go every weekend as he had intended—and had stopped at the mall to purchase a blue and silver tie to wear with his blazer before coming back. Despite his awful introduction to Breakvale, he felt rather attached to the town and its people; he even accidentally called it "home" while visiting with his friends back in Charleston, and much to his own surprise, felt at ease with the notion. In fact, were it not for the occasional loneliness he experienced at night while sleeping alone in a bed made for two, he might have even had the mind to stay longer than his four-year contract. Breakvale seemed to possess some ineffable, magic quality that left him unable to resist its charm. It didn't take him long to understand what Roxanne meant about why people don't want to leave Breakvale.

He had adapted, as well. He didn't even realize it had happened until he found himself a regular patron at Roxanne's and recognized one night while playing a round of pool with Roxanne and two other patrons that he'd actually made friends. It was a cheerful thought, especially since he never thought he'd be able to make a genuine connection with anyone in Breakvale. Like his students, many of Breakvale's residents were genuinely good and honest people. It was like living in Mayberry, he thought, if Mayberry were possessed by a secret-hoarding monster. Roxanne had become, in many ways, Grayson's guide to Breakvale. She knew the history of the town and of its people and connected Grayson to it in ways he would never have all on his own. She had a laid-back, down-to-earth charm that made her approachable and feel trustworthy—it's what made her such a good bartender. Roxanne was also a great supporter of the high school and its sports teams.

It was 5:30 p.m. on Friday night, and the entire town of Breakvale packed themselves into the little football stadium to witness the big Homecoming game between the Stallions and the rival Tigers. Sitting in the bleachers, midway up and dead centered on the fifty-yard line, Roxanne stood up and waved at Grayson to catch his attention. She had saved him a seat—her father's seat—that she reserved every year during the football season. Grayson waved back at her and marched up the bleacher steps to join her.

"You look sharp," she remarked, taking in the sight of him in his navy blazer and black aviators. "Nice tie."

"Thanks," he grinned.

He took his seat next to her, handing her a bag of popcorn and a soda, which she accepted with a cheer. Grayson thought he had seen team spirit before, but this assembly surpassed anything he had ever imagined. Dozens of parents sat eagerly in the stands, clad in blue and silver. There was sparsely any other color to be seen. The players had yet to take the field, but already the students were gregarious and chanting.

“Is this normal?” he asked, leaning into Roxanne’s ear to be heard.

“Yes,” she replied. “This is just about the biggest event of the year. I think most people around here care more about this than the Super Bowl.”

When the players finally took the field a few minutes later to begin warming up, the cheers from the stands were deafening. A man’s voice rang out over the loudspeakers.

“Ladies and Gentlemen, will you please rise for the singing of the national anthem,” he said.

The entirety of the stadium stood up in almost perfect unison. Hats were removed and hearts were covered. Two students marched to the fifty-yard line carrying a tall pole topped by an enormous American flag. Behind them walked a girl that Grayson recognized as a student from his fifth-period class. She began the national anthem and sang it with clarity and perfection. When she finished, the crowd erupted with cheers and appreciative clapping. The flag was marched away and the players took their places on the field.

Roxanne leaned over to Grayson’s ear. “You see that balding, heavy-set fella standing there on the track? The one with glasses? That’s Doc Weaver. He’s the only doctor we’ve got. You know that building on West and Elm? That’s his office. The man still makes house calls like it’s the fifties,” she informed. “Anyway, that was his youngest girl singing the national anthem.”

“Oh wow, I didn’t know. His daughter is in one of my classes. I haven’t needed a doctor, so I guess I never thought about the fact that there’s not a hospital here,” Grayson said.

“Yeah, the doc is great and all, but if you’ve got any kind of serious condition, you better hope you can make it to County Medical forty-five minutes away,” Roxanne joked.

"Here's to hoping," Grayson laughed.

It was an exciting game almost right from the kickoff. Though he had never cared much about football, he was enthralled by the drama that unfolded on the field in front of him. Looking down at the cheerleaders on the track, he saw Alexis at the back of the cheer squad, clapping and shaking pom-poms with such vigor that the tinsels mixed into a dizzying flash of blue and silver. He leaned into Roxanne's shoulder and pointed to where Alexis stood.

"You see that girl there at the end?" he asked, indicating Alexis.

"Mmhmm," said Roxanne. "Alexis Carter."

"She's in my first-period English class. She's sharp, and one of my favorites."

Roxanne nodded. "Her parents are Jim and Mary Carter. They run the local hardware store."

Grayson cocked an eyebrow. "Really? I didn't know."

"They're pretty quiet people. Very reserved. They don't do much except run the store and attend church. Jim's a deacon in the church and his wife runs the Sunday school class for the little kids," Roxanne said.

"That actually makes a lot of sense," said Grayson.

Roxanne turned her head and gave Grayson a curious look.

"My second day here Alexis approached me wanting to talk about something she said she couldn't tell her parents about."

"What was it?"

Grayson hesitated for a moment.

"I'm not gonna tell anyone," she said, rolling her eyes. "Anyway, Jim and Mary don't come into the bar."

Grayson leaned into Roxanne's ear. "She had sex with her boyfriend and was feeling some mixed emotions and anxiety about it."

"Oh, damn. If Jim found out about that he'd blow his top. Poor girl. They are nice people mostly, but holy hell can they be judgmental," said Roxanne.

Grayson shook his head. "You know, when she initially came to me wanting to talk about it, she said she had a secret that she couldn't keep, something she had to say out loud. At first, I thought she was just anxious because it was so personal. But now I wonder if she was also so desperate to tell me because she was afraid of the Beast?"

Roxanne thought about it for a moment. "Maybe. It's been known to target children in the past for their secrets, but it's never killed a child before. Only adults."

"Interesting," Grayson said, deciding not to press deeper, but to save that topic for a larger discussion later. "Either way, we haven't talked about it since. I didn't really feel like it was appropriate to be the first to bring it back up. I hope she figured it out."

"Oh, to be a teenager again," Roxanne said, throwing Grayson a side-eyed look.

"No thank you," he said, rolling his eyes.

The first half ended with the Stallions down by three. It had been such a close game right up to halftime. Breakvale High's small marching band was warmly received as they took the center field and gave an impressive and enthusiastic performance. When the players returned to the field twenty minutes later, the cheering grew louder and stronger than it had been all night. It was a tight second half. Despite a touchdown by the Tigers, the Stallions managed to tie the game in the third quarter thanks to a fumble from the Tigers' quarterback. The Tigers' defense refused to give any ground, making it a slow march down the field in the fourth quarter. The closer their team got to the end zone, the harder the Breakvale crowd cheered. It was in the last forty seconds that the game was decided. It was fourth and twelve from the forty-two-yard line, and the Stallions dispatched their kicker for a risky field goal attempt, but the Stallions were down by two and out of options. Some in the crowd cheered quietly, some bit their lips, while others still clenched tightly the arms and thighs of those next to them. The kicker took his shot. All eyes were on the ball as it arched high and went long, sailing smoothly between the goalposts. The stadium erupted into thunderous cheers and applause. As the teams congratulated one another and the crowd continued to cheer and revel, Grayson stood up and turned to hug Roxanne.

"Going somewhere?" she asked.

"Yeah, I volunteered to chaperone the dance. I've gotta get over there before students start showing up," he said, hugging her. "But that was amazing! Thank you for inviting me up here with you."

"I come here every home game. If you're bored on a Friday night, come join me," she offered congenially.

Grayson left the stadium and walked up the hill toward the school building. The gymnasium had been decorated with what felt like an obscene amount of blue and silver, with streamers, balloons, and tinsel clinging to almost every available surface. A large cloth backdrop had been set up for pictures near the entrance, and a volunteer photographer busied herself with setting up a lighting rig. A few of the other faculty members were already there setting up the food and drink stands while others were testing the sound system. In the far corner of the gym, the

DJ glowed in the light of his laptop computer as he queued up his music. Principal Daggett stood near a makeshift stage at the opposite end of the gym overseeing the microphone rigging. He spotted Grayson and waved him over, and Grayson dutifully approached.

"Grayson! What do you think? It's a fine set up, don't ya think?" he boasted, flashing a proud smile. "Only the best for our best and brightest."

"It is certainly something special," he remarked.

"Say, you wouldn't mind helpin' out there and untangling those extension cords, would ya?" he asked, pointing toward a knotted mess of orange cords on the floor by the stage.

Grayson set about untangling the cords. Looking around the room, he felt that the decorations were actually rather garish, but with the lights dimmed low, perhaps the students wouldn't notice. Then again, he thought, it's unlikely they'll care about much beyond their own interactions with their peers. As he stood there untangling the extension cords, he turned his attention to Principal Daggett, who seemed unusually distracted. He watched the principal zip back and forth, checking in with each group of faculty and volunteers, seemingly desperate to ensure that every detail was precisely executed. It was a frenzied kind of pace that betrayed his otherwise calm and easy-going manner. No doubt tonight must be important to him.

By nine o'clock the students started shuffling in. Grayson was happy to see that many of the students had ditched the blue and silver spirit attire and embraced a wider variety of colors and patterns. By ten o'clock, all the students had arrived and the photographer was breaking down. The students mostly seemed to be enjoying themselves, and the occasional cheer would break out from the middle of the gym floor as one student or another performed an especially impressive dance move. Once in a while, the DJ would play a slow jam, and students would pair up with friends or significant others and dance hand-in-hand or wrapped in an awkward embrace.

Standing against the wall while monitoring the students, Grayson thought about his own Homecoming experiences. He attended the Homecoming dance all four years, and while he always managed to have a good time, when a slow song came on, and it was time to find a partner, it felt like a knife to the heart. Not because he had to dance with his best friend Liz, but because he couldn't dance with the boy standing two couples over: Derek Tomlin, Grayson's first boyfriend. The idea of dancing with another boy in any sort of romantic way seemed impermissible in a place like Charleston; and while he was thankful to have grown up in an age when having a boyfriend in high school was possible, it still felt like a cruel injustice.

Glancing across the room, Grayson spotted Alexis in the corner with her boyfriend, Drew. They were cuddled up next to each other and trying to talk over the music. He watched as Drew discreetly brushed her inner thigh first and then one of her breasts. She looked up at him, and they both stood still for a moment, then he leaned in to speak something into her ear. She nodded and smiled, then took him by the hand and led him toward one of the side exits. Grayson knew immediately what they intended to do. He waited a moment to see if any of the other volunteers noticed their exit, but when no one seemed to pursue them, he let out a hefty sigh and chuckled as he walked toward the exit and out the door after them.

The back of the gymnasium was dark, and the air was cool outside, especially compared to the swelter happening in the gym. There were only two dim lights at either end of the building.

Grayson looked around but couldn't see either student. He propped the door open with a piece of broken cement and stepped out into the grass. There was a large, wooded area behind the gym. He walked a little way into the long line of trees, listening quietly for the sound of rustling leaves or raging hormones. He thought about calling out their names but decided that even if they heard him, they weren't likely to respond. All he could do was smirk and shake his head as he walked back into the gym.

***

Drew and Alexis walked hand-in-hand through the thickly wooded hill behind the school. A waxing moon floated high in the sky, obscured by a thick cloud bank that scattered the light and left the pair in nearly complete darkness. Drew eagerly pulled Alexis further along up the hillside, weaving them through the trees until he found a suitably concealed area well out of sight from the school building. Alexis appeared less enthusiastic.

"Drew, it's freezing out here," she complained. "Why are we all the way up here?"

Drew took off his blazer and draped it around Alexis's shoulders. He rubbed her arms in an attempt to warm her and then sat down in a pile of leaves. The moon peaked out from behind the clouds, casting a pale light across her face and causing her homecoming dress to glimmer ever-so-slightly. To Drew, she had never looked more radiant.

"I'm not very good at this kinda stuff," he admitted. "But I know it's been kinda hard on you. The sex, I mean. Like, with your emotions and stuff. I love you, Alexis. I wanna make you feel better. So…how?"

Alexis sank down next to Drew and began to cry.

"Oh. Hey, hey, hey. What's wrong?" Drew asked, unsure whether to touch her.

She sobbed quietly for a few moments, before finally managing to choke out the words, "I'm pregnant."

Drew sat back, temporarily stunned at the news. He leaned in and, at last, put his arms around her. "Are you sure?" he asked.

"Yes. I've taken the test three times. I just don't understand how. We used condoms. I just…I don't know what to do," she sobbed.

Drew leaned in closely to her face and wiped the tears out of her eyes. "Hey, it's gonna be okay. We'll figure it out. My parents will help, and I'll get a job, and we can get married and find a place—"

"We're too young for this Andrew!" she barked. "Don't you understand? I don't wanna be married. I want to go to college. I wanna leave this stupid fucking town and never look back."

Drew backed off from her and took a deep breath, hurt and confused at the sudden rejection.

"What are you saying?" he said finally.

"I don't know! I don't know, Drew. It's just…it's all wrong, and I don't know what to do."

A sudden, loud, popping noise echoed through the trees, like the breaking of twigs underfoot. Drew and Alexis both looked up and around. For a moment, everything was still, and then they heard the crunching leaves. Drew stood up.

"Drew—"

"Shhh," he whispered to her. "Stay there."

He pulled out his phone and triggered the flashlight, then took a few steps forward in the direction of the sound.

"Hello? Is someone there?" he called out.

He held his phone up high to cast a wide beam but didn't see anything. He walked a little further, looking around and behind some of the trees and downed logs. A raccoon suddenly sprang out from behind a log and skittered up a nearby tree. Drew exhaled a breath of relief.

"It's just a fucking raccoon," he called back to Alexis. "Alexis, it's just a raccoon."

He turned back around, but Alexis was gone. He called out for her, but there was no answer. His heart sank and his pulse quickened. He screamed out for her. There was no answer. Panic welled up inside him. He stood there, rooted to his spot, paralyzed by fear. Drew spun around, flashing his light in every direction. He heard a strange growl rumble from somewhere near him. Before he could identify its source, he felt something strike the back of his head, and he collapsed into the pile of leaves beneath him.

5

Grayson decided to take an impromptu trip to Charleston again, having made the long drive immediately after the Homecoming dance, just so he could spend one Saturday evening visiting with a couple of friends and catching up on the nightlife he missed out on while living in Breakvale. He was exhausted, but his soul was refreshed, and he turned up early to school on Monday morning feeling rejuvenated and ready to have a great week. As his students shuffled in, he took notice of the disturbed and concerned looks on several of their faces as they whispered in hushed tones to one another. When the final bell rang, he took note of two particular absences. He waited two more minutes before closing his classroom door.

"Where are Drew and Alexis?" Grayson asked, knowing that someone would have heard if they were sick or playing hooky.

The room was silent.

"They're missing," piped up one of the girls sitting in the front row.

"What do you mean they're missing?"

"They didn't come home after the dance. No one's heard from them," she continued.

"They probably got a motel room and ditched out for a couple of days," speculated one of the boys at the back.

Almost as if on cue, there was a knock at the door. Grayson opened it to find Principal Daggett standing in the doorway, looking particularly distressed and disheveled. He motioned silently for Grayson to step out into the hallway and close the door, then led him around the corner where two police officers stood waiting.

"Grayson, this is Chief Danbury and his deputy, Lisa Thorne," Principal Daggett introduced.

Grayson shook both of their hands, taking note of Chief Danbury's appearance. He looked every bit of the police officer stereotype, right down to his wide-brimmed hat and thick mustache. Deputy Thorne, on the other hand, had her long blonde hair pulled back into a tight ponytail that spilled out of the mesh back of her baseball cap and trailed down to her shoulder blades. She had a thin, strong frame, and carried herself in a way that made her already sharp facial features appear even more tough and intimidating.

It was Chief Danbury who spoke first.

"Mr. Ender, you were one of the chaperons at the Homecoming dance Friday night, is that correct?

"I was," he said, nodding.

"Where were you this weekend?" he asked, his eyes looking unflinchingly at Grayson.

"I went back to Charleston for the weekend. I was with friends and my folks all weekend. They can verify it. This is about Drew and Alexis, isn't it? They're missing."

"That's right," said Deputy Thorne. "Their parents reported them missing Saturday morning when they didn't come home."

"I literally just heard about it from my students. I had no idea until a few moments ago," said Grayson. "Listen, I saw them leave the dance Friday night. I watched them slip out the back door in the gym and go behind the school."

The officers exchanged glances. “Did you follow them outside?” the chief asked.

“Of course I did,” said Grayson. “But by the time I got across the gym and out the door, they were nowhere in sight. I assumed they snuck off into the woods to have sex.”

“And that was the very last time you saw them?” Chief Danbury asked.

“Yes.”

“You didn’t think to go after them or to report it to Mr. Daggett?” Deputy Thorne inquired, her brow stern and furtive.

“Well, no, honestly,” Grayson said. “It was dark. These kids have grown up here. I just assumed they knew where to go and what they were doing. They would’ve just hidden from me anyway until I gave up looking. Besides, we both know that if I’d stopped them, they would’ve just gone elsewhere later to do it.”

Chief Danbury’s phone began to ring.

“Excuse me,” he said, answering it as he walked a few feet down the hallway to take his call privately.

Deputy Thorne pulled out a small scratch pad. “Can you tell me what they were wearing last when you saw them?” she asked.

As Grayson began to describe their Homecoming attire, the chief walked somberly back up the hallway toward them. Principal Daggett took note of his expression first and immediately began to tear up.

“No. No, no. Sheriff?” he said, his voice beginning to break.

Grayson and Deputy Thorne both paused to look at the chief.

“That was Stanley. Andrew McIntosh’s body was found floating in Kitt’s Creek this morning by a couple of fishermen,” he said.

Principal Daggett spun on his heels and turned away from the group, visibly distraught by the news. Grayson stood there in stunned silence, unable to fathom the death of a student he'd seen alive and well barely more than forty-eight hours previously.

Chief Danbury turned to his deputy and spoke softly. "The boy's parents are on their way to the station to make a positive identification. I need you to meet 'em there. I'm going to check out the dump site."

"Wait, was there any sign of Alexis?" Grayson asked.

"No. I've got a couple of volunteers organizing a search party," stated Chief Danbury.

"Whoever killed Drew might be keeping her alive," Grayson said.

"Let's hope so, Mr. Ender."

Chief Danbury reached out and placed his hand on Principal Daggett's shoulder to console him. "Dale, now I'm not trying to tell you how to do your job, but I think it'd be best if you got a hold of Dr. Thomas and sent these kids home today and maybe cancel the next couple of days. A lot of parents are gonna panic and keep their kids home anyway."

Principal Daggett shook his head in agreement. "I'll go call now," he half-muttered as he walked away.

Deputy Thorne looked Grayson directly in the eyes. "You're not a suspect at this time, Mr. Ender. But I would also ask that you remain in Breakvale for the time being, in case we have questions."

"That's fine," he replied. "I have nothing to hide."

"Secrets have a way of bubbling to the surface around here," Chief Danbury cautioned, putting on his sunglasses. "Truth is Life, Mr. Ender."

The pair turned and walked away, leaving Grayson behind in his quiet bewilderment.

***

Dr. Thomas took Chief Danbury's advice and dismissed school immediately, with classes canceled for at least two days, or until a proper amount of time for grieving had passed. By late in the afternoon, the entire town had been made aware of Drew's death and Alexis's disappearance. There was palpable tension in the air all across town, and nowhere was that more apparent than at Roxanne's diner, which had become a makeshift headquarters for the search parties. Grayson stood at the end of the crowded bar with Roxanne, listening to Deputy Thorne give instructions to the next wave of volunteers and organize them into three groups, with each group assigned an officer to lead the search party.

Grayson was assigned to the search party responsible for scouting the mountainside adjacent to Kitt's Creek where Drew's body was discovered. Roxanne walked around the end of the bar, pulled a flashlight out from behind it, and handed it to him.

"It'll be dark soon on the ridge. Be really careful," Roxanne said gravely.

"You're not coming?" Grayson asked.

"I've already told my employees they can go out with the search parties. I'm staying here to hold down the fort," she explained. Grayson turned to leave, but Roxanne took him by the shoulder and leaned in closely to whisper. "Listen to me. Deputy Thorne said it looked like the kid had some blunt force trauma to the head and might've been strangled to death. Right now, a lot of people are assuming it was the Beast of Breakvale that might've killed him. But the Beast has never killed a child before. Something isn't right. Just be careful."

He paused for a moment. "I will."

The search parties set out, loading up in the beds of several pickup trucks, and drove eastward out of Breakvale and up into the mountain ridge. They crossed over one of two bridges that spanned Kitt's Creek as they ascended the only paved road up into the mountainside. Grayson learned from one of the other men in the truck bed that Drew's body had been found at the second bridge only a few miles south, and for as long as he'd been in the water, they assumed his body was dumped upstream. Or the body was tossed into the river by the Beast. Opinion among the others in the truck seemed split on the culprit and the reason for his murder. The convoy of trucks and vans came to a stop on the right shoulder of the road in single-file order. Two dozen people, equipped with flashlights, phones, whistles, and firearms of all kinds, began the slow, tedious process of combing the forest in rapidly failing light for any signs of Alexis.

Grayson spotted Principal Daggett as he stepped out of one of the vans parked a few vehicles down and jaunted over to join him.

"Principal Daggett!" Grayson shouted, trying to get his attention.

Principal Daggett spun around and gave a gentle wave. "Grayson. Please, just call me Dale. Glad to see you out here."

"How could I not?" Grayson replied. "I never should have let them go."

"You can't go blamin' yourself. You couldn't'a known," Dale said, resting his hand gently on Grayson's shoulder. "Besides, you're here and we're gonna find that young girl. Come on, walk with me."

The pair brought up the rear left of the search party, flashlights trained to the ground, scouring for any piece of Alexis or any clue to her whereabouts. They said nothing to each other for a long time, until Grayson finally broke the silence.

"I heard that Drew was suffocated to death," he said, eyes still fixed on the ground.

"Who told you that?" Dale asked.

"Roxanne. She apparently heard it from Deputy Thorne," he replied.

"I hadn't heard that yet. What kind of monster would strangle an innocent kid like that?" Dale replied.

"A lot of people seem to think it was the Beast of Breakvale," Grayson said.

Dale was quiet for a moment. "Maybe. It's never hurt a kid before."

They were quiet again for several minutes.

"Do you think it was the Beast?" Grayson pressed.

"I don't know what to think, to be honest," Dale said. "It's a fact'a life that people come up dead once or twice a year around here because of that damned thing. But never a kid. Never a kid."

A whistle rang out, sudden and shrill, through the trees. Dale and Grayson looked at each other.

"Someone found something," Grayson said. He pointed down the ridge toward the creek. "Over there."

He and Dale followed the others quickly but carefully down the hillside, joining a small group that had gathered around the discovery. It was a necktie. Grayson recognized it immediately.

"That's Drew's tie," he said to Dale. "I saw it on him at the dance."

One of the police officers came over and began moving people away from the area and photographing the object and surrounding ground. Within minutes the necktie was bagged as evidence. Grayson approached the officer and confirmed that he had seen Drew wearing that same necktie at the dance. There was no blood on the tie that Grayson could see, and he wondered if this tie could have been used to strangle Drew to death. Strangulation seemed to Grayson like a peculiar way for the Beast to kill someone, but then he didn't really know much about how it claims its victims.

Within minutes, the search resumed, but this time the party moved outward in a radial fashion from where the necktie was discovered. The sun had fully set over the western ridge by this time, blanketing the search party in total darkness except for the flashlight beams and the light of the moon when it occasionally peeked out from behind the clouds. After several more hours of searching, Chief Danbury made the decision to stop for the night. A few volunteers chose to continue looking on their own, but most loaded back up into the vehicles and returned to town. Grayson hitched a ride with Dale and requested that he drop him off back at the diner to pick up his Jeep. When they arrived, he was surprised to see that the lights were on and the bar was still open. Grayson stepped inside to find a dozen people drinking coffee, talking about the next location they would search. Roxanne waved Grayson over to the end of the bar.

"I heard Martha Jones found Drew's tie," Roxanne whispered.

"Yeah, how did you know?

"She called her nephew, Mason, who was sitting here when he got the call," she explained.

"I see. And that's why you're open at two in the morning?"

"I'm staying open for as long as people are out searching. These people need coffee. And I've got the only place in town with coffee that's also big enough for everyone coming and going."

"You've had a long day," Grayson said.

"Not as long as Alexis's parents," Roxanne replied, nodding over her shoulder to an older man and woman sitting at one of the tables with a large map of the town sprawled open on it. They were flanked by a few other people, all of whom were either talking with Alexis's father and pointing to the map or comforting his often-weeping wife.

"I wouldn't go over there if I were you," she warned, seeing Grayson ponder whether or not to say something to the grieving parents. "Jim's a powder keg right now. He threw a glass against the wall about an hour ago."

"Thanks for the warning," Grayson paused. "You're a saint for doing this."

"Just trying to help. This town might be fucked up, but it's still home," Roxanne said with a slight smirk. "You should go home. Get some rest. The search will continue tomorrow morning. Deputy Thorne will be here at six to start coordinating the searches again."

Grayson nodded in agreement; he was exhausted and felt like Roxanne's dismissal was the permission his conscience needed to slip away to rest for a few hours. He shot Roxanne a quick salute and went home to sleep.

***

The morning came early. Grayson was so accustomed to waking up early for work that even after only sleeping a few hours, he was wide awake. He returned to the diner for a quick breakfast before joining another search party. He was not surprised to find that the diner was already crowded when he arrived. It appeared that Roxanne had managed to slip away from the bar at some point, because she was wearing a different outfit from the night before, and her hair was pulled up into a ponytail that stuck out the back of her baseball cap. She spotted him in the doorway and waved him on over.

"How about a cup of coffee?" Grayson said, taking one of only two empty seats at the bar.

"Sure thing," Roxanne said. "You want some food? I have a kitchen staff again."

"Eggs and bacon?"

"Comin' right up."

Roxanne shuffled over to the window behind the bar to put in the order. Grayson looked around the diner. Alexis's parents were gone, probably out searching again already this morning. He recognized a few of the kids in the diner as high school students, likely accompanying their parents, hoping to find their lost friend. He hadn't seen any students out last night, and something about seeing these kids now crushed him. He tried to imagine, for a moment, what he would have done if one of his friends had gone missing like this, but he couldn't fathom it.

Roxanne came back with a cup of coffee for Grayson and set it down in front of him. "Coffee is free for the search party," she said. "You're on your own for breakfast." She winked at him and moved down the bar to take care of some other patrons.

The phone behind the bar rang. Roxanne jumped immediately over to answer it. The bar grew increasingly still as more people took notice of Roxanne on the phone, watching as her face shifted from a wide-eyed and eager expression to one of shock, and then sadness. She nodded a few times, confirming something with whoever was on the other line, and then hung the phone slowly back up on the receiver. She turned to face the now silent crowd.

"That…that was Chief Danbury," she said, clearing her throat for what she had to say next. "They found Alexis this morning. She's dead. They found her in a ravine east of the power plant. The chief wants me to tell all of you thank you for everything you have done."

A few people burst into tears at the news, though most just sat silently in their seats as they tried to comprehend the news. Roxanne disappeared around the corner into the kitchen. Grayson stood up to follow her and wasn't surprised to find her misty-eyed and sniffling inside the doorway.

"Are you okay?" he asked.

"As okay as any of them, I guess. It's horrible," she said through gritted teeth.

Grayson paused for a moment. He realized she almost looked more angry than sad.

"There's more, isn't there?" he leaned in. "What didn't you tell them?"

Roxanne took a slow breath. "They didn't find her body in the ravine, Grayson. They found her head. Just her head."

Grayson's heart dropped to his stomach. "Has this ever…has the Beast—"

"No, never. It's never happened like this before. It's never decapitated someone. I don't know what to think. The Beast doesn't normally kill someone so brutally. But there hasn't been a murder here in forty years. I just…something isn't right, and I don't know what to do."

"Maybe there's nothing you can do. It sounds like this is a law enforcement issue now."

Roxanne turned her head away, tears dripping slowly down her cheek. She took a deep breath and wiped them away. "Pull it together, Roxanne," she muttered to herself.

"It's going to take some time for everyone to work through this," Grayson said. He thought for a long minute and then continued. "You said the Beast only ever takes one or two a year. If it was responsible for the kids' deaths, then it should be a long time before it happens again, right? So, if there's nothing else we can do, we could at least try to figure out why it chose kids this time."

Roxanne stopped for a moment to think about the implications of what Grayson had said. "You know what, you're right. But how do we do that?"

"I don't know. Not yet, anyway. But you know more about this thing than almost everyone here. And research is something of a specialty for me. Between the two of us, surely we can figure this out," Grayson said encouragingly.

Roxanne nodded in agreement, slowly at first, then more aggressively. "Yes. Yes. We can do this. For Alexis. And for Drew." She reached out and hugged Grayson. "Thank you. Listen, I need to get back to work, but come back by later if you're free and we can talk more."

"I can do that."

Roxanne wiped her eyes a final time, then slipped past Grayson and went back to working the bar. Having lost his appetite, Grayson left a ten-dollar bill on the bar next to his coffee cup and proceeded to return home to try to get some more rest. On the drive back, he marveled at how accustomed he had become to this strange town; first a mysterious monster and a schoolteacher who disappeared, now two dead students. It just didn't make any sense. The only thing he knew for sure was that he had stepped right into the middle of something that he couldn't ignore or run away from.

6

School resumed the following Thursday. The day began with a surprise announcement from Principal Daggett that there would be an assembly during second period, no doubt to discuss the deaths of two students, and to address safety protocols.

The students were mostly solemn as they walked into the auditorium. Pictures of Drew and Alexis were projected onto a large roll-down screen at the back of the stage. Grayson stood at the back of the auditorium, observing the students as they shuffled in. While all the students were mourning the loss of two of their friends and classmates, there was now a tangible fear that any one of them could be next.

Principal Daggett took the stage to begin the assembly. Standing behind a wooden podium, he shifted uncomfortably in his spot, adjusting his tie and straightening his blazer.

"Good morning, everyone. There's no easy way to say this, so I'll be forthright. As I'm sure you all know, two of your classmates were recently found dead after disappearing from the Homecoming dance last Friday night. The bodies of Andrew McIntosh and Alexis Carter were recovered from the woods east of Kitt's Creek. This is an absolute tragedy, as no young person should ever have their lives cut so short. Many of you are probably scared and confused, and I'm certain we are all experiencing tremendous grief at their loss. For the next few days, all students who wish to talk about their feelings may be excused at any time to speak with the school counselor. You don't have to grieve in silence. Before we continue, we will now have a two-minute silence, to honor the memory of Drew and Alexis."

Principal Daggett set a timer on his phone and laid it on the podium in front of him. He then bowed his head, prompting the students and staff to do the same. The two minutes of silence seemed to last an hour. When, at last, his phone buzzed, everyone returned their attention to the stage. Principal Daggett cleared his throat.

"There are still many things we don't know yet about how and what happened to Drew and Alexis. That's why, as of right now, Dr. Thomas and I have agreed to put new safety measures in place. From now on, no student will be allowed to leave school grounds without an adult present. Any student needing to leave during the day will check in with the office and will only be allowed to leave with a parent or guardian. During sporting and other school events, all students will be restricted to the area of the building where the event occurs. Any student found wandering the halls or outside will receive an in-school suspension. Letters will go out today to your families explaining the change in policy. This is for your safety."

Grayson watched a few students lean over and whisper to their friends. It was apparent that some of them already felt that the new rules were overly restrictive, and he wondered whether their fear of the Beast would be enough to keep them in line. Principal Daggett also seemed to take note of the whispers.

"Some of you might feel like this is a harsh reaction. But I'll be damned if any of you are gonna meet this same fate while I am your principal. You might not like it, but again, this is for your protection. Here in Breakvale, we have a motto. What is that motto?"

"Truth is Life," the students spoke in unison.

"That's right. Truth is Life. Now we don't know what kind of secrets these two might have had," Principal Daggett asserted, pointing to the pictures on the screen behind him. "But remember truth and honesty are valued above all else here in Breakvale. They are the keys to life. If you always act with honesty and integrity and follow the rules, no harm will come to you."

Grayson stood there listening to the principal, dumbfounded at the blatant victim-blaming he had just heard. What began as a nice memorial quickly spiraled into the kind of bizarre behavior he had become accustomed to, but this seemed highly inappropriate, even by Breakvale standards. Even more incredibly, as Grayson surveyed the other staff members' reactions, he seemed to be the only one visibly bothered by the principal's words.

Principal Daggett continued. "Now, before you return to class, if any of you have any information about Drew and Alexis that you feel might be helpful, or if you would like to see a counselor now, you may remain here in the auditorium. God bless us all."

He waved his hand quickly to indicate that the assembly was dismissed before exiting the stage. As the students all stood up, the solemn silence shifted to hushed gossiping and rumor-mongering as they shared with their friends their own thoughts and speculations about their deceased classmates and the new rules. As the last of the students were herded out of the auditorium, the history teacher, Mrs. Newsham, approached Grayson.

"There's a candlelight vigil being held at the church tonight in memory of the two departed students. Will you be attending?" Mrs. Newsham asked.

"I didn't know anything about it," he confessed.

"Pastor Arthur announced it during his sermon last Wednesday night. I know you don't go to church, but I thought you might like to attend. It starts at seven," she said.

Grayson was momentarily irked at her judgmental tone but kept his composure. "Of course, I'll be there," he said.

The assembly ended just twenty minutes into his conference hour, and without anything better to do, Grayson followed some of the other faculty into the teachers' lounge. He crossed the small room to the water cooler by the window and sipped on a cup of water while a few of the teachers delved into gossip. Mr. Rigby, the P.E. coach, and Mrs. Wells, the Home Economics teacher, both lit cigarettes and took long, reflective drags.

"It's a damn shame about Drew," Coach Rigby finally said. "He was a hell of a ball player."

"Mmm," said Mrs. Wells while taking a drag. "Damn shame. Course, and I don't mean to be crass or nothin', don't wanna speak ill of the dead, but seems to me that him and that girl were up to no good."

"Oh? How's that now?" Rigby replied through a cloud of cigarette smoke.

Mrs. Wells leaned in close and spoke in a hushed voice. "Well, now I heard from Doc Weaver's wife, Marybeth, that the Carter girl," she leaned in closer and spoke with emphasis. "She had an S.T.D."

Grayson stood facing the window, listening to them gossip away. He clenched his fists and felt his knuckles tighten. He crushed the water cup in his hand like he wanted to crush both of their judgmental heads.

"Is that so?" Coach Rigby grunted.

"Mmhmm," Mrs. Wells smugly. "I dunno what them kids done or what they didn't do, but I know that maybe if that Drew boy had been in church more maybe they might not have been taken by temptation. You know that's the only way she woulda got an S.T.D. Alls I'm sayin' is maybe they'd still be alive if they didn't have that shame to hide. That's all I'm saying."

Grayson couldn't take it any longer.

"Are you fucking kidding me? Do you even hear how fucking ridiculous and awful you sound?" he snapped.

Mrs. Wells stood up from her seat. "Excuse me? I know you are not talkin' to me like that."

"Yeah, I am talking to you like that. Two students in this school are dead. Dead. We don't even know how. And you have the fucking nerve to sit here and blame them for it?"

"Listen, pal, I think you need to calm down," Coach Rigby warned, taking a step toward Grayson with his hand raised.

"I don't need to calm down. This is absurd. I can't believe I'm hearing this from a teacher. Where's your fucking compassion?" Grayson fumed.

"Look, you're new around here," Rigby began, "So I'm gonna give you a pass for talkin' like that. But you need to understand that this is how it is in Breakvale. People die. Now it's a damn shame, but that's just how it is. If they hadn't been keepin' secrets, maybe they'd still be alive."

Grayson stood there in stunned silence for a moment. "You know what? Fuck your complacency. And fuck you. Both of you."

As Grayson stormed out of the faculty lounge, Coach Rigby and Mrs. Wells both exchanged glances before taking another long drag and returning to their gossip.

The rest of the day passed by without further incident, though Grayson was sure that he had made himself public enemy number one among the rest of the staff for going after his colleagues like he had; he didn't regret it though, and if he had the opportunity, he decided, he'd do it again. Maybe, he joked to himself, he'd ask the pastor later for forgiveness.

The final dismissal bell rang and Grayson's students packed up and filed out of the classroom. As he packed his own material away and prepared to head home, he heard a knock at the door. It was Principal Daggett. Grayson knew immediately what he wanted.

"If you've come to ask me to apologize, I'm not going to do it," he said without looking up from his desk.

"Well now, I heard you had a little altercation with Coach and Mrs. Wells this morning. I was just comin' to get your side of things," said Daggett.

"I'm sure it happened pretty much how you heard it," Grayson said dismissively. "They sat there and blamed Drew and Alexis for their deaths. They were kids, Dale. It wasn't right, and I spoke my mind. I stand by what I said."

"Well, that may be so, but I gotta talk to ya all the same," Daggett replied, inching carefully closer to Grayson's desk. "Look, you're still kinda new here. I know things here seem pretty strange, but it's how it is."

"With all due respect, sir, that's bullshit," Grayson objected, looking up and locking his gaze with Principal Daggett's own concerned stare. "It doesn't matter what they did. They were kids, and they didn't deserve to be mutilated."

"I understand how you feel, Grayson," Daggett said diplomatically. "Maybe we're all just so used to it we're a bit numb to it all. Now I admit that the Beast taking two kids is very unusual, but they were both seventeen, after all. Nearly adults. The Beast might not care about age like we do if it thought those kids were already behavin' like adults. All the same, this is the price we pay here to have the kind of perfect little town that we do."

Grayson shook his head. "I'll be honest, Dale. This town is fucking insane. I'm not even sure why I'm still here, except that these kids deserve to have someone here who cares about whether or not they're going to turn up dead tomorrow morning."

Principal Daggett sputtered trying to find his reply. "Now I'm not so sure that's a very fair attitude to have. Everyone here cares about these kids. We all care a lot about each other in Breakvale. Every one of us. That's why I felt I needed to come talk to you. We all gotta look out for each other."

"Well, they sure didn't seem to care much about those kids in the lounge earlier," Grayson retorted.

"They mean well, they do," Principal Daggett said. "I think maybe this all shows we need to have more compassion and understanding for each other. Them and you."

Grayson scoffed.

"Now listen, I know," Principal Daggett urged, lowering his voice. "All I mean is that maybe it'd be a good idea for you not to ruffle any feathers. We all gotta look out for each other."

"Be a team player," Grayson muttered sarcastically.

Principal Daggett smiled. "Yeah, exactly. We gotta make sure we can all work together. You wanna protect these kids? So do I. And the best way to do that is to make sure we can all get along and work together."

Grayson buried his face in his hands and let out a heavy sigh. "Alright, look, I'm not going to apologize. I meant what I said.

But I will try very, very hard to maintain a positive relationship with them going forward."

"That's the spirit!" Principal Daggett cheered, taking a relaxed step backward. "You don't have to go say you're sorry or nothin'. But maybe just write 'em a little note or somethin' burying the hatchet. You're the English teacher, right? I'm sure you can write something that sounds... I dunno, like an olive branch or something."

"Yeah, sure I can do that," Grayson relented.

"Good stuff. Glad to hear it. I knew we made a good choice bringing you on board," Principal Daggett said. "Listen, I gotta get home to the old lady. I expect I'll see you at the vigil tonight?"

"Yeah, I'll be there."

"Alrighty. I'll see ya there."

Grayson sat alone at his desk for a moment. Sure, I'll write them a note. Tell them they can kiss my ass, he thought.

***

Grayson was thoroughly unprepared to pay a visit to the church for the candlelight vigil. Ever since his strange and awkward visit from Pastor Arthur, he had managed to avoid him and the church all together. In a town where everyone treated truth like a religion and the Beast like some kind of supernatural peacekeeper, the thought of listening to a sermon seemed entirely unpleasant. Under the circumstances, however, he knew that this was one instance where he could not avoid it.

The First Baptist Church of Breakvale sat on the northeastern outskirts of town, so near the power plant that its towering smokestacks cast a long shadow across the church grounds in the setting sun. Grayson arrived ten minutes early, only to find that he was already late. The small parking lot was filled to capacity, and many more vehicles were lined up in neat rows on the grass. Hundreds of people were gathered on the lawn in front of the church building. He found a place to park in the grass at the end of a row near what looked like an old well house, then joined in at the back of the crowd as candles were being passed around and lit. A man and woman that Grayson didn't recognize offered him a candle and lit it for him. The people in the crowd spoke to one another in quiet voices. Some were crying, others were laughing at what he hoped were fond memories.

At seven o'clock sharp, the pastor ascended the steps of the church and stood in front of its two massive wooden doors. He was dressed in a gray three-piece suit and had combed his wispy, silver hair down neatly. He was followed by a man that Grayson recognized as Ross McCrory, the associate pastor, who stood on the next step down. The pastor raised both hands to hush the crowd, which instantly fell silent.

"Brothers and sisters of Breakvale, I thank you for coming tonight to honor the memory of our two lost lambs, who have been called home to be with our Lord God in eternal peace. Andrew and Alexis were both members of this congregation since birth. Their parents are here with us tonight. Will you please come up?" he urged, gesturing toward the steps in front of him. The two sets of parents, each struggling to contain their emotions, stepped up and in front of the crowd. "When one member of our congregation hurts, we all hurt, and tonight our hearts ache for you. While their loss will be felt deeply and painfully for the rest of our lives, we may rejoice in the knowledge that we shall be reunited with them once more in the kingdom of God. As your family aches, please know that all of these people gathered here tonight open their arms and hearts to you. You may step back down now."

As Drew and Alexis's parents returned to the crowd, one of the mothers burst into hysterical tears, though Grayson couldn't see who it was. Pastor Arthur seemed unfazed by the display of emotion and continued on.

"As you all know, our way of life in Breakvale is unique, and the values we hold above all others, truth and honesty, are fundamental to this way of life. The tragic loss of two of our children reminds us that these values must remain at the core of who we are and how we serve others. Secrets can be disastrous things in any community, but here in our own, they carry a tremendous price. Each year, we are reminded of that price, but this year, the cost feels particularly steep. But to live in paradise, sometimes sacrifices must be made. The Carter and McIntosh families have paid that price for us this year. Remember this and keep them in your hearts and in your prayers as you tuck your own children into bed each night. God bless us all, and may the Lord guide us in all we do. Truth is Life."

"Truth is Life," the crowd echoed back.

A woman from the crowd stepped up to Ross and whispered something in his ear. He, in turn, approached Pastor Arthur with the message. Pastor Arthur nodded his head.

"I understand that our esteemed mayor is here with us tonight and would like to make an announcement. Mayor Wallace, the platform is yours," said Arthur, stepping down next to Ross.

A tall man in business attire emerged from the crowd. Grayson realized that he had yet to meet the mayor of Breakvale. The man appeared to be about the same age as Pastor Arthur, though he had a heavier build, a full head of dark brown hair, and thick facial hair. He waved briefly to the crowd before fixing himself to the spot where the pastor had stood.

"Good evening, everyone. As your mayor, I want to express my absolute condolences to the families mourning tonight from this terrible tragedy. As Pastor Arthur said, it's up to each one of us to ensure that we're living truthful and honest lives every day. Breakvale is a small place, and a loss like this affects us all. Every year we must cope with loss, and if I'm being honest, it never gets any easier. Like the good pastor also said, it's the price we pay to live in such a wonderful place. Nowhere else in the world is there a town as peaceful, or happy, as ours. Where there is no crime, and everyone cares for one another like family. The foundation of this happiness is our core tenement. I know many of you are concerned by the sudden deviation from years past. After all, it's always been adults before. Never our children. Now, Drew and Alexis were both approaching adulthood, that's true, but as your mayor, I share your concern, and don't want another one of our children to pay the price for our security. That's why I have decided to implement a seven o'clock curfew for all children, until such a time as we have an opportunity to understand why two children were chosen. Parents, your children should be at home by seven o'clock every night unless accompanied by an adult. Consider this a fresh opportunity to spend time with your children, to ensure their homework is tended to, and that they are safe under your guardianship. To the Carter and McIntosh families, I am so sorry for your loss. I will do everything in my power to ensure this does not happen again. Truth is Life!"

"Truth is Life," echoed the crowd.

The mayor stepped down and back into the crowd. Pastor Arthur stepped back up to deliver a sermon. Grayson noticed

Ross's eyes scanning the crowd, and their gazes locked for a moment. There was something in Ross's expression that suggested he was uncomfortable, though Grayson wasn't sure why. He nodded at Ross, offering a hello and acknowledging his stare. As quickly as it happened, Ross turned his head away and fixed his gaze back on the pastor. *Strange*, Grayson thought, *but no surprise*. Ross seemed the sheepish type who would be embarrassed by accidentally making eye contact with someone.

Grayson lingered for only a few minutes more before he finally couldn't listen to the pastor drone on with biblical recitations anymore and decided to quietly leave. On the drive home, he realized that he had not seen Roxanne in attendance, though perhaps she wasn't able to find coverage for her to leave the bar, since basically the entire town was already at the vigil.

The more that Grayson reflected on the speeches that both the pastor and the mayor gave, the more unsettled he felt. It wasn't necessarily the content of the speeches that made him uneasy, but the crowd's complicity in it. He knew that the people of Breakvale believed strongly in the Beast, but he had never seen the strength of that faith in such numbers before, and it steeled his resolve to figure out the truth behind why two children were dead because of it.

7

Two months had passed since the Homecoming incident, and the town of Breakvale seemed to return to its normal routine. Grayson had become so preoccupied with helping his students deal with the emotional trauma of losing two classmates and having to prepare his students for their mid-term exams, that it left him with little time to dive deeper into the mystery of the Beast. No one in Breakvale had reported seeing the creature, and there was an optimistic attitude around town that it wouldn't return for quite some time. The mayor's curfew had taken effect in that time as well, and since almost everyone had respected it, and with no reported sightings of the Beast, the curfew was declared a success at keeping the children safe. He had heard a rumor from Roxanne that the mayor was considering making the curfew permanent; and though he had privately questioned whether something as simple as a curfew had actually prevented the Beast from attacking more children, without more substantial evidence, Grayson reasoned that it certainly couldn't hurt to keep it in place a while longer.

Grayson had also heard from Roxanne that the official investigation into Drew and Alexis's death had essentially been halted. There were no witnesses and no new leads, and since the community had seemingly made up its collective mind that the Beast was responsible for the attacks, Chief Danbury was forced to render the case inactive. It seemed to Grayson that it was easier for the people of Breakvale to forget the entire atrocity than to try to explain it rationally. He was unhappy with the chief's decision to close the investigation, but took some small consolation in having completed mid-terms with his students, and was entirely elated to be on winter break. He finally had an opportunity to do absolutely nothing except relax at home and restore his physical and emotional well-being.

On this particular Friday night, Grayson decided that meant spending the weekend at home lounging on the couch in his boxers and a t-shirt and binge-watching Law & Order. He was partially into his eighth episode when there came a knock at the door. He got up and looked out the little peephole. It was Ross McCrory. Grayson chuckled as he opened the door.

Ross's eyes widened at the sight of Grayson in his underwear and his face flushed red with embarrassment. He quickly averted his gaze.

"It's just underwear, Mr. McCrory," Grayson said with an ornery smirk. In that moment, he took a rather perverse delight in making Ross McCrory uncomfortable. "I wasn't expecting company. What can I do for you?

Ross sputtered for a moment before becoming coherent. "I was hoping to talk to you about…I mean, do you mind if…umm. I'm sorry, could you, uh, could you put on pants please?

"They're basically shorts. Do you want to come in, Mr. McCrory?" Grayson asked.

Ross nodded slowly, still looking away. "Yes, please, I...I was hoping to talk to you about something."

Grayson opened the door wide and motioned for him to enter. "I'll go put on pants. Give me a sec. Make yourself comfortable."

He disappeared into his bedroom. Ross perched uncomfortably on the edge of the couch, looking around at the sparsely decorated living room and nervously fidgeting with a button on his jacket, until Grayson returned wearing jeans and a hoodie.

"Better?" he asked.

Ross nodded again. "Thank you. I'm sorry. I…I know this is your home and you can wear whatever you want, I just wasn't…"

"No need to explain," Grayson waved dismissively. "What is it you want to talk about?"

He took a seat at the opposite end of the couch, slouching comfortably into its cushions. Ross appeared contemplative for a moment before speaking, though he felt fairly certain he already knew what Ross was going to say next.

"Mr. Ender, I know you're not from around here. There's not an easy way for me to ask this. It's just…you've seen things and lived things that people here in Breakvale aren't really used to. I mean, I don't know, I've just heard some rumors. You know what they say about rumors…anyway, I was just wondering if it was true. If you were, you know…"

"If I was what?" Grayson asked, narrowing his eyes.

"If you were...I mean, are you...?" Ross trailed off as he struggled to bring himself to say the words. He sprang up from his seat. "I'm sorry. I shouldn't have come and bothered you like this."

Ross started toward the door, but Grayson jumped up after him. "Now wait a minute! You came here with some kind of purpose. Come sit back down," he demanded.

Ross awkwardly returned to his seat.

"Now. Am I what?" Grayson asked more forcefully.

"Gay?" Ross whispered softly.

"Am I gay?" Grayson chuckled. "Why was that so hard for you to ask?"

"Well, it's not really any of my business. I just...I heard stuff, like I said. People talking," Ross tried to explain.

"Who? Who's been talking? Where did you hear that?"

Ross looked visibly uncomfortable. For a moment, his mouth hung open wide as his mind did somersaults trying to figure out his response.

"Look, I'm gonna save you some trouble. Yes, I'm gay. But it really isn't anyone's business but my own," Grayson stated. "I'm sure someone around town's figured it out by now. But what I need you to understand is that I'm here to teach, and I don't need a bunch of religious nutjobs, no offense, chasing me out of town like I'm Frankenstein's monster."

Ross nodded feverishly. "No, of course not. We're all very glad you're here. It's just that I needed to know if the rumors were true."

"Well, they're true," Grayson responded. "But now you have to do something for me. I need you to keep that information to yourself. You're bound by some kind of religious confidentiality thing, right?"

Ross gave a faint, nervous chuckle. "I'm not like a priest or anything. Oh! But yes, of course, I promise I won't breathe a word of it to anyone."

"I know you won't," he said casually. "I think the guilt would eat you alive."

An extremely awkward silence fell over them.

"Was that it? That's all you wanted to know?" Grayson asked at last.

"I'm sorry. I feel like this was really inappropriate of me to barge in on you like this and make you uncomfortable in your home," Ross apologized.

"You're fine. I'm not uncomfortable. Besides, I wasn't doing anything except watching television."

Ross stood up again. "Thank you, Mr. Ender. I'll leave now so you can get back to your evening. And I promise I won't tell a soul."

"I know. I trust you," Grayson said.

Ross opened the door and took a hurried pace toward his car. Grayson watched as he jumped in his sedan and pulled away. When the taillights had disappeared around the corner, he closed the door and locked it.

"Oh boy," he muttered. "That poor guy's in for it."

He sat back down on the couch and resumed watching his show. Despite the sudden excitement of Ross's visit, it didn't long for him to get too cozy on the couch under his favorite blanket and accidentally slip off to sleep.

He'd only been asleep for a few minutes when the power went out in his house, pitching the living room into total darkness. As he slept there unaware on the couch, six inky black tendrils emerged from the ceiling above Grayson's head and oozed slowly down toward his face. The tendrils coiled around his face and body, until they completely enveloped him. The crimson eyes of the Beast glinted in the darkness as they appeared from somewhere in the void of its mass, before falling in line with Grayson's own eyes and sinking beneath his eyelids.

Grayson walked hand-in-hand with someone through a thickly wooded hillside. A waxing moon floated high in the sky, obscured by a thick cloud bank that scattered the light and left the pair in nearly complete darkness. He eagerly pulled the person further along up the hillside, weaving them through the trees until he felt like he'd found the place where he should stop. He looked behind him at the person whose hand he had been holding. It was Alexis.

"Drew, it's freezing out here," she complained. "Why are we all the way up here?"

Grayson didn't pause at the mention of the name and instead took off the blazer he was wearing and draped it around Alexis's shoulders. He rubbed her arms in an attempt to warm her, then sat down in a pile of leaves. The moon peaked out from behind the clouds, casting a pale light across her face and causing her homecoming dress to glimmer ever-so-slightly.

"I'm not very good at this kinda stuff," he heard himself saying, though not understanding the words. "But I know it's been kinda hard on you. The sex, I mean. Like, with your emotions and stuff. I love you, Alexis. I wanna make you feel better. So…how?"

Alexis sank down next to him and began to cry.

"Oh. Hey, hey, hey. What's wrong?" he asked, hesitating to touch her.

She sobbed quietly for a few moments, before finally managing to choke out the words, "I'm pregnant."

Grayson sat back, temporarily stunned at the news. He leaned in and at last put his arms around her. "Are you sure?" he asked.

"Yes. I've taken the test three times. I just don't understand how. We used condoms. I just…I don't know what to do," she sobbed.

Grayson felt himself lean in closely to her face and reach up to wipe the tears out of her eyes. "Hey, it's gonna be okay. We'll figure it out. My parents will help, and I'll get a job, and we can get married and find a place—"

"We're too young for this Andrew!" she barked. "Don't you understand? I don't wanna be married. I want to go to college. I wanna leave this stupid fucking town and never look back."

Grayson recoiled at the attack and took a deep breath. He felt hurt and confused at the sudden rejection.

"What are you saying?" he said finally.

"I don't know! I don't know, Drew. It's just…it's all wrong and I don't know what to do."

A sudden, loud, popping noise echoed through the trees, like the breaking of twigs underfoot. Grayson and Alexis both looked up and around. For a moment, everything was still, and then they heard the crunching leaves. Grayson stood up automatically.

"Drew—"

"Shhh," he whispered to her. "Stay there."

He pulled out his phone and triggered the flashlight, then took a few steps forward in the direction of the sound.

"Hello? Is someone there?" he called out.

He held his phone up high to cast a wide beam but didn't see anything. He walked a little further, looking around and behind some of the trees and downed logs. A raccoon suddenly sprang out from behind a log and skittered up a nearby tree. He exhaled a breath of relief.

"It's just a fucking raccoon," he called back to Alexis. "Alexis, it's just a raccoon."

All at once everything went dark. Grayson blinked his eyes, and suddenly, he was standing next to Alexis's body. She lay motionless on the ground with her eyes closed. He could feel something in his left hand, but he couldn't make his head turn to see what it was. With his right hand, he bent down and picked up a large rock without ever taking his eyes off of Drew.

He watched Drew turn back around and call out for Alexis, but there was no answer. He heard him screaming out for her but knew there would be no answer. Grayson felt a rush of adrenaline swell up inside of him. His heart began to beat rapidly. He quietly circled around Drew, stalking him in his footsteps. He stayed low to the ground as he watched Drew spin around, flashing his light in every direction until he stopped with his back to Grayson.

This was his moment. A low, excited, animalistic growl reverberated in his chest until he couldn't hold it back anymore. Grayson sprang up from his hiding spot, swung the rock with intense ferocity and struck Drew on the back of his head, causing him to collapse into the pile of leaves at Grayson's feet.

Grayson shot straight up. He was drenched in a cold sweat. He looked around the room, trying to discern if he was still dreaming or if he had woken from his nightmare. He was still on the couch. He pulled his phone from his pocket and clicked it on. It was almost nine in the morning; he had slept for nearly ten hours, but felt dizzy and slightly ill, and as if he hadn't slept at all. He felt the sickness bubble up inside his stomach, and he dashed into his bathroom. He slammed the toilet seat up and hurled into the bowl. After two more strong waves of nausea, he finally felt his skin cool and his stomach settle. He stood up, flushed the toilet, and then stumbled into the kitchen to pour himself a glass of water.

He shuffled into the living room, eased down onto the couch, and clicked on the television. He lay there, unable to think about anything except the nightmare, until he eventually drifted back to sleep.

***

"I'm telling you, it was unlike any dream I've ever had before," Grayson insisted, sipping his cup of coffee while seated in his usual spot at the end of the bar. "The details…everything felt so precise."

It was late in the afternoon of that same day, and Grayson decided that he couldn't keep the details of the nightmare to himself. After his rough awakening, he managed to sleep peacefully for a few hours before going to Roxanne's bar to discuss his troubling dream with her. After losing the contents of his stomach, he felt a ravishing hunger and ordered "The Best Damn Steak in Breakvale," as it was listed on the menu, and which was apparently sourced from the local butcher.

"Did the medical examiner indicate whether she was pregnant or not? Did Deputy Thorne mention it?" Grayson asked.

Roxanne shook her head. "No, and it makes everything more horrible if it's true. It could be the reason they were attacked. So that's what you think you saw? Them getting attacked?"

"Kind of…I think so? Like, at first, I was Drew. I was seeing everything from his perspective. And then suddenly I wasn't. Somehow, it switched, and then I was looking down at Alexis's body and was stalking Drew like some kind of animal."

"Like a predator," Roxanne added.

"Yeah. Exactly. But I couldn't see myself, or whatever I was. I couldn't control my own body. Like, I was consciously aware that what I was seeing and doing wasn't me, but I couldn't do anything different. It was like being inside a movie or being locked into a roller coaster ride that I couldn't get off of. I don't know if that makes any sense at all."

Roxanne pursed her lips and thought a moment before speaking. “I suppose it does. Kind of like an out-of-body experience, right?” she suggested.

Grayson nodded over his coffee cup. “Exactly.”

A bell dinged in the window behind Roxanne and she spun around to grab the plate, which she plopped down in front of Grayson. The smell of the steak made his stomach grumble in anticipation, and he wasted no time cutting into it as he continued to talk over bites of steak.

“I suppose it’s possible you saw their murders,” Roxanne posited. “Maybe you have some kind of latent psychic power that was triggered when the Beast attacked you. I mean, you were in its thrall for a really long time.”

“I don’t know about psychic powers, but maybe I was seeing things from the Beast’s perspective?” Grayson pondered. “But if that were the case, why was I in its body and Drew’s body? How could it have known his perspective?”

“I dunno. I mean, we don’t really know much about this thing. But we do know it has a way of getting into a person’s head,” Roxanne contended. “Maybe it somehow extracted Drew’s memory before killing him, and you saw flashes of both?”

“Maybe…” Grayson said, chewing a mouthful of steak. “But, like, why now? That happened months ago. Why would I suddenly be seeing all of this now? I haven’t had any contact with the Beast since the first time here in the diner.”

Roxanne leaned against the bar and spoke more quietly. “Listen, I’ve got some books upstairs that belonged to my dad, and I think one or two of them deal with old legends and stuff. It’s been a while since I’ve even looked at them. But maybe we *should* take a look at ’em? See if we can find some answers?”

"That's a great idea. It's a starting point," Grayson said. "We should also see if the library has any books or records on it. Maybe old newspaper articles or something?"

Roxanne nodded. "Good thinking. When do we do this?"

"The library is open again on Monday?" Grayson suggested. "Can you escape the bar for a little while in the afternoon?"

Roxanne turned and leaned into the kitchen window.

"Hey Keith!" she shouted. "You're running the show Monday afternoon. I got some business down at the library."

"You got it, boss!" Keith shouted over his radio from somewhere in the back.

Roxanne turned back around with a subtle grin. "Sometimes it's good to be the boss."

There was a small break in conversation while Grayson finished up his food and Roxanne took some drink orders. When she circled around to clear his dishes, he stopped her.

"A while back, you said you'd only been visited by the Beast once before and that that was unusual. Why is that?" he asked.

"Why is it unusual? Or why just once?" she fired back.

"Both, I suppose?" Grayson said.

She sat the dishes up in the window and turned back to him. "I don't have anything to hide. The Beast came once and did to me what it did to you. But since then, I've lived my life like an open book. Guess I don't have any juicy secrets for it to suck on."

"But others do, that's what you're saying?"

"Absolutely. This whole town's motto, Truth is Life, it's a load of bullshit. Everyone in this town has secrets. People here like to pretend that they're perfect or pious, but they've all got shit swept under the rug," she shrugged.

"Like who?"

"Take Officer Stanley for instance. He has a big online gambling problem. Joe McEnroe, the guy who owns the feed store, is addicted to pornography. Sue Henson, she's got a pill problem. And everyone but Mr. and Mrs. Beall seems to know that they are cheating on each other. Word gets around town. Especially in the town's only bar. I'm telling you, I hear it all." Roxanne said with a wink.

"Huh. How long ago was it when the Beast visited you? And what did you reveal to it?" Grayson inquired.

Roxanne gave a heavy sigh, then called the waitress over behind the bar. "Hey Kay, watch the bar for me, will ya?"

Roxanne motioned for Grayson to follow her and they took a seat at a table in the corner.

"So, here's a thing you don't know about me," she began. "I used to be something of a wild child. Growing up in Breakvale isn't so bad, but as a teen, I hated it here. I couldn't wait to get out. But as I'm sure you've probably figured out, this town has a funny way of keeping people around. I got pretty restless and mixed up in some bad stuff. Not really much for a rebellious kid to do around here except drink and make friends with the wrong crowd. The drinking and the partying eventually led to drugs. I did make it out of Breakvale, for a while. Traveled the state, hitch-hiking mostly, scoring whenever I could and sleeping with anyone for just about anything."

"Oh. Oh boy," Grayson murmured.

"Yeah, oh boy. I'm not proud of it, but it's a part of me," Roxanne acknowledged.

"And that was the secret that the Beast wanted from you? That you were doing drugs?" Grayson speculated.

"Oh no," Roxanne laughed. "That was no secret. Everyone in Breakvale knew about Old Man Dawes's miscreant daughter. I caused my dad a lot of grief and heartache back then."

"What about your mom?" Grayson asked.

"She died when I was ten. A horse she was riding got spooked and threw her off. Broke her neck. Killed her pretty much on impact," Roxanne said, looking down at her hands.

"I'm sorry," Grayson said, feeling guilty now for asking.

"It's alright. It was a long time ago," Roxanne looked back up at Grayson. "Anyway, I finally overdosed one night and ended up in the hospital. They managed to track down my dad. He came up and brought me home. Made me sober up. Well, he tried anyway."

"What happened?"

"That's where the Beast comes in," Roxanne started. "I was sitting down here, at this very table actually, and it slithered up out of the ground like it does. It made me confess how I really felt. That I was guilty of being a huge disappointment to everyone, that I was ashamed of myself. Of my behavior. And that I blamed my dad for my mom's death. He kept pushing her to learn how to ride. She was so afraid of it, but he wanted to ride together. Anyway, I had been holding on to that anger and resentment for so long that after it all finally came spewing out, I was numb. But my dad never gave up on me, and eventually, we rebuilt our relationship."

"Oh wow," Grayson said. He thought for a moment. "So, in a weird kind of way, the Beast actually changed your life, like, for the better."

"It was terrifying and so painful at first. But yeah, it kind of did," Roxanne nodded. "We had some good years together before he passed away."

"May I ask how?"

"Pancreatic cancer. He was a tough old bird. Never complained about pain. By the time we knew anything was wrong, it was too late," Roxanne said, looking down at her hands again.

"Gosh," Grayson said. He reached out and put his hand on hers. "I'm really sorry."

She placed her other hand on top of his, then looked back up at him and smiled. "It's okay. I made my peace with it. He knew I loved him. And I know he loved me. That's as much as I could've asked for. But when he died, he left everything he owned to me, including this bar. So now I run it in his memory. You see that picture," Roxanne pointed to a small 8x10 photo hung on the wall at the opposite end of the bar. "That's him. I put that there so we can see each other every day, and so he can keep an eye on things still."

Roxanne winked at Grayson. They smiled back at one another and simply enjoyed the warmness of the moment without saying anything else.

The bell above the door rang suddenly, and Roxanne looked up to greet the incoming customer. Grayson noted the surprised look on her face and turned around to see Pastor Arthur standing in the doorway, surveying the room.

"Oh, this oughta be good," Roxanne whispered.

When he spotted Grayson and Roxanne, Pastor Arthur made his way over to their table.

"Mr. Ender. Ms. Dawes," he greeted, acknowledging both of them with a tip of his hat. "A member of the congregation spent the better part of ten minutes extolling the virtues of your establishment's pot roast. As I was in the neighborhood, I thought I might stop in and order some to go."

Roxanne laughed. “You're kidding? All this time I've owned the bar and you've never once set foot inside. Now, all of a sudden, you finally come in, and it’s for the pot roast?” she teased. “You don’t have to take it to go, you know. We’ve got plenty of tables to eat at.”

“I’m afraid if I stay any longer, I’ll miss my evening programming,” he replied. “I’d sure like to know what it would take to finally convince you to come visit me on Sundays, Ms. Dawes.”

“Ah, pastor, you know I give my crew Sundays off to be with their families, so they can go to church. If I leave, who’s gonna run this bar, huh?”

“Of course, of course,” he said with a tiny smile. He turned to look at Grayson. “And how about you, Mr. Ender? I saw you at the candlelight vigil. You kept your word that you would come to church if it was for your students. I'd like to hope that what you heard might change your mind about me. Perhaps we can even say it’s water under the bridge, and I could convince you to come at least once.”

Grayson gave a nervous chuckle. “Sundays are my day of rest, I’m afraid. After teaching a bunch of teenagers all week, my rest days are important.”

“What could be more restful than to hear the Word of the Lord in His house? It is cleansing for the mind and the spirit,” Pastor Arthur extolled. “It really would be good to see you. Tomorrow, perhaps? Since the kids are all on Christmas break. Surely you have had several days of rest already?”

Grayson groaned internally. He had just let the pastor back him into a corner on this one.

"You got me there, pastor. You're right, of course. I suppose one Sunday couldn't hurt. For the kids," Grayson reluctantly surrendered.

"Delightful! Very delightful," Pastor Arthur exclaimed, clapping his hands together enthusiastically. "Nine o'clock in the morning, Mr. Ender. I'll look forward to seeing you there. Now, I really should be getting on my way. From whom do I order?"

Roxanne pointed to the waitress at the bar. "She can take your order right over there at the bar."

"Truth is Life," Pastor Arthur said. He tipped his hat once more, then stepped over to the bar to order his food.

"Fuck. I guess I should be going as well," Grayson grumbled as he stood up from the table. "It seems I now have an early morning ahead of me."

Roxanne smirked. "You have to be careful with that one. He's old, but he's sharp. Sometime later you'll have to tell me what the water under the bridge is."

"With pleasure. It's a story," Grayson rolled his eyes. He stepped around the table and hugged Roxanne. "Thank you for sharing all this with me tonight. I'll see you on Monday, yeah? Two o'clock, after the lunch rush?"

"Sounds good," she affirmed.

Roxanne stepped over to the bar to continue entertaining Pastor Arthur as Grayson slipped out the door and headed home feeling completely duped.

8

Grayson slept on the couch again and woke up early with a stiff back from the uncomfortable position he ended up in for most of the night. He spoke briefly on the phone with his parents as he made himself ready, both mentally and physically, to attend the church service. His parents were taking a small vacation in Nashville and seemed to be having a very good time. He hung up the phone and, for a moment, remembered the times when he and his parents would go to Nashville together. It had been so long since the last time they'd visited Nashville together that his memory of the city seemed faded and distant. Then again, so many memories of his life before Breakvale felt that way. With a resigned sigh, he grabbed up his Jeep keys and forced himself out the door.

As he expected, the parking lot was packed for the morning service. Grayson managed to find an open spot in the very back corner of the lot and walked the distance to the church building. He approached the front steps of the old church and was greeted by several friendly smiles from other churchgoers. As he got closer to the entrance, he noticed something that he had not noticed in the darkness during the vigil: several strange symbols above the heavy wooden doors. They weren't characters that he was familiar with; they almost resembled glyphs of some kind carved into the wooden paneling above the doors. He stood in his spot for a moment looking up at the symbols, until the sound of Pastor Arthur's voice yanked him from his thoughts.

"Grayson, my child!" he bellowed from the top step. "I'm very glad to see you've come."

Grayson approached him and shook his hand. "You were quite persuasive."

He smiled and turned to Ross, who had been standing quietly beside him. "You remember my associate pastor, Mr. McCrory?"

"I do," Grayson said, trying to conceal a smirk. He extended his hand for Ross to shake. "How are you, Mr. McCrory?"

Ross shook his hand with surprising firmness. "I'm good thanks. It's nice to see you here."

Pastor Arthur motioned for Grayson to enter the church as he continued shaking hands and greeting more church members as they arrived. Grayson crossed the threshold into the church and was immediately flooded with memories of church from his youth. The sight of the pews, with the velvet red cushions, and the light flooding in from the enormous windowpanes—all of it reminded him of being ten years old, sitting in the pew next to his parents, bored to tears and just wishing for the time to go by quickly so he could play on his teal Game Boy Color. The church somehow even smelled the same, like dust collected in the velvet cushions and the old Bibles stashed in wooden pockets on the backs of the pews, and then something else—rosewater, maybe—effervescing from some of the women in the congregation.

He took a seat near the back, more out of necessity than choice, as the pews toward the front were already crowded. Several more minutes passed before Pastor Arthur and Ross McCrory proceeded up the aisle. Pastor Arthur took his station at the pulpit and Ross sat in a seat off to his left. From where

Grayson was sitting, he could see Ross very clearly, and the two made eye contact several times. Each time they locked eyes, Ross would quickly glance away. The cat-and-mouse game endlessly delighted Grayson and proved to be a form of entertainment during an otherwise dull sermon. He had already decided that he had little interest in attempting to listen to Pastor Arthur's pontificating. Instead, he stared out the window, watching the wind rustle the tops of the trees along the hillside. He could see part of the power plant at the top of the hill, with its tall stacks gently puffing out clouds of vapor. Rays of sun permeated the church windows, warming the velvet fabric of the pews, and warmed Grayson, too. Pastor Arthur droned on about something in Corinthians, but Grayson couldn't focus on it. He felt like a fat house cat basking in a bay window. His eyelids drooped heavily down, and before he could even try to fight it, he felt them shut firmly.

Grayson's eyes snapped back open. He was in his apartment. It was dark outside, and all the lights were off. Despite the pitch-black rooms, he walked confidently through the house. Something propelled him through the living room and down the hallway until he stopped at his bedroom door. As if on command, his bedroom door swung open. He could see someone lying in his bed, covered to the neck with the comforter and head buried in the pillows. He wondered why someone would be sleeping in his bed. He moved forward into the bedroom. A familiar exhilaration began to stir inside of him. He felt a rush of adrenaline. He'd felt that rush before. He felt vicious and powerful. He glided silently to the bedside and ripped the covers back. A woman lay there in his bed. She woke at the sudden disturbance, then screamed as she witnessed Grayson standing beside her in the darkness.

Grayson's eyes snapped back open again. He came to while screaming, just as the woman had been screaming. He was back in the church. Pastor Arthur stopped his sermon as the entire congregation turned to look at him. Feeling foggy and embarrassed, Grayson stood up and apologized for the disturbance. He scooped up his jacket and hurried out the door.

"Maybe he felt the Holy Ghost," Arthur joked, and the congregation chuckled. Seemingly unconcerned, they returned their attention in unison to Pastor Arthur.

Grayson spent the remainder of the day at home. He was certain he had received another dream vision like before. The emotions he felt in this dream were consistent with how he felt in his previous dream about Drew and Alexis, though this time he didn't attack the woman in her bed. He wondered if he simply had woken up before he could attack her, or if an attack even took place. He struggled with the larger looming question of why he was suddenly receiving these flashes of memory in his dreams. He attempted to re-trace the path he took in his dream. Apart from a few decorations, everything looked precisely the same, leaving Grayson with another clue to suggest that his home had been Emily's home before she disappeared. He knew from Roxanne that the school had set her up in The Sparrows, so it wasn't unrealistic to think that the property manager would simply put him in her empty unit. Perhaps, he thought, seeing the Beast in her room startled her enough to make her flee Breakvale and disappear once and for all.

Grayson stood in his bedroom, lurking over his bed trying to recapture the feeling of his dream, when he heard a rapid, urgent knocking at his front door. Who the hell could that be this late? he thought. The banging continued as he sprinted to the door to answer it. No sooner than he opened the door, Ross McCrory sprang through the entryway. He grabbed Grayson by the face and kissed him.

Grayson took a step backward in shock.

"*Get inside*!" Grayson demanded, closing the door behind him. "What the *fuck* was that?"

Ross's face was pale, and for a moment all he could do was stammer. When he collected himself, he finally was able to explain.

"The Beast. It…it came to me. While I was at home. It made me say stuff, made me realize stuff, that I didn't…I couldn't…um, I'm sorry. I'm not making a lot of sense."

Grayson motioned for Ross to sit down on the couch.

"Okay, wait, so the Beast did that thing it does and made you confess…confess that you have some kind of crush on me?" Grayson prompted, attempting to clarify.

Ross nodded, his pallid face spotting red in his cheeks.

"I see. Well. Honestly, this is only kind of a surprise. I had a sneaking suspicion…"

"I'm sorry. It's stupid, I know. I just…I am really, really confused right now, and I don't know what to do. I can't talk to anyone. John wouldn't understand. He would say it's wrong. I know it's wrong—"

"No, now wait a minute. It's not wrong. What the hell do you mean it's wrong? Listen to me, there is nothing wrong with you." Grayson said.

"But the Bible—" Ross started.

"Fuck all that," Grayson rebuked. "Sorry, I know it's important to you. Look, we can come back to that debate later. I want to know if you're okay though. Did the Beast hurt you? Like, are you injured?"

Ross shook his head. "No, I'm fine. It didn't hurt me."

"Tell me what happened."

"Do you have anything to drink?" Ross asked suddenly.

"Um, yeah," Grayson said. "Soda, water, juice?"

"No, I mean a *drink*," Ross corrected him.

"Oh, uh, I think I have some whiskey?"

"Please!" Ross said.

Grayson chuckled and went to the kitchen and poured two glasses of whiskcy on the rocks for them. When he returned, Ross took the first one and swallowed it in a single gulp. He recoiled and made a disgusted face but took the second glass from Grayson's hand and took a smaller sip. Grayson just sat speechlessly next to him.

"I needed that," Ross said, slouching back into the couch a little and trying to relax. "I was just at home eating dinner by myself. Then it came through the wall and started talking to me. It has this really awful, scary voice. Then it kinda reached out, I guess, and touched my head, and then next thing I know, I'm just confessing these feelings about you. Like, ever since you came here, I just had this weird feeling about you. Not like bad weird, but good weird, and I didn't know what to think. Then the more I thought about it, the more I guess I realized that I liked you. But that's wrong. Well, no not wrong. But I'm not supposed to feel that way or think thoughts like that. But then the Beast just sorta ripped it all out of me. After I confessed it all I came over here because I didn't know what else to do."

"Wow. Okay. So...uh. Lots to unpack there. But I'm glad you came," Grayson said. "I want to help you however I can."

"Do you feel the same way about me?" Ross asked directly.

"Uh, well. I guess I don't. I mean, I don't really know you," Grayson replied.

Ross's expression shifted slightly, and Grayson could see that he was trying to hide his disappointment. Ross took another sip of the whiskey.

Grayson smiled, trying to look encouraging. "But, like, just because I don't know you doesn't mean I don't like you. You seem very sweet. And look, this is a lot newer for you than it is for me. You've got a crush I think, and if you've never had a crush on a guy before...well, I guess Breakvale isn't really the most accommodating for guys like us, is it?"

"No. I mean, I've never admitted something like this out loud. I don't know anyone else like you. Like us, I guess," Ross responded.

"Exactly. So don't look so crestfallen. This is a huge thing for you. I think the best thing for right now is to be a friend to you and help you through it," Grayson suggested, reaching out and putting his hand on Ross's hand in comfort.

"I could use a friend," Ross admitted, smiling slightly. He sipped down the rest of his whiskey and handed both glasses to Grayson. "Could I get another?"

Grayson laughed. "I'm coming back with two. One is for me this time."

"Yeah, sorry," Ross said, blushing a little. "Do you mind if I hang out here for a while?"

"Of course. Stay as long as you want," Grayson said.

He left and returned with two more drinks. The pair sat on the couch in the living room and talked for several hours. It became increasingly apparent that Ross had repressed his sexuality for a long time because of his personal faith and because of growing up in Breakvale, but he somehow wasn't consciously aware of it. Maybe he buried it so deeply that even the Beast couldn't detect it as a secret until he started having feelings for Grayson. Ross had a gentle, childish innocence about him, which seemed to only further shield him from himself. Grayson also discovered that Ross was a lightweight; he was completely inebriated by his fourth drink. Grayson cut him off after that, but by 1 a.m., Ross was still far too intoxicated to drive home.

He was practically falling asleep when Grayson offered him a ride home, but Ross meekly asked to spend the night, as he was still too afraid to return home alone. Grayson obliged and offered Ross his bed for the night. He helped to steady Ross as they walked into his bedroom to lay him down to sleep.

"You wanna take your shoes off?" Grayson asked.

Ross had already closed his eyes by the time his head hit the pillow. He nodded.

Grayson took his shoes off and sat them at the foot of the bed. He sat down on the empty side next to Ross. "I'm going to sleep on the couch. Wake me up if you need anything okay?"

"Stay," Ross muttered, eyes still closed. He reached out and wrapped his arms around Grayson, trying to pull him down further onto the bed.

"Ross. Ross, I don't," he began in protest. Ross pulled harder; his grip somehow iron-clad despite his intoxication. Grayson gave up on struggling. "Oh, okay. Alright. Just for a little bit."

Grayson lay there silently for a short while. When he heard Ross beginning to snore gently, he attempted to free himself from Ross's clutches but disturbed him each time. Eventually he, too, began to get comfortable and, despite every light still on in the bedroom, closed his eyes and drifted off to sleep.

Grayson's eyes snapped back open. He was in his apartment. It was dark outside, and all the lights were off. Despite the pitch-black rooms, he walked confidently through the house. Something propelled him through the living room and down the hallway until he stopped at his bedroom door. As if on command, his bedroom door swung open. He could see someone lying in his bed, covered to the neck with the comforter and head buried in the pillows. He wondered why someone would be sleeping in his bed. He moved forward into the bedroom. A familiar exhilaration began to stir inside of him. He felt a rush of adrenaline. He'd felt that rush before. He felt vicious and powerful. He glided silently to the bedside and ripped the covers back. A woman lay there in his bed. She woke at the sudden disturbance, then screamed as she witnessed Grayson standing beside her in the darkness.

Grayson felt his body lurch forward to pounce on top of her. He struck her across the face. She struggled to fight him off, thrashing under the weight of his body. He grabbed her by the wrists and pinned them to the bed. The same low-pitched growl emanated from somewhere in his throat, and it terrified her. She fought harder and screamed again. Grayson watched his hand reach out and strike her across the face once more. The woman began to cry as she twisted and writhed in the bed. He struck her several times in a row with both fists and with each punch, she fell limper until she was finally rendered unconscious. Grayson reached down to unzip his pants, ripped her underwear apart, and then assaulted the woman as she lay unconscious in her bed. He groaned and growled with each rabid thrust. He watched his hands reach up around her neck and strangle her until he finished. His conscious mind was shocked and appalled at the atrocity he had just committed, but he could also sense the immense, disgusting satisfaction that this monster felt.

Grayson felt his body drift backward up off of her. He stood over the woman, staring at her empty husk of a body. He turned around and zipped up his pants, then seemed to float into the bathroom. He turned on the water and splashed it on his face. He looked up and saw himself in the mirror. The reflection staring back at him was of his own familiar face, except that his eye sockets were black and hollow, with two small, red gleaming orbs shining through in place of his eyes. He crossed back into the bedroom, pulled Emily's body down on the floor, and began to strip the bed sheets.

His head snapped back at the sound of rustling below him. Emily had pulled herself to her knees and was searching in the dark for something. Grayson took a step backward and felt his hand reach down to his side. He withdrew a gun from a holster and fired two shots at Emily. The first bullet missed, striking the wall behind her. The second shot pierced her shoulder, and she slumped down to the ground. He stood over her, watching as her blood pooled on the carpet, waiting to see if she would move again. He knew he should feel bad, but all he could feel was power and excitement.

He rolled her body out of the way and moved the nightstand. He searched for a moment until he spotted a hole in the wall near the baseboard. He pulled out a large pocket knife and dug around in the drywall until he found the bullet lodged inside. He popped it out and slid it into his pant pocket. Grayson's arms reached out and dragged the bed over by a foot so that the frame would cover the bullet hole, then neatly placed the nightstand back next to the bed.

Grayson awoke with a jolt, covered again in the same cold sweat. The sunlight poured in from the bedroom window, but for a moment, he wasn't sure whether he was truly awake or still dreaming. The sudden commotion also woke Ross, who, after a groggy and delirious second, didn't realize where he was. The pair looked at each other, each panicking for a different reason.

"We didn't…" Ross began.

Grayson tried to regain his composure and focus. "No, no you passed out. I was going to sleep on the couch but you kind of grabbed me and wouldn't let go."

Ross turned red immediately. "I am so sorry. I don't know what I'm doing. I shouldn't be here," he panicked.

"Hey, it's all right. You're fine. Everything is fine. Nothing happened," Grayson reassured.

Ross closed his eyes for a minute and then flopped back down onto the bed. Grayson remembered suddenly that it was Monday and frantically pulled his phone from his pocket to check the time.

"Fuck. Shit. Shit. Uh, Ross, hey, I don't mean to kick you out the door, but I have to get to school. Class starts in fifteen minutes."

"Oh, oh no!" Ross said, springing back up. He tried to fumble his way around but fell back into the bed.

"Are you okay?" Grayson asked.

"I think I might still be drunk," Ross said, squinting at Grayson.

"Listen, I have to go. You stay here and sleep. When you feel better, you can leave. Just lock the door behind you. Help yourself to anything you want in the kitchen. Except maybe the whiskey," Grayson smirked.

Ross just nodded. "I think that's a good idea," he murmured. Then he quickly added, "Wait…isn't it winter break? There's no school."

Grayson stopped dead in his tracks. He realized that Ross was right, so he turned around and flopped back down on the bed. He let out a hefty sigh.

"Are you okay?" Ross asked, his eyes still tightly shut.

"I had a very crazy dream, that's all," Grayson said.

Grayson lay there for several minutes before rolling off the bed and onto the ground. He located the hole in the wall next to the bed frame. It looked exactly like the hole he dug the bullet from in his dream. He stuck his finger in the drywall and dug around, hoping maybe to find a bullet, but there was nothing there.

He heard Ross begin to snore from above him and laughed. He stood back up and shuffled into the kitchen to make some breakfast for himself and his hungover guest before his meeting later with Roxanne.

***

The Breakvale Public Library was a small, two-story brick-and-mortar building that once served as City Hall. It still maintained most of the town's public records in a separate office, including the microfiche copies of the town's now-defunct newspaper.

The two had taken up residence at a little, round table in the corner of the library behind some of the taller bookcases where they could discuss their matters privately, and Grayson spent the better part of twenty minutes recounting his dream in exact detail for Roxanne.

"The way you describe this woman...it sure does sound like Emily. That's exactly what she looked like. What the hell is going on with you?" Roxanne whispered.

"I don't know. This dream felt the same, like I was out of control of my body. But the attack was so different. It was…violent. Way more violent," Grayson recounted.

"Attack is hardly the right word, Grayson. Rape and murder, that's what it was," Roxanne corrected him.

"I feel disgusting, Roxanne. Like, I know that wasn't me, but I was still there. I could feel it. All of it. And whatever it was took sadistic fucking pleasure in it," Grayson confessed.

Roxanne took him by the hand. "No, no, you can't think like that. You can't blame yourself. That thing...it wasn't you doing that. You were only seeing it."

"I still don't know what I'm seeing, though. Is it a vision of the Beast attacking people? Is it someone else? Or both? And why me? Why all of a sudden?" Grayson said with increasing exasperation.

"I don't know. But somehow, you're seeing these things, these glimpses into people's deaths. You have a chance to make things right," urged Roxanne.

"Yeah, but how? It's not like I can go to Chief Danbury with explicit details about their deaths. I'd sound like a lunatic. Plus, I'm an outsider. He'll immediately assume I'm somehow involved. Or guilty of the crimes altogether. Remember, I was the last person to see Drew and Alexis alive," reminded Grayson.

Roxanne frowned. "I guess that's true."

"Still, it's hard to ignore the evidence that there's something more going on. These dreams, or visions, or whatever they are, keep pointing me around like some kind of nightmarish scavenger hunt. First, I found the key to my desk drawer taped inside my nightstand and evidence that Emily knew she was in danger, and now I've seen two separate attacks in vivid detail that seem to match up with reality," Grayson said.

"I wonder if the Beast accidentally created some kind of link with you when it interrogated you. Maybe it's broadcasting these visions to you and it doesn't even know it," Roxanne speculated.

"Maybe. The only way to know for sure is to keep looking for answers," Grayson said. "Speaking of which, I'd like to look through these books if you don't mind, while you comb through the old newspapers."

Roxanne withdrew two books from a bag hanging off her shoulder. She handed the two tattered books to Grayson.

"Sounds good. I'll be upstairs if you find anything," she said, then left for the microfiche lab.

Grayson placed both books in front of him. One was titled *Spirits & Legends of the Americas*, and the other *Myths & Symbols*. He began with *Spirits & Legends of the Americas*. He flipped open the hardcover and skimmed the table of contents, looking for anything relevant, but didn't see anything of immediate interest. He flipped to the back of the book to look through the appendices. Mid-way down a table of keyword terms, something caught Grayson's attention.

"Shadow beings," he whispered to himself, flipping immediately to the first page number listed.

The section that included the information on shadow beings was part of a larger chapter on something called elementals. Grayson had no idea what an elemental was. The paragraph described in detail a kind of being that seemed to fit the Beast's characteristics. It read:

"Like other ancient earth spirits, elemental shadow beings are said to appear in various shapes, including the general shape of a person, of an animal, or even amorphous forms such as a dense fog. Some may have sharp or distinct features, such as abnormally long bodies or appendages. Many people also report shadow beings as having red eyes. They are distinct from ghostly shadow beings (see Chapter 3 on page 42 for more information). Many cultures have myths describing shadow beings, though not all cultures agree on the shape or behavior of a shadow being. Some shadow beings, for example, are said to approach unsuspecting victims by sliding around on the ground or crawling across the floor toward them, while others report their ability to hover or fly. Some shadow beings are also said to appear before people in their sleep, causing sleep paralysis, night terrors, and insomnia. Still, some other cultures report that shadow beings have the power to enter the minds of unsuspecting victims and possess them or drive them to irrational madness."

Grayson bookmarked the page and continued to thumb through the book. He backed up to the beginning of the section about elementals. After forty-five minutes or so, he switched books and began to read through *Myths & Symbols*. He spent nearly another hour carefully combing through the book, looking for any information that might be relevant, but he ultimately came up empty-handed. This book was too broad and didn't seem to have any helpful information about symbols related to shadow beings or elementals, and what little information the book contained about shadow beings was already covered in more detail by the other book.

Grayson was looking at pictures of Native American symbols and sigils when Roxanne returned to the table, appearing eager to share something she had found.

"You must've found something good," Grayson said.

"Well, not exactly. Not anything definitive, but it sure is interesting," Roxanne began. "So, the newspaper records really only go back to the forties, so that's where I started. I looked through every headline and major article that I could find, just kind of keeping an eye out for anything that might seem related to the Beast."

"What did you find?"

"Nothing," Roxanne responded. "But that's just it. There was nothing written about the Beast at all. Not until this little article I found about a power plant worker who fell to his death in seventy-seven. He was up on a catwalk when he fell thirty feet and broke his neck. But get this, an anonymous eyewitness claimed to have seen a creature matching the Beast's description interacting with him while he was on the catwalk. The witness claimed that he was hiding and couldn't really see exactly what happened, but either the man jumped out of fear or was pushed over the railing by the Beast. But ever since that incident, the town paper has reported on every single instance of a death attributed to the Beast until they stopped reporting it in twenty-fourteen when the newspaper shut down."

"Holy shit!" Grayson exclaimed.

"I know! But honestly, this raises more questions than it answers," Roxanne said. "First of all, both apparent suicides and missing persons were attributed to the Beast when there was a lack of clear evidence to suggest anything else. But there are also records of some pretty brutal deaths attributed to the Beast. Not unlike what happened to Alexis and Drew. Honestly, Grayson. I grew up here. I remember some of these deaths from when I was a kid. I never read the newspaper, so I never knew they kept records like this. I can't believe I never bothered to look into this sooner."

"Well, it's like you told me, when you're here, you just kinda take this stuff for granted and don't really question it," Grayson reminded.

As Roxanne shifted in her seat, a small charm on the bracelet around her wrist flipped over. Grayson stared at it intently. He'd seen this symbol before, but he couldn't quite place it.

"Wait, Roxanne, hold on. I've seen that symbol. I just saw that symbol," he said suddenly. He reached for the copy of *Myths & Symbols* and began to thumb hurriedly through its pages until he found what he was looking for. "That bracelet. Where did you get it?"

"It was a gift from my father. He gave it to me after I got sober," Roxanne disclosed.

"Do you know what that symbol is?"

"No. Dad just said it was a charm to keep me safe. It belonged to my mom until she passed away. Ironically, she wasn't wearing it the day she was killed," Roxanne noted.

"I'm not sure it would've helped. I think that it was only meant to keep her safe from one thing," Grayson whispered. He turned the book around to reveal a symbol on the page matching the one on her charm bracelet.

"Look," Grayson pointed. "It's the same symbol."

"A symbol of protection to ward off intrusive earthly spirits," she said, quietly reading from the book.

"You said that you've only been visited by the Beast once. Did your dad give that to you after you were visited?" Grayson asked.

"Yeah, he did," Roxanne said softly. She leaned back in her chair. "I never knew. He never said."

"Maybe he was concerned that if you knew, it wouldn't work or something," Grayson suggested. "That symbol on your bracelet might be why you've never been visited again."

"Yeah, maybe," she replied slowly, lost in her memory.

Grayson also thought for a moment. "I know I've seen this symbol somewhere else before. Where was it?"

"I've never seen it anywhere else," Roxanne said. "Not that I can recall, anyway."

Grayson spent several moments trying to plunge the depths of his memory for an answer, but when at last he decided the information wasn't coming to him, he gave a defeated sigh. Then it struck him.

"The church!" he exclaimed. "There were a bunch of symbols. Roxanne. I've seen that same symbol carved above the door of the church. That's where I saw it."

Roxanne sat up in her chair. "I haven't been to that church since I was a teenager. I would never have connected the two together."

Grayson's mind began to connect dots so fast that he could barely get the words out of his mouth.

"Rox, before that was the church, it was the schoolhouse, right? It was literally the first building built in Breakvale. Remember that story you told me about your great-granddad? How he said that the original settlers here woke something up from deep inside the earth when they started mining? There's a reason your dad kept these books and gave them to you. He was on to something. Look at this!"

He grabbed up *Spirits & Legends of the Americas* and hastily flipped to the section on elemental shadow beings. He read it aloud for Roxanne, who similarly began to connect the threads of Grayson's theory.

“What if it was the Beast that they woke up?” Grayson speculated. “What if the Beast was out for revenge? Someone who knew that might have carved the symbols on the church to keep it out and keep people safe.”

Roxanne sighed. “Unfortunately, all the records from that time are completely lost or destroyed.”

“Well, we've got some more questions for sure, but Rox, this is a win! This might be the first actual evidence of what this thing is,” Grayson celebrated.

“Agreed,” Roxanne said. She opened her mouth as if to say more but stopped herself. “I’m starving honestly. Let’s go back to the bar. Keith is on the grill today. I’ll have him make us lunch.”

9

It was the day of the winter solstice, and the weather had turned frigid to herald winter's arrival. A cold front swept across the state, dumping several inches of snow on both Breakvale and Charleston, where Grayson had gone home for the holiday season. Knowing the road into Breakvale, he expected it would be several days after Christmas before he had any desire to make an attempt to return, even in his Jeep. Inclement weather always made him a nervous driver, and even after driving for more than a decade in the winters of West Virginia, he still feared sliding off the road and being stranded in a ravine, especially on the near-abandoned roads leading to Breakvale.

The Christmas season gave Grayson the opportunity to spend some much-needed time away from the murders and supernatural monsters of Breakvale and instead delight in the company of his family and old friends. Even though he had moved from Charleston only four or so months ago, it felt like a decade had passed. *Time sure does move differently when you're trying to evade the wrath of a mind-reading monster*, he thought. He even discovered a few new gray wisps of hair that had crept into his bangs and the sides of his head from the sheer stress of it all.

Returning to Charleston and seeing his friends again made Grayson realize how distant he had become; he hadn't spoken to many of his friends in months, and each conversation with them began with the same scripted apology. While his friends didn't seem to mind, it bothered him that he should have to make these apologies at all. It wasn't until he was away from Breakvale that he realized how consuming the town can be; it put it into strange perspective just how easily the residents of Breakvale can become isolated, and suddenly he understood how, even in the digital age, a place like Breakvale, with all of its strange occurrences and gruesome secrets, could go unnoticed by the wider public. Despite being in the company of old and trusted friends, Grayson felt as though he couldn't discuss the Beast or the murdered students with any of them. Even if they did believe his stories, he reasoned, it would only endanger the lives of curious or concerned visitors to Breakvale.

While this trip home was about escaping Breakvale, determined as he was not to let it occupy more of his thoughts, Grayson knew there was one final detail he needed to clear up before going back. He had agreed to visit Seth for a drink and to catch up. This was also going to be his opportunity to deny the Beast of Breakvale any more satisfaction. They sat alone together on Seth's couch, having had dinner and moved on to an evening cocktail, looking at the pictures Aaron had taken during their trip to Turkey.

"You guys look like you're having a great time," Grayson remarked as they flipped through the photos.

"We definitely did have a great time," Seth replied. "Aaron loved the architecture, so a ton of these photos are just pictures of buildings. Temples, marketplaces we went to, minarets...I think they're called?"

"What was your favorite part?" Grayson asked.

Seth gave a nervous chuckle. "Honestly? Leaving," he said. "It's not exactly my ideal place for a vacation. I spent most of the time there terrified that someone would see we were a couple and cause a scene. Never happened, thank God. But we didn't touch in public basically the whole time we were there."

There was a long silence. "Were the beaches nice at least?" Grayson asked.

"Oh, the beaches were great. So, I guess there's that," Seth said with a shrug. "I dunno. It was good. Like, it was nice spending time with him away from everything, just him and me. It was definitely a dream trip for him, and I was glad to be a part of it."

"That's nice at least," Grayson said thoughtlessly as he took a sip of his drink.

Seth looked at Grayson, and their gazes met for a moment. Grayson wagged his eyebrows as he took another sip to fill the silence.

"So, any hot guys in Breakvale?" Seth asked suddenly.

Grayson laughed. "I wish you could see just how few."

"No scruffy daddies?"

Grayson shook his head.

"Come on," Seth said, his eyes sparkling as he teased his friend. "You're telling me that in a backwoods town like that there's not at least one hot guy with a plaid shirt and a beard?"

"You're asking me if there are any hot lumberjacks, and the answer is absolutely and definitely no. Definitely none my type."

For one brief moment he imagined how Seth would react to the town of Breakvale and its strange folk. He wished he could show him. The thought of losing him to the Beast was a sobering one, though, and he shook it from his mind.

"In fact, for a long time I thought for sure that I was the only gay in the village," Grayson joked.

Seth's eyebrows perked up. "Oh?" he said curiously. "So, there is someone? Maybe?"

"Maybe," Grayson said hesitantly. "It's complicated though."

"When is it not fucking complicated?" Seth replied. "It's fucking boonies West Virginia. Let me guess...he's on the down low?"

"Yes, in a manner of speaking. I'm not even sure he's a hundred percent gay. But he's definitely not not gay. And definitely not out," Grayson replied.

"Does he live at home with his parents?" Seth asked.

Grayson realized he didn't actually know much about Ross. "Not sure, to be honest. It hasn't come up. But I don't think so."

"What's his name?" Seth asked.

"Ross."

"And why do you suspect he's gay?" Seth drilled.

Grayson paused and blushed a little as he tried to fight back a smirk. "Because he came knocking on my door late at night and kissed me in the doorway and then ended up passing out in my bed."

"Yeah, alright that's pretty good evidence," Seth nodded. "Nothing happened though?"

"God no. He's way, way too new. I'm absolutely the first person he's come out to. And I'm pretty sure I'm the first person he's kissed," Grayson speculated, sipping more on his drink. "I was not gonna be this guy's first time when he just came out to me. And also not we'd been drinking."

"Smart move," Seth nodded.

"Oh, and also he's the junior pastor for the only church in town," Grayson mumbled from behind his glass.

"He's what?" Seth screeched.

"Yeah. It's a whole thing. I actually don't even know what's going on. All I know is that he showed up a few nights ago at my door kissing me and telling me how he was all confused and stuff. Honestly, I have no idea what to do," Grayson admitted.

"Gray, I'm gonna be honest man, I know you're probably, like, super lonely down there, but this sounds like a recipe for disaster," Seth opined. He stood up and took their empty glasses to the kitchen to fix another round of drinks. From the other room, he said, "In a small town like that, just feels like it's gonna end badly."

Grayson slouched back in his seat. "Yeah, I know. You're right. But like. He's kinda cute, in this doe-eyed, terrified puppy kinda way. He's grown up in Breakvale his whole life never knowing any different and thinking he's weird or defective. Don't I owe it to him to at least help him find himself and figure stuff out?"

"Sure," Seth shouted back from the kitchen. He came sauntering back into the room with two tall drinks. "Just don't fuck and or date him. Being someone's first never ever ends well."

"We were each other's firsts," Grayson retorted.

"Yeah, and fucking look at us now," Seth said playfully.

"Fair," Grayson nodded, playing along but feeling a little stung. "We're at least still friends though."

"Because we are mature, well-adjusted gays that got lucky with supportive parents," Seth said. "All I'm saying is you're better off just coming up here to Charleston once a month to get your fix and stick to porn and shit when you're stuck in hicktown."

Crass as his point was, Grayson knew Seth was right, though it didn't exactly make him feel less ambivalent about Ross. Grayson sipped for a long moment on his drink while Seth fussed with the couch pillows around him to make himself more comfortable.

"So, you and Aaron, you guys are doing better then?" Grayson asked at last, hoping to shift the topic of conversation off his own love life.

"I guess. I mean yeah, sure. Things are good," Seth shrugged again.

"That doesn't exactly sound convincing."

Seth sighed. "It's just...I dunno. Do you ever feel—"

"Like a plastic bag? Drifting through the wind—"

"Shut the fuck up," Seth smirked, smacking him across the shoulder. "No, do you ever feel like you're just kind of doing something because it's easy or convenient? Not because it's what you want, but like, because it's safe?"

"No, honestly, not really. Seems like I never do stuff the easy way," Grayson laughed. "But I think I get what you mean. You're not happy exactly, but you're not so unhappy that you feel like something has to change."

"Yeah, I mean I guess that's it. Like, I love Aaron. But I don't know if I'm...in love with him still," Seth admitted.

"Ah yes, that old cliché," Grayson winked.

"Ugh. I know," Seth groaned, sinking down into the couch and covering his face with a pillow.

"Like, he's always gone it feels like. He works nights and I work days and we rarely have a day off together," Seth said, his voice muffled by the pillow. "We haven't even had sex in like two months. He's always tired. And I'm always tired. I'm just tired."

"Yeah, I get it," Grayson said, his face partially obstructed by his cocktail glass as he took a long, slow sip.

An inordinately long silence fell over the pair as they sat there on the couch together, Seth's face still buried in the pillow as Grayson swigged the remainder of his liquid courage. At last, he put his glass down.

"Seth, I've gotta tell you something. It's important and it doesn't mean anything but I just gotta get it off my chest. Also, this is like, kinda hard to say so I'm just gonna say it and then you can ask questions if you want," Grayson began, then took a plunging breath. "I don't think I'm really totally over you. And I'm not saying that I want to get back together or anything. We've been split up for a few years and you're with Aaron and I would never want to come between you guys, but like, I definitely still love you and have feelings for you, and I'm not quite sure what to do about it. But I don't want to keep it a secret anymore and just felt like I needed to say it."

Seth lay there in silence. After a few moments, Grayson said, "I know it's a lot to take in. Also, I'm sorry if this is, like, awkward or whatever. This isn't some ploy to like get back together or sleep with you or anything. I just wanted to be honest and tell you the truth."

When Seth gave no reply, Grayson pulled the pillow off of Seth's face to find him completely incapacitated.

"Goddammit, Seth," he huffed. He slapped him several times on the leg. "Wake the fuck up asshole."

Seth stirred and attempted to set up before slumping back down. "Did I fall asleep?" he managed to mutter.

"Yes! In the middle of me talking to you, you jerk," Grayson said.

"What did you say? Sorry man," he replied.

Grayson rolled his eyes. "Don't worry about it, nothing important. Come on, let's get you to bed."

He helped his friend up from the couch and stagger sleepily into this bedroom. Seth hugged Grayson and thanked him with a kiss on the cheek before collapsing onto the bed. Grayson's heart stirred for one restless moment, fluttering at both the kiss and the thought of lying there next to him. He considered just snuggling up with him for a momentary glimpse of what used to be. Aaron wouldn't be home for a few more hours, and he could blame it on the drinks if he needed an excuse. Grayson stood in the doorway, looking at Seth sprawled out on the bed, his figure illuminated by the light filtering in from the hallway.

Even in the darkness, Grayson could trace his physique through his clothing, and he could feel himself getting excited at the thought of seeing Seth naked again. A loud, hard snore shook Grayson from his trance, and he thought better of the desire burning in his chest. He turned around, put on his coat and shoes, and locked the door behind him, locking himself out of temptation in the process. He sat in his car for several minutes, his mind reeling from all the emotions he'd just experienced. He was thankful, at least, that the rush of adrenaline he experienced had made him feel alert enough to drive home.

***

Grayson felt the crunch of snow under his boots as he staggered out of the bar. The cold wind bristled against his cheeks and a little snow settled into his hair. Thank God, he thought, it's so fucking hot in there. From somewhere behind him, he heard his friend shouting.

"Are you sure you're okay to drive?" the voice called.

Grayson slipped on a patch of ice and nearly fell but was able to steady himself. "Yeah, I'm good," he hollered back.

The light that illuminated his path dimmed and disappeared as the door to the bar closed behind his new friend. He dug around in his coat pocket until he found his keys and fumbled with them a while in the dark until he unlocked his vehicle. He managed to hoist himself up into the cab and slammed the door on his foot. He yelped at the shock and the pain, and pushed the door back open, swinging his heavy boot into the vehicle. *Gonna feel that tomorrow*, he thought. He went to start the engine but dropped his keys. He patted across the seat in an effort to find them, then reached down to the floorboard to feel around. When at last he'd found them near the gearshift, he made two unsuccessful attempts to insert the key into the ignition. On the third, he turned the engine over, and his truck wheezed into life.

He looked up from the ignition and turned on his headlights. Ten feet in front of his truck, the Beast loomed menacingly in the headlights. It looked seven feet tall, seeming to glide across the snow-covered parking lot as it approached his truck. He felt its glowing red eyes stare at him, gleaming from within some depthless, black void. Grayson felt a sting in his neck. His breathing quickened as his heart raced from watching the Beast drift closer to the front of his truck. His vision grew blurry, and he lost control of his eyelids as they sagged involuntarily shut.

For a moment everything was pitch black. Suddenly, his body felt cold, and he felt a pain in his mouth like he'd been punched. He could feel his pulse throbbing in his face, and it burned. He could feel his eyelids and focused on them, managing to regain control of their muscle function. He struggled for a moment to pry them open until a small amount of light finally crept in and he was able to focus his blurred vision. He tried to look around but couldn't see anything more than candlelight and some flickering shadows cast upon a rock wall. Grayson tried to sit up but couldn't. He looked over at his left arm. It was strapped down to something. He looked across his chest and to his right arm. He was completely restrained. He looked up a little and tried to wriggle his body and fight against his bondage but was completely immobilized. He tried to open his mouth to scream and felt a searing pain as he tried to move his lips. He slammed his head back against the cold, hard slab, and the excruciating pain he felt made him dizzy.

A figure stepped out of the shadows and into his blurred line of sight. The figure's face was obscured by a large black hood, and Grayson could only see their chin.

"Lie still. Don't struggle," the figure said, his deep voice commanding and familiar. "And don't try to speak. You'll rip the stitches. I don't want to have to do it a second time."

Grayson attempted to scream, but all he could produce was a muffled, guttural cry that rumbled desperately in his throat. He flailed against his shackles once more, trying to pull himself free.

"Struggle all you want," the figure said. "You're only going to wear yourself out."

The figure disappeared from his sight. Grayson attempted to relax himself, trying to slow his heart rate. He looked around the room, hoping to find some answer. The walls were stone and bare. Was he underground? The only light in the room emanated from the tall, sallow candles dripping wax down long, slender spires lined up orderly against the stone walls. There was an entryway in front of him, maybe twenty feet away, with dimly lit stairs that let up somewhere. Maybe that was his exit, if he could just get free of these straps. He attempted once to shake them loose but failed. The panic welled up inside his chest again. His face hurt so badly. He could feel his breath stinging the wounds on his lips each time he exhaled from his nose. This time his vision grew blurry from the tears in his eyes as he fought the sickening pain in his face and a creeping sense that he was about to die.

Grayson tried slowing his breathing again to remedy the stinging in his lips, but his tears managed to drip into the corners of his mouth, and the salt burned his wounds worse than any pain he'd ever felt in his life. Then he heard the chanting. Like a low sing-song rumble from somewhere up the darkened staircase, he heard their voices. He tried to listen but couldn't understand what they were saying. As the chanting grew louder, he heard their footsteps against the stone staircase. There had to be several of them. He knew he had no chance. He knew he was going to die. He closed his eyes tight and began to pray quietly in his mind, not for rescue, but salvation.

Grayson kept his eyes closed and listened as he heard the chanters enter the chamber. He couldn't bring himself to open his eyes. He could feel them standing around him, surrounding him like a caged and wounded animal. They continued to chant until the same deep, commanding voice from minutes earlier rang out and brought them to a silence. He squeezed his eyes shut even tighter. Please God, don't make me suffer anymore.

Grayson opened his eyes, blinking away the darkness until he could make out his surroundings. He was in his bed at his parents' home. For a moment, he couldn't discern whether what he was seeing was real or not until, finally, he mustered the strength to sit up. His heart still pounding, he let out a long, slow sigh. It was another nightmare—or worse yet and more likely, it was another vision. He felt around his nightstand for his phone and clicked the screen on. It was 3:15 a.m. He felt sick again.

He stood up and shuffled down the hallway and into the bathroom, where he flicked on the light and sat at the toilet until the nausea passed. He flushed the toilet and crossed to the sink to wash his hands. Grayson looked up in the mirror. His body went cold. He reached up with a wet hand to touch his mouth. Across his top and bottom lips were seven faint, red spots, exactly where the stitching had been in his nightmare. He shut his eyes firmly, then opened them, trying to blink the hallucination away, but the spots remained.

"Goddammit I'm too tired for this shit," he cursed to his reflection. "I'll panic tomorrow."

He flicked off the bathroom light and stumbled back down the hall to his bedroom, where he collapsed into the bed, rolled himself up tightly in the comforter, and forced himself back to sleep.

It was noon by the time Grayson roused himself again. The sunlight beat through the window curtains, which he had deliberately drawn closed to avoid being woken prematurely; he needed the rest, even if it meant sleeping in and making life harder for himself when school was back in session. That was a problem for future Grayson, he reasoned.

He had managed to lose his phone somewhere in the bed after forgetting to plug it back in when he woke up at three in the morning. Then he remembered the spots on his face. He jumped up out of bed and hurried into the bathroom down the hall. His eyes immediately fixed on his lips as he flicked the bathroom lights on. The spots were gone. Grayson sighed a breath of relief, but his mind wandered through the possibilities. Had he imagined the spots? Was that also part of the dream? As he looked down at the counter, he received his answer: his phone was still sitting on the edge of the sink, right where he left it after carrying it into the bathroom with him earlier that morning. He picked it up, turned off the lights and went back to his bedroom and flopped down onto the bed.

Grayson clicked his screen on to find a missed call from Roxanne. Immediately his heart dropped. He had to call her back, but he already knew what she was going to say. After a few rings, Roxanne picked up.

"Grayson, there you are! Listen, I've got to tell you—"

"A man's gone missing, hasn't he?" Grayson said, his eyes closed tight as he braced himself for confirmation that it wasn't just a nightmare.

"How'd you know?" Roxanne asked.

"I dreamed about it last night, Rox. Not dreamed. It was more real than that. I saw it. Another vision. I saw it happen. I felt it happen," Grayson stressed, trying to fight back tears. "It was someone with a truck. He was abducted outside your bar. Someone was worried about him driving home because he was drunk, but he insisted he was fine."

Roxanne was silent for a moment. "Yeah, yeah Grayson that's right. He's been missing since the night before last. Last anyone saw of him he was leaving my bar to go home."

"Who is it?" Grayson asked through a lump in his throat.

"Mikey Seevers," she said.

"Seevers...like our little grocery store?" Grayson asked.

"Yeah. It's their oldest son," Roxanne revealed.

"He's not a kid though. It was a man in my vision."

"Mikey is thirty-two. He helps his parents run the grocery store," she replied.

Grayson sat up. "Rox, he's dead. I'm just almost sure of it. In my vision I was him. Mikey. I stumbled out of the bar and got into my truck and when I started it and turned the lights on, I saw the Beast in front of my truck. But then I, like, passed out. And I woke up in some underground room with a bunch of candles and I was strapped down to this, like, stone table, I think. And my mouth was sewn shut."

"Grayson, that's horrible," Roxanne gasped.

"There was some man there, but I couldn't see his face. He stitched my mouth shut. Mikey's mouth. And then I heard chanting, and more people came into the room, but I couldn't look. All I could do was pray to God for it to end quickly and for me not to suffer."

"What happened then?"

"I don't know. I woke up before anything else happened. I thought maybe it was just a nightmare, but last night after I woke up, I went to the bathroom and looked in the mirror and saw these red dots on my face, like, right where the stitches would've been. And now today the spots are gone, and I thought maybe it was all just a fever dream until I saw you called me. Then I knew it wasn't. I just knew."

Roxanne didn't say anything for a long time.

"I'm so sorry, Grayson," she finally offered.

"It's okay. I don't...I don't understand what it all means, or why I'm seeing these things. But they're all connected somehow, I'm sure of it. And it's not just the Beast anymore. I'm telling you, Rox, there are people mixed up in this, too. Working with the Beast maybe. And it could be anybody," Grayson predicted.

"You should stay in Charleston. Grayson. Don't come back here," Roxanne pleaded. "As long as you're away from Breakvale, you're safe."

"I can't. I can't stay away, Roxanne. Somehow, I'm receiving these visions even from hundreds of miles away. And I still don't even know or understand why. No matter where I am, this thing can still haunt me. Besides, it feels like things are escalating,"

Grayson said. “The only way to stop these visions and stop the disappearances is to figure out why it’s happening. And maybe save some lives in the process.”

“You don’t have to be the hero, Grayson.”

“I’m not trying to be a hero. I just want answers, and I want these horrible images out of my head. I’m coming back to Breakvale in a few days. I’m going to spend Christmas with my family, then I’ll be back.”

“Yeah, take your time,” Roxanne urged. “I hope you reconsider staying in Charleston. But if you do come back, I want you to know you’re not alone. We’re in this together, to the end.”

“I know. You’re the only person I can trust,” Grayson said earnestly. “Listen, Mikey’s body is probably gonna turn up in a day or two. I don’t know where. But I’m sure it will.”

“When it does, I’ll let you know,” Roxanne said. “I gotta go. Lunch rush. But listen, you have a good Christmas and you spend time with your family. Don’t rush. Breakvale will be here when you’re ready to come back.”

Roxanne hung up the phone. Grayson clicked his screen off and slumped back down into the bed, unsure of how, exactly, he was going to have a good Christmas anymore.

10

On the road back home to Breakvale, Grayson thought really hard about turning around and going back to Charleston. He already missed his parents and the safety of his childhood bedroom there. He missed Seth, and even though he knew that Seth didn't hear his confession, he felt better having openly expressed his feelings about him. While he didn't like to think of himself as a pessimist, he couldn't help but wonder what might be waiting for him back in Breakvale. Going back this time felt different, like he was going into battle; but he felt a renewed sense of purpose. For some reason he, and he alone, had unique insight into what was happening, and he thought—hoped—that maybe it would help them uncover the truth.

Grayson survived the descent down into the valley, sliding on the snow and ice only once, though it was enough to jump-start his heart, and rolled up to Roxanne's diner around nine o'clock in the evening. Maybe if he were lucky, Keith would still be there and willing to fix him something to satisfy his growling stomach. He put the Jeep in park, then stepped out and stretched for a minute after the long drive before heading inside.

The bar was quiet. One man sat alone at a table in the corner drinking a beer and watching the television. Hearing someone come through the door, Roxanne looked up and beamed at the sight of Grayson's face. She scampered around the end of the bar and ran up to hug him. This caught Grayson off-guard, since Roxanne had never greeted him like that before, but he was happy to receive the jubilant welcome all the same.

She stood back but continued to brace his shoulders. “I’m glad you’re back. You look...rested.”

Grayson laughed. “Well, that’s good I look it, because I definitely don’t feel it. Actually, I’m starving. Is Keith still on the grill by chance?”

“No, it’s been a slow night, so we shut the kitchen down about thirty minutes ago. There’s still some pulled pork left, though. I can whip up a sandwich for you,” Roxanne offered.

“I love you. That would be amazing,” Grayson said.

“Take a seat at the bar. I’ll be right back,” she said, running off to the kitchen.

Grayson took a seat at the bar. Roxanne came back in a few minutes carrying a plate of food, which she slid down the bar to him before pouring him a glass of water. When she returned, Roxanne sat the glass down in front of him and leaned in low against the bar.

“Mikey’s body never turned up,” she whispered. “Right now, the chief is acknowledging that he’s gone but won’t speculate anymore about it. I think he’s worried about stirring everyone up again.”

“Probably for the best,” Grayson acknowledged, talking through a mouthful of food.

“The official story is that he had a friend pick him up after he left the bar, and is on a little trip with them because, get this, Mrs. Seevers got a text message from him on Christmas day saying that he had one of his buddies from Morgantown come to get him and they were spending the holiday up in Cleveland,” Roxanne said, cocking one eyebrow in suspicion.

"What? And the chief believes that?" Grayson asked.

"Not for a second," said Roxanne. "At least, not privately. The Seevers are worried, but they think it's true and that he'll come back. Mikey's got a bit of a habit, so it's not uncommon for him to just up and disappear for a while."

"But the chief suspects foul play?" Grayson asked.

"That's what he told me. Again, he doesn't wanna get people panicked for no reason, so he's going with this story, but privately, he and Lisa are doing their own little investigation, trying to run down his friends and find any connections to either Morgantown or Cleveland," Roxanne said.

Grayson sighed. "There're thousands of acres of forests around here. Old mining shafts. The river. His body could be anywhere. If it hasn't turned up now, I don't think it's going to. It's just really strange that all of these disappearances are connected to the Beast, but so far only half the bodies have been discovered. Officially, Emily is still a missing person, just like Mikey. But Alexis and Drew's bodies were left someplace where they could be found. It doesn't make sense."

Roxanne smirked. "It does make sense if you consider the possibility that they are separate circumstances."

Grayson gave her a puzzled look. "What do you mean?"

"Think about it. What if...what if the bodies of the kids were found because that's what the Beast wanted? Like it was remorseful about the fact that they were kids," she said.

He thought about it for a moment, then shook his head. "That doesn't explain what I saw in my vision though. I saw actual people in my vision committing some kind of awful, like, ritual thing with Mikey."

"I know. But you also saw the Beast in your vision before waking up on the table. Maybe they were two separate people...or aren't otherwise connected?" suggested Roxanne.

"I dunno," Grayson said hesitantly. "It sure seemed like I was the same person. But maybe not."

"You've shifted perspectives before. Remember how, in your one vision, you started as Drew and then shifted to the Beast? Maybe it was like that?" Roxanne said.

Grayson grunted and hung his head. "That's the frustrating thing about these visions. They don't make any fucking sense. Everything is speculation."

Roxanne looked up and waved as the man sitting in the corner bid them both goodnight and left the bar. As soon as the door closed, Roxanne leaned back in.

"There's something else, though," she said excitedly. "So, you know his truck was parked outside the bar for a few days before the chief had it impounded. The doors were locked but…his back window was open a little."

Grayson sat up straight. "What did you do?"

"I had a little look inside it myself, obviously."

"And?"

"And I had to get a long pole to hit the unlock button from the window. But once I was inside, I started snooping around. Look what I found," Roxanne said. She withdrew her phone from her pocket and flipped to a picture she had taken, then set the phone down on the bar in front of Grayson. "It was under the driver's seat."

"It's a syringe."

"Yep. Here's the thing. Mikey's struggled off and on with heroin addiction for the better part of his adult life."

"Wait, so what did you do with it?" Grayson asked.

"I left it there. His car is technically a crime scene. No telling what was in it, if it was heroin or not. I asked Danbury yesterday if they found anything in the truck and he said they found some evidence that he might have been on drugs. Said they sent stuff off to the state crime lab to have it tested but said it could be a while before they got any results," Roxanne said, putting her phone back in her pocket.

"Jesus. Roxanne, what the fuck is going on?"

"Things have never been like this before. Like, what's happening in this town right now is totally unprecedented. Honestly, you picked a really shitty time to move here," Roxanne said through a strained laugh.

"No kidding," Grayson scoffed. "What's our next move?"

"I don't see that we have one yet. Maybe do some more research or wait to see if Mikey turns up. Or if you have another vision," suggested Roxanne.

"I'm not wild about that one," Grayson said.

"I don't know that we have much of a choice. With any luck Mikey will come back and be fine, and maybe the kids will be the end of it after all," Roxanne offered. "Hopefully we won't see the Beast again for a long time."

"Here's to hoping," said Grayson. "But all the same, I'd feel better if we were more prepared."

"Agreed," Roxanne said.

Grayson stood up from his chair and donned his jacket from the seat back. "In the meantime, I'm exhausted from the drive, and I think it's time to sleep."

Roxanne nodded. "Yeah, I'm gonna close down. Go home, get some rest. Get yourself ready for school next week. Aren't you excited to go back?" she snickered.

"Why'd you have to go and say something like that," he groaned. "I'm not ready to go back. I don't wanna."

Roxanne laughed.

"Oh, what do I owe you for dinner?" Grayson asked, reaching for his wallet.

"Nothing," she objected. "You get the family discount, anytime you want. Just don't tell anyone."

Roxanne winked at him as Grayson reached over the bar to give her a hug, then left to head home.

***

The next few days passed without incident, though no one had heard from Mikey, and his body had yet to turn up. Grayson sat at home binge-watching *Star Trek: The Next Generation* when he heard a knock at the door. He stood up and walked over to look through the peephole at who would be visiting him at ten at night on a Thursday.

"Goddammit," he muttered to himself. He went back to his bedroom to put on his pants. When he came back and opened the door, Ross stood there on his darkened doorstep, barely illuminated by the streetlights, but beaming at the sight of Grayson. "Come on in, man."

Ross slipped through the door as Grayson closed and locked it behind him. He stood next to the door, unsure of what to do with himself until Grayson instructed him to take off his boots and have a seat.

"What's going on, Ross?"

"I'm sorry to come so late. It's just that I like coming when it's dark out. You know?" Ross explained sheepishly.

"So no one sees you. I get it," Grayson replied.

Ross took off his coat and laid it over the arm of the couch as he sat down next to Grayson. “I was wondering if maybe we could kinda talk?”

“Sure, what’s on your mind?”

Ross paused for a moment to gather his thoughts. “Well, it’s just that I’ve been doing some thinking. You know, about the other night?”

“When you kissed me,” Grayson confirmed.

“Yeah...I... I’m just having a hard time, you know, trying to figure out why God would make me like that if it was such a bad thing?” Ross admitted.

Grayson exhaled. “You’re struggling to reconcile your faith with your sexuality. I get it.”

“I kept reading and reading and praying to God for guidance, but I didn’t get an answer. Well, then, I thought maybe I just gotta find answers some other way. So, then I looked up gay porn and, God help me, I wasn’t ready for how excited I got because it felt dangerous, and then I got really aroused and then I felt really ashamed and I’m just really confused and I don’t know what’s wrong with me,” Ross concluded breathlessly.

“Wow. That was. A lot,” Grayson stated. “Okay, first of all, there’s nothing wrong with you. Let's get that clear right now. Look, we can have this conversation, but I need to lay some ground rules, got it?”

“Okay?”

“First of all, I don’t want to hear you say anymore that there’s something wrong with you, because there’s not. Second, I don’t want you quoting any scripture at me. Believe me, I know all the verses, I know everything the Bible has to say about homosexuality, and there’s nothing you can say that will convince me that it’s bad.”

"Okay," Ross agreed with a strained look on his face.

"Good. Now then, let's talk about the actual, real history of the Bible and how it was made," Grayson began, preparing himself for a lengthy lesson that for years he had mentally prepared to have one day.

The pair sat talking on the couch for the better part of three hours. It seemed to Grayson that there were two very distinct people sitting in front of him. There was the Ross that was clinging to his faith for guidance and understanding, and the Ross that desperately wanted to break free from his religious identity and embrace his sexuality, even though it terrified him. Seth was right: this was a fiery car crash waiting to happen. Yet, as Ross sat there in front of him talking about his faith, Grayson couldn't stop his mind from drifting toward more romantic and sexual thoughts about the boy in front of him. *It* was *a good kiss*, Grayson thought. *Am I just lonely and horny, or do I actually find him attractive?*

"Do you know what I mean?" Ross asked, snapping Grayson back to reality.

"Yeah, absolutely. I get it," Grayson affirmed, though he had no idea what Ross had said. He stood up. "Do you want a drink?"

"No, no I don't think that would be a good idea," Ross said, shaking his head. "I don't want to fall asleep here again."

"Would that really be such a bad thing?" Grayson replied.

Ross's face went flush. "Well no, I didn't mean it like that. I just meant that I don't want to be an inconvenience."

"Relax. It was a joke."

"Right," Ross said, feigning a weak laugh.

Grayson sat back down, this time moving closer to Ross on the couch. "Look, Ross. I know that this is really hard for you. It's easy for me to be glib because I don't have the same concerns that you do, and I've been out since I was, like, sixteen," he said gently. He reached out and put his hand on Ross's knee. "Your situation is different, but that doesn't make it impossible. Lots of gay people are able to find a balance between their faith and their sexuality. You can, too. You just need to be patient with yourself and find your understanding. Your relationship with God is unique and it's your own. It's not what John Arthur tells you it should be. It's between you and God. Everyone else can fuck off."

Ross sat there for a moment considering Grayson's perspective. Several times he opened his mouth to speak, but didn't say anything as the wheels continued to turn in his mind. At last, he put his hand on Grayson's and smiled.

"Thank you. Honestly, I'm still not sure how I feel. But I do feel better being able to talk to someone. You know, other than Him," he said, pointing a finger toward the ceiling. "You're very kind for letting me come here and talk about all this."

"Of course. Gonna be honest, I don't think there's anyone else here you could talk to about it," Grayson laughed.

Ross stood up from the couch and smiled. "I should be going. I've interrupted your evening long enough," he said.

Grayson looked puzzled. "You don't have to go if you don't want to. You can stay."

Ross shook his head. "No, I can't. I feel like I've bothered you enough already."

"Nonsense," Grayson replied. He gestured toward the television. "Do you watch Star Trek?"

"Can't say I do."

"Why don't you stay a while and watch some with me? I'll fill you in on what you need to know."

"I'll stay, but maybe just for an hour or two. I shouldn't stay the night here again," Ross countered.

"Yeah, that's fine. I'd enjoy the company."

Grayson scooted into the corner of the couch and motioned for Ross to come sit next to him. Ross eyed him for a moment before he sat back down, making sure he kept some distance between them. Grayson cracked a smile.

"Ross. We don't have to if you don't want to, but we can cuddle if you want. Sometimes it's nice to just be physically close to someone. Besides, you've already slept in bed next to me. It's not that different."

For the first time all night, Grayson saw Ross flash a fleeting, genuine smile as he slid closer and pressed himself into Grayson's body. Grayson wrapped his left arm around Ross's waist, drawing him a little tighter in.

"Ross. I can feel your heart racing," Grayson said gently. "Breathe."

"Sorry. It's just all really new," Ross replied.

"You're okay. Everything is okay."

He told Ross all about the TV show's characters and explained the premise, then started the episode over. As they sat there together, Grayson felt morally dubious. Secretly, he craved the physical affection, though he wasn't sure yet whether he felt any real affection for Ross; however, he knew that behavior like this would only make Ross grow more infatuated with him. Maybe for tonight, he thought, he would just let it be.

It didn't take long, only an episode and a half, before Grayson could hear Ross snoring peacefully next to him. He looked down at Ross's face and watched him sleep. *He really is very cute*, Grayson thought. Maybe he was being too pessimistic that kindling something with Ross would only end in disaster.

After their talk, he felt as though Ross had really taken his advice to heart. With a little time and some patience, who knows what could happen. Grayson tilted his head back and closed his eyes, imaging what a potential future could look like. It didn't look so bad.

Grayson was midway through another episode when he felt his phone vibrate twice in his pocket. He reached in and pulled it out, careful not to wake Ross, and clicked the screen on. He had a text message from Seth. Grayson opened the message. It was a long one:

Hey Gray, I need to tell you but wasn't sure how, so I figured I'd just text you. I was awake the other night when you told me all that stuff you felt. I just didn't know what to say so I pretended to be asleep. I'm really sorry. I should have told you then but it was so sudden that I kinda was blindsided. Anyway, the thing is, I still really care about you too. I think about you a lot. Ever since you told me that stuff, sometimes I'll be cuddling with Aaron and I'll pretend it's you there with me, and it feels good. I know that probably sounds fucked up. And it's not fair to either one of you. But it's how I feel. I know you're living in Breakvale and you're gonna be there awhile, and I've got my own stuff to figure out here. I just want to say I love you and I hope this doesn't change anything between us because maybe someday we can try again. So yeah, just reply to this when you can, or you don't have to. I just felt like you deserved to hear the truth from me, too.

Grayson re-read the message several times, taking in each word, fighting back frustrated tears. He clicked his screen off and let his phone drop onto the carpeted floor. He didn't want to look at it anymore. It wasn't fair, he thought, not fucking fair at all.

Seth heard every word and couldn't bother being honest with him after he had bared his soul to him. And yet, here he sat with this guy asleep against him, a scared boy who was trusting him implicitly, who had just bared his soul to him, and who he had manipulated into staying just so he had someone to cuddle with.

Grayson felt the irony like a dagger in his chest. He took a deep, slow breath and exhaled. Fuck it. I could fucking die tomorrow. Who knows in this town, he thought. While he didn't know yet what he was going to say to Seth, he decided that, for now, he was just going to have to take it one day at a time.

11

The body of Mikey Seevers never turned up like Grayson and Roxanne thought it would, and by the end of February, Mr. and Mrs. Seevers had given up hope of ever seeing their son again. Officially, Chief Danbury had closed the investigation and labeled him a missing person, though he continued to suspect foul play. The chief disclosed to Roxanne that the syringe she found in Mikey's truck had traces of heroin, leading him to conclude that Mikey ended up on the losing end of a bad drug deal.

It had also been months since the Beast last appeared to anyone, reassuring some and worrying others around town. At the bar, Roxanne heard whispers of conversations between friends. People in Breakvale were beginning to grow suspicious that another attack might be imminent, as if their quiet life in Breakvale had been too generously given. On more than one occasion, Roxanne overheard patrons at her bar confessing their secrets to one another, providing insurance against a visit from the Beast. Even their use of the town motto— Truth is Life— could be heard more frequently with each passing day.

Grayson had noticed a similar trend among his students. He frequently heard his students talking amongst their friends, sharing small secrets that they had kept. The students seemed acutely aware of the fearful climate in Breakvale. No one wanted to end up like Alexis or Drew. It was in many ways painful for him to watch them struggle with the omnipresent threat of death, which manifested itself unexpectedly in numerous ways, the most heartbreaking of which were the poems the students wrote during his unit on poetry. More than three-quarters of his students wrote about or alluded to the brevity of life or the danger of keeping secrets in Breakvale. Some directly referenced the Beast, others chose allegory, but they all told Grayson the same story: the children feared they could be next. Tragically for them, he thought, it was a fear that was well-founded.

Grayson arrived at school early to finish running off copies of an exam for his upper-class students on The Grapes of Wrath. As he walked down the hallway to his classroom, some dedicated early birds were already present and working hard to decorate the school for the upcoming Spring Fling. He admired their resiliency in the face of a constant existential threat. He rounded the corner into his classroom and was startled to find a pallid-looking Principal Daggett perched on his desk. Grayson instinctively pulled the door closed behind him.

"Dale, you look like hell. What's going on?"

Daggett's eyes glistened as he struggled to fight back some tears. "I think there's been another one."

Grayson's heart sank. "Another student's gone missing?"

"We don't know for sure," Principal Daggett said.

"Who?"

"Her name's Tina Wilson. Her daddy's ol' Jimmy Wilson that lives up the hill toward the plant."

Grayson wracked his brain trying to place the name with a face. "I don't think I know her."

"You wouldn't. She's a senior and already took what English she needed. Spends most of her time with Mrs. Wells learning Home Economics," Daggett explained.

"What happened to her?" Grayson pressed.

"Got a call from the chief about half an hour ago. Tina Wilson didn't come home last night. She was out visiting a friend and was supposed to be home by eleven. She normally comes right on home, so her daddy fell asleep and didn't think nothin' of it. When he woke up this morning, she wasn't there. He always drops her off at school before goin' on to work. The chief is out lookin' for her now."

Grayson didn't know what to say. When Mikey went missing, he'd had a vision about his disappearance, but he hadn't received a vision about this girl, so he couldn't be sure she was missing. Then again, he didn't have the vision until a little while after Mikey disappeared—not that he could tell any of that to Principal Daggett.

Principal Daggett turned his face away and began to sob. Grayson stood up and instinctively reached out to hug him.

"She's friends with my boy, Mr. Ender. What's he gonna say when he finds out she's missing? He's gonna break down, I just know it."

Grayson was shocked. "I didn't...Dale. Fuck. I didn't know you had a son."

"He's eighteen, just graduated last May. Tina's one of his good friends. She's been over for dinner lots of times. I watched them grow up together. I can't...I can't lose another one," Principal Daggett choked through tears. "I can't lose another one."

They stood there in an embrace for a long minute, until Principal Daggett pulled away and wiped his eyes. He sniffled for a moment then cleared his throat.

"I'm gonna call a staff meeting at the start of first period. We gotta get ahead of this. If another one of these kids has gone missing, it’s gonna scare the hell outta all the rest of ‘em. Someone's gonna notice she’s gone.”

Grayson nodded. “You’re right. But we need to wait until Chief Danbury has had a chance to look for her before we make a school-wide announcement. No sense in panicking them now.”

Principal Daggett stood up and cleared his throat again, extending his hand out. Grayson shook it affirmatively.

“We’re gonna figure this out. Now, I gotta go figure out what I’m gonna say to the rest of the faculty. Tell your kids they’re gonna do some quiet reading or something this morning. Thanks again. You’re a fine man, Mr. Ender. I’m glad you’re here. Truth is Life,” Principal Daggett uttered as he opened the door and strode out into the hallway.

Grayson had little time to prepare anything. Moments after Principal Daggett left, his students began shuffling into the classroom and taking their seats. He leaned against his desk as they filed in, saying good morning and waving to each blissfully unaware face, and dreading that they may be about to receive the exact news they’d been fearing since last fall. When the final tardy bell rang, Grayson stood up from his desk.

“Good morning, everyone,” he began jovially. “We have a small change of plan this morning. I know everyone was expecting a test, and we’re still going to have it, but I heard from Principal Daggett that there’s going to be a faculty meeting pretty soon this morning, and you’re going to be on your own for a while. So, what I want everyone to do is work together to fill out the multiple choice and short answer part of the test first, and then do your essay portion individually. Does everyone understand?”

His students exchanged confused glances for a moment but nodded or otherwise acknowledged his instruction. Grayson walked around the classroom handing out the tests as the intercom chimed signaling an announcement.

“Will all faculty please report to the office conference room for a short meeting?” Principal Daggett’s voice rang out. “All students are to remain in your classrooms until your teachers return.”

The students looked around at each other, their expressions a mixture of surprise and bewilderment. As Grayson stepped out the door, he gently reminded his class of the test’s rules and then slipped out the door. Other faculty members began to emerge from their classrooms, sporting expressions of similar bewilderment at the unorthodox and impromptu staff meeting and whispering speculatively among themselves as to what the meeting could possibly be about.

The office conference room was small and could not comfortably accommodate everyone. Grayson stood at the back of the room by the door as the last few faculty members shuffled in and took standing positions against the walls. Principal Daggett was the last one in and closed the door behind him.

He took a deep breath. “There’s no easy way to say this, so I’m just gonna say it,” he began. “I received a call from Chief Danbury this morning before school started. One of our senior girls, Tina Wilson, Jimmy Wilson’s daughter, has disappeared without a trace. The chief wasn’t sure at first whether something might’ve happened to her, but I just spoke to him a minute ago, and he said they found Tina’s bike in a ditch about halfway up Oak Dale Road. He thinks maybe she was snatched off the road last night while she was riding her bike home in the dark. As of right now she’s still missing.”

For several long seconds no one said a word. It was the sound of Mrs. Wells bursting into hysterical tears that broke the silence. Another teacher held her in her seat as she cried, and several other teachers became visibly emotional.

"So, what are sayin', Dale? The Beast snatched another one of our kids? The third one in a year?" demanded Coach Rigby, his face flushed red in anger. "What's that girl done to get herself snatched by the Beast?"

"I dunno Coach. You all know as much as I do now," Principal Daggett said. "We don't know anything except no one can find her."

Mrs. Wells shot a distressed glare at Coach Rigby. "That girl ain't done nothin'! She ain't done nothin'! She wouldn't hurt a fly. She's a good girl. A good, Christian girl."

"Mrs. Wells, I'm sure Coach didn't mean anything by it," Principal Daggett assured. "Look this is obviously very hard on all of us. A lot of us have children, some of them are even friends of Tina's like my boy, and I worry about these kids like they're my own. So rarely do we lose a child, and never three in a year. I'm as torn up about it as all the rest of you. But I called you all in here 'cause we need a plan. We gotta all be on the same page about what we're gonna tell the students."

"They're gonna find out eventually," Mrs. Newsham said.

"Are we supposed to just pretend like we don't know this girl's probably dead in a ravine or floating in the river by now?" said one of the other teachers.

"Now listen, all of ya!" Daggett snapped. "I talked to Dr. Thomas. She and I agree that it would be best if the students had a chance to hear it first from their family or from Pastor Arthur…"

Grayson felt suddenly lightheaded. He closed his eyes and the sound of Principal Daggett's voice, of all the voices in the room, began to fade out until there was nothing. Nothing except the scent of damp earth. He forced his eyes open.

It was dark. He could smell mud. He tried to sit up, but his head was dizzy and pounding and he fell back against the ground. It was soft and wet. He dug his fingertips into the earth, and it squished between his fingers. He was lying in the mud. Grayson could hear the sound of dripping water. He tried to roll over but couldn't muster the strength. He laid his head back again and relaxed into the mud with a soft moan. He closed his eyes.

Suddenly Grayson found himself staring down a low tunnel, walking toward the darkness. He was walking into a cave. He had a flashlight in his hand, and he clicked it on. His boots squelched in the mud as he explored further into the cave until his light caught something on the ground in the darkness. As he approached, he felt a rush of exhilaration swelling up inside of him. He knew this feeling. When he got close enough, Grayson cast the beam of light down on a young girl lying there in the muck. Right where he left her. He clicked the flashlight off.

Grayson awoke on the floor of the conference room. Coach Rigby was kneeling down next to him as other faculty members looked over the coach's shoulder at him lying on the floor.

"Hey there buddy, where'd you go?" Rigby asked, flashing a concerned smile.

"What happened?" Grayson mumbled, sitting up with the coach's assistance.

"You passed out all of a sudden," Rigby informed him.

"I...uh. Yeah, I guess so," Grayson said, trying to gather himself.

"Where's Nurse Cline?" Principal Daggett hollered from somewhere behind the rest of the faculty.

In another couple of moments, the door to the conference room opened and the nurse came in. She bent down and took Grayson by the chin.

“Did he hit his head?” she asked.

“I don’t think so. He was leanin’ against the wall and just kinda fell down,” Rigby stated.

Nurse Cline took out a small pen light from her pocket and flashed it in Grayson’s eyes. “Yeah, alright. Help me get him on his feet.”

Nurse Cline and Coach Rigby helped Grayson stand up and guided him over to a chair vacated for him by another faculty member.

“He’ll be alright,” the nurse said. She put her hand on his shoulder. “Have you eaten anything today?”

Grayson shook his head. “No. I was gonna eat during my conference period.”

“Probably just low blood sugar. He got a little woozy,” Nurse Cline diagnosed. She looked around at all of the staff members, taking particular note of Mrs. Wells’ exasperated state. “What’s going on here, anyway?”

“Tina Wilson’s gone missing,” Rigby informed her.

“Tsk. Another one? How horrible,” Nurse Cline said somewhat dismissively. She looked over at Principal Daggett. “He’s not used to the stress of stuff like this happening. Might be a good idea to send him home for the day. He’s not doin’ anybody any good like this. Call me again if you need me.”

Principal Daggett nodded in agreement as Nurse Cline left the conference room. He cleared his throat to call everyone’s attention.

“Alright, so we’re all clear on how this is gonna be handled?” Daggett asked, looking around the room. When no one spoke, he continued. “Right, remember everybody, not a word to your students. Truth is Life.”

“Truth is Life,” the faculty echoed collectively.

“Okay, now everybody get back to your classrooms,” Principal Daggett commanded.

The faculty began to shuffle out of the room, some still casting concerned looks back at Grayson as they passed. Coach Rigby remained by his side until Principal Daggett came over and put his hand on the coach’s shoulder. They nodded affirmatively at each other, then Coach Rigby left the room. Principal Daggett knelt down next to him.

“I think the nurse is right. You ought to go on home. Don’t worry about your classes. We’ll get someone to cover for you,” Daggett said warmly.

“They, uh, they’re doing a test. I let them work together on the first part and then do the, uh, the essay individually,” Grayson muttered, still trying to process everything that had just happened.

“We’ll take care of ‘em, don’t worry,” he reassured. He helped Grayson to his feet. “Are you okay to drive? I can have Linda take you home.”

“No, no that’s not necessary. I’m fine. I’ll get home okay. I think I just need to lie down a while,” Grayson said.

The conference room door swung open, and one of the other teachers came in holding Grayson’s bag and his coat. She handed it to Principal Daggett and left. He placed the belongings on the conference table.

“I had Stacey go get your things. This is it right? I think it’s all I saw you come in with?” asked Daggett.

"Yeah, yeah that's it," Grayson said, standing up. He donned his jacket and slung his bag over his shoulder. "I'm gonna go now. I'll be back tomorrow. Thanks again, Dale."

"Don't mention it," he replied, clapping Grayson on the shoulder. He walked Grayson to the door and waved him an encouraging goodbye.

Grayson crossed the parking lot and got into his Jeep, where he sat for a moment reflecting on his vision, trying hard to remember every detail he could still see and feel. He turned the engine over and took off out of the parking lot. Thankfully, Principal Daggett bought into his sickly charade. He felt just fine, but knew he didn't have a minute to waste if he was going to find the missing girl.

Grayson drove straight to Roxanne's bar. Maybe she would have an idea of where to look or which caves to search in the area. He knew that now was the time to tell Chief Danbury about this vision before it was too late, but he needed to be sure he'd listen, and he hoped that Roxanne's word would be enough to convince the chief.

Grayson parked his Jeep behind the building and hustled through the door. Roxanne looked up from behind the bar. She could see the look on his face and immediately circled around to intercept him.

"What's going on?" she asked.

"Can we talk in the back?"

She led him into a small office off the kitchen. Grayson sat down at the desk as she locked the door behind them.

"Okay, you're freaking me out. What's going on?" she asked again.

"Another girl's gone missing," he said.

"What? Fuck. Who?"

"A girl named Tina Wilson."

"Jimmy Wilson's girl," Roxanne acknowledged, running her fingers through her hair and tucking it behind her ears. "He was just in here with her for dinner a couple nights ago. What happened? Wait, how do you know about this? Was it another vision?"

"Hold on, one at a time. Yes, there was a vision, but I found out from Dale Daggett, who heard from Chief Danbury this morning. Apparently, Tina was out at a friend's house last night and was supposed to come back but never did. Then the chief found her bike this morning in a ditch someplace near her house. Dale called all the faculty in for a meeting basically to tell us that no one really knows yet and not to say anything to the students because the administration doesn't want to be the one to have to tell these kids that another one of their classmates is gone and probably dead."

"Jesus."

"They want the kids to hear it from their parents or from church or something. But while we were in the meeting, I apparently passed out, and while I was out, I had a vision that *has* to be about Tina Wilson. I saw her."

"Is she still alive?"

"I don't know. Maybe? In the vision, at first, I was her. I was on the ground lying in some mud. I'm pretty sure I was in a cave of some kind. I could hear, like, trickling water. And then it shifted, and I was something or someone else. I had a flashlight, and I remember shining it on her. And then I got that same feeling I had before in my other visions, like I was excited getting ready to attack. Then I came to and that was it."

Roxanne was silent for a moment as she took in all of the information. "So, she could be alive, or she could be dead. If something was in that cave with her, if the Beast was there, she might already be dead."

"Yes."

"But wait, what would the Beast need with a flashlight?" Roxanne asked.

"It doesn't need a flashlight. I don't think it was the Beast this time," Grayson revealed, shaking his head.

"Okay, so what do we do? This is coal mine country. There's at least a dozen abandoned mines around here and maybe a hundred caves just within an hour of Breakvale. She could literally be anywhere," Roxanne said, squatting down and leaning against the wall.

"I know. I didn't see enough to be able to narrow it down. It just looked like a cave," Grayson said. He paused. "I think...I think it's time I told Chief Danbury about these visions I've been having, and I thought maybe if you corroborate my story, maybe he might believe me. At least enough to consider searching the caves and stuff in the area."

Roxanne sighed. "I dunno, Grayson. The chief...he's a good person and he takes the Beast stuff seriously, but I'm not sure if he'll believe that you've been somehow psychically receiving visions about it. Though, you've been right every time. I'll call him down here if you want. If you feel like this is the right move, I'm behind you all the way."

Grayson nodded. "I think we should go down to the station, though. Too many people coming in and out of the bar. It might draw unwanted attention. Can you get away for an hour or so?"

"Yeah. The chief is probably out around town looking for Tina, though. I'll call him and have him meet us there," she said, standing up and taking out her phone to place a call. She spoke to the chief for just a moment, telling him she had information about Tina, and he agreed to meet them down at the station. Roxanne hung up and turned to Grayson.

"He'll be there in fifteen minutes," she said. "Let's go."

They walked back through the kitchen and into the dining room. As they passed Kay behind the bar, Roxanne pulled her aside.

"I've got an important errand to run. I'll be gone about an hour or so. Can you run things while I'm gone?"

"Sure, hun, no problem," Kay said, pouring out three cups of coffee as she smacked her chewing gum.

Grayson drove them both to the station, though he had never been there before and had to rely on Roxanne for directions. The station was empty inside except for Officer Stanley, who was manning the desk. They waited for Chief Danbury to arrive, but didn't have to wait long. He walked through the station door without saying a word and beckoned for Grayson and Roxanne to follow him into his office. They perched uncomfortably on the seats in front of his desk.

Chief Danbury just looked at them both. "So, now, Roxanne, you said you had some information about Tina. Somethin' you couldn't tell me over the phone?"

"Yes, well, Grayson has information," Roxanne said cautiously. "But I need you to know that everything he's about to tell you is true. You've known me my whole life, chief. I'm telling you, I believe him. Please just hear him out."

The chief sat back in his chair, already unamused by whatever he was about to hear. Grayson spent the next half hour recounting each vision in precise detail to the chief and answering his questions about each crime scene. When at last he had finished telling Chief Danbury the details of his most recent vision about Tina Wilson, and that he was certain she was being held captive in a cave somewhere, the chief didn't say a word. He stood up, walked over to the coffee pot and poured a cup of coffee, then returned to his desk.

"That's an awful lot of specific knowledge about each of the crime scenes. I'm gonna be honest, Mr. Ender, I know that strange things happen in Breakvale, but I gotta tell ya, this is a *strange* one. And if it weren't for Roxanne sittin' right here next to you tellin' me that she believes you, I'm not sure I wouldn't arrest you right here and now."

"Believe me, I know how it looks, chief. That's why I didn't say anything until now. The visions always happened after it was too late to do anything. But not this time. That's why I felt like I had to tell you. Maybe there's a chance we can still save Tina."

Chief Danbury thought for a minute. "There's just one problem. There's an awful lotta caves and old mines around here. That girl could be in any one of 'em, and I don't have the manpower to go searching through each one. Believe me, I want to find this girl. Her daddy's a good friend of mine. But that's a tall order trying to mount that kind of search."

"How can we help, chief?" Roxanne asked. "I'll open my bar like last time, help coordinate search teams."

"I'm gonna call the mayor. I was hoping I'd be able to run her down this morning and get her home safe. But if what you're sayin' is true, that you think it's a person behind this and not the Beast...well, that makes this a lot more dangerous for Tina. If whoever kidnapped her catches on that we might be close to finding her, she's liable to end up dead real fast, and it'll be because of us."

Grayson hadn't thought about it like that. If they rallied the whole town for a search party, her abductor might get nervous and dispose of her quickly. He'd watched enough crime dramas to know that, statistically, the first forty-eight hours were the most critical, and that search parties would be an easy way for her abductor to insert themselves into the investigation. What small hope Grayson had that they would find Tina alive was suddenly snuffed out.

"What I need for you to do right now, the both of you, is to go on back home and stay tight-lipped about all this," Chief Danbury instructed. "Roxanne, we may need to use your bar as a headquarters again if the mayor decides to launch a search party. Can you be ready for it if we need it?"

"All I need is a phone call and I'll be ready," she said.

"As for you, Mr. Ender, if you have any more of these, uh, visions, I want to know about 'em right away, you got that?" the chief stipulated.

"Yessir. I'll call you right away," Grayson affirmed.

"Good. Go on home now. Remember, not a word."

They stood up and exited the station. Roxanne and Grayson walked silently back to his Jeep. Once they were inside, Roxanne turned to Grayson.

"Something doesn't feel right," she asserted.

"With the chief?"

"With this whole situation," Roxanne said cautiously. "Call it woman's intuition, but I just have a sort of uneasy feeling about all this."

Grayson drove Roxanne back to the bar and dropped her off. On the drive home, he started thinking about his vision, trying to call back the details he could remember while he was lying there on the ground. It was a fruitless effort though; he couldn't recall any details at all except for the feel and smell of the cave floor.

At home, Grayson stretched out on the couch and took to watching re-runs of *Criminal Minds*. He'd done enough for one day, he reasoned, and if the mayor authorized a search party, he could have some long days and nights ahead of him. The TV droned on in the background, but as he lay there, all he could think about was Tina in that cave, frozen there in the cold mud, afraid and knowing that she was about to die alone. It made him think about all the poems his students had written. It could just as easily have been one of them. He closed his eyes and tried to shut the thoughts out entirely.

12

A low rumbling roused Grayson from his sleep. The auto-sleep timer on his television had shut it off, leaving his apartment completely dark, except for the small amount of light filtering through his window from the streetlamps outside. He looked around his living room for the source of the sound but couldn't see anything. He sat up. He could hear the rumbling again, low like a growl, emanating from somewhere down the hallway. He tip-toed quietly across the living room to the light switch. He flicked the switch up, but the room remained dark. He heard the growl again, this time more clearly. He was not going to go down the dark hallway. Absolutely not.

Grayson backed away slowly toward the front door, keeping his eyes trained on the hall in front of him, watching for any sign of movement. He backed midway into the living room and watched a dark shadow dart from his bedroom to the study across the hall. He felt his body go cold in terror. There was something in the house with him. He turned to run for the front door and wrenched it open. The Beast stood there lurking in his doorway, its piercing red eyes gleaming in their desolate void. Grayson stumbled backward and fell onto the living room floor. The Beast shrieked and swelled in size, its black tendrils spreading out in every direction as it glided over and above him. It reached out with one long, arm-like shadow toward his face before unfurling a single, finger-like digit that touched his forehead.

Grayson's head convulsed against the carpet as what little light was visible faded from his sight. Suddenly he was behind the wheel of an old Cadillac. He was on the old outer road headed toward the power plant. He knew this road; he had driven it before. He heard rustling in the back seat. He glanced up in the rearview mirror. There was the same girl he'd seen in the cave, bound by duct tape and tightly gagged with some kind of cloth around her mouth. She tried to scream, but the sound was muffled. The girl thrashed in the back seat, trying to break free from the tape binding her arms and legs. Grayson pulled a pistol from his lap and reached over the seat to point it at her.

"Shut the fuck up now. You stop that nonsense. Ain't nobody gonna hear you screamin'. All you're gonna do is piss me off," he growled.

The girl in the back seat screamed even harder through the muffle and then began to cry. Grayson reached over and turned the radio up louder to drown out her wailing. Conway Twitty played on the radio. It was his favorite song, and he sang along in a fanatical, off-key voice.

"'Hello darlin'. Nice to see ya. It's been a long time, you're just as lovely, as you used to be,'" he sang. He turned around and shouted at the girl in the back. "Sing along goddammit. Hello Darlin'. It's a classic. Sing it with me. 'I'm doin' alright, except I can't sleep, I cry all night till dawn…'"

Grayson looked back over his shoulder to find the girl's face buried in the cloth seat, sobbing quietly to herself. "Ah forget it. You're too young to know anyway."

He kept the radio blasting, singing along to the old country cassette tape as it played. As Grayson approached the power plant, he took a left turn onto a dirt road leading up a hill. Away from town and without the streetlights, his headlights struggled to cut a visible path in the darkness, and he leaned over the steering wheel, squinting to make out the road ahead. In a few minutes the road came to an end marked by a large stop sign nailed to a wooden fence. Grayson drove the Cadillac off the road and through a gap in the fence.

"Won't be far now, we can get out and stretch those pretty little legs of yours," Grayson said, shouting at the girl in the back seat.

He had enough time to sing one more song at the top of his lungs before pulling up to an old abandoned mine shaft. Grayson put the car in park and got out. He opened the door to the back seat and pulled out a pocketknife.

"Now you listen close, girly. I'm gonna cut you free. But you just be real good and don't do anything stupid or I'll shoot ya right here and now. Ya hear me?" Grayson warned.

The girl whimpered and nodded. Grayson reached into the back seat and used the pocketknife to cut the duct tape binding her and legs. He grabbed her by neck and pulled her out of the car, holding the gun against her back.

"March it. Right ahead there," he commanded.

He guided her in front of the beaming headlights toward the entrance of the mine shaft. A large, wire-metal gate blocked the entrance, and a single door was barred with a padlock. He took a key from his pocket and handed it to the girl.

"Unlock it and gimme the key and lock," Grayson demanded, pressing the barrel of the gun into her back.

The girl continued to sob quietly as she fumbled with the lock.

"Hurry up now!" he barked.

The girl removed the padlock and handed the lock and key to Grayson. He swung the metal door open, then grabbed a fistful of her hair and forced her into the cave. He marched her at gunpoint down the tunnel, her sniffles and barely contained sobs echoing through the shaft. When they got deep enough in for him to be satisfied, he stopped her.

"That's far enough," he rasped. "Turn around and face down the shaft."

The girl whimpered and did as she was told. Grayson withdrew a syringe from the breast pocket of his denim button-up. He bit the cap off and plunged the needle into her neck. The girl let out a single, muffled gasp and collapsed into the mud below.

Grayson bolted up straight from the floor, looking wildly around his living room for the Beast, but everything appeared to be normal. His lights were back on, and the front door was closed and locked. He braced himself on his television console to get to his feet. He knew that road, and he knew where Tina was—at least, he hoped she was still there. He grabbed his car keys from their spot on the console, grabbed his phone, and dashed out the front door.

The clock in his Jeep read 11:48 p.m. He'd been unconscious for more than twelve hours. He revved the engine and peeled out of the parking lot. He couldn't chance slowing down or causing an accident by driving through the center of town, even though it was the most direct route, so he followed the path he had taken in his vision. It was a narrow back road that followed the ridgeline along the river and skirted the west of Breakvale. Grayson raced down the road, trying hard to keep a watchful eye on the switchbacks barely lit by the moon and his headlights. He slowed down only for a moment to pull his phone from his pocket and dial Roxanne. The line rang for several seconds before it picked up.

"Grayson, what's going on? I've been trying to call you all night," Roxanne said.

"Roxanne, listen, I had another vision. I know where Tina is. Or at least where she was. I'm going there now. It's an old mine shaft with a big metal door barring the entrance—"

Grayson paused as a pair of headlights that had been well behind him suddenly caught up to him, blinding him as he glanced at them in the rearview mirror.

"Hang on, Rox, some asshole is blinding me with their fucking headlights."

He flipped his rearview mirror up to cast the light off and accelerated to get away from them.

"Call the chief. Tell him to meet me there. I'm almost there."

"Meet you where, Grayson?" Roxanne said urgently.

The headlights behind Grayson closed the distance between them until he could see the boxy front end of the car. Grayson sped up. The car behind him matched its speed.

"Rox, I think someone is following me," Grayson said, a note of panic rising in his voice.

"Grayson, where are you? Tell me where you are!" Roxanne's voice cracked.

"I don't know the name of the road. It's the one west of town that looks over the river. I'm headed toward the power plant—"

The car behind him smashed into the back of his Jeep, causing him to lurch forward and hit his head on the steering wheel. He started to swerve but was able to keep control of the steering wheel. He tried to right the Jeep when he felt another impact from behind push his Jeep forward. As they approached a curve in the road, the car behind him rammed into the corner of his Jeep one final time, sending Grayson veering off the road as it sped on. He tried to keep control of the Jeep but couldn't react fast enough as it hit the gravel of the shoulder. He jerked on the steering wheel to try to steady it, but the force flipped the Jeep onto its side, and it rolled down the hill, smashing its way into the ravine below.

***

Grayson's head throbbed. He tried to raise his head but couldn't hold it up and it fell back against something soft. Still, he groaned at the pain.

"You're awake," a voice said from somewhere in the room. "You were in an accident. Don't go movin' around."

His vision was a little blurry, but as he blinked, he was able to make out a person, a man, standing at a table to his right. There was something bright above him. A light. It hurt to look at it directly, and Grayson had to close his eyes and look away.

"You're lucky you have good airbags and that you were wearing your seat belt. That sure was a nasty little accident you had," the man said.

"Where am I?" Grayson strained to ask.

"You're safe, Mr. Ender. Don't worry," the man said.

He didn't recognize the man's voice. He opened his eyes a little and looked around, trying to blink his vision into focus. He could see the floral print on the wallpaper. It was old and kitschy. There was a counter of some kind, with drawer handles on its face, and jars sitting on the countertop. Grayson squinted hard to discern what was in them. They looked like sticks and something white he couldn't quite make out. On the floor was a pile of something black that looked like clothes and a pair of boots, but he couldn't figure out exactly what they were. His eyes felt heavy, and he closed them for a moment. He could hear the man doing something. He could hear what sounded like metal. Then Grayson heard shuffling feet, and he opened his eyes to see the man approaching him.

"You really shouldn't have gone pokin' around where you didn't have no business pokin' around. But that's alright. We can still make the most of this yet," the man said.

Grayson opened his eyes wider. He watched the man's face come into focus as he stepped into the light. He knew that face. He'd seen him around town before.

"Doc Weaver?"

"Yeah, it's me alright," Doc Weaver said with a chuckle.

"What's going on? Where am I?" Grayson asked, an uneasy panic setting in.

"Never you mind that. Now I heard you been receivin' visions and whatnot," Doc Weaver mocked. "That you think they're gonna lead you to that missing girl."

Grayson tried to sit up, but the doctor pushed him back against the examination bed.

"Hold up now, hoss. Just stay where you are. Everything's gonna be alright," said Doc Weaver. "Now I wanna know how you've been receivin' these visions."

"I don't know what you're talking about," Grayson lied.

"Don't bullshit me, boy," the doctor snapped. "I know you know what I'm talkin' about."

"I have no idea what you're talking about. What visions? I don't have any visions," Grayson said, trying to sound convincing.

"Alright, alright. If that's how you're gonna be," Doc Weaver grumbled. He turned around to grab something from a metal tray behind him. "It don't really matter. I was just curious as to how you knew what you did. But if you don't want to tell me that's fine. You're too late to save that girl anyway. I already had my fun with her. And let me tell you boy, she was real fun."

The doctor turned back around with a syringe in his hand. He leaned in close. "Don't fight me now, it's only gonna hurt you." He held Grayson's head down and injected the contents of the syringe into his neck. As Grayson began to fade out, Doc Weaver leaned in and whispered into his ear.

"Too bad you couldn't save her. She screamed real good. It was fun. And you enjoyed every minute of it."

***

The cool breeze off the ridgeline stirred Grayson awake. The full moon was directly overhead, providing enough light that Grayson was able to make out the trees around him, though he struggled to completely open his eyes. His head hurt badly. He tried to move, but his muscles were stiff, and he felt a twinge of pain in his ribs. He remained still for a moment and tried to focus on his breathing. Grayson looked around. He was outside, in a forest somewhere. Then he felt something in his hand. He was holding something. He raised his hand up just enough to look down. For a second he couldn't tell what it was. He screamed and tried to toss it as far as he could, but it just stuck to his hand before falling to the ground next to him. His left hand was covered in dried blood.

He'd been clutching a human heart.

The sudden rush of adrenaline and fear overcame the pain he felt from moving as he sat up and struggled to get to his feet. He looked down at himself to find he was completely covered in blood that had dried and crusted onto his clothes. He didn't know what to do. He staggered a few feet down the hill but stopped when he noticed a person leaning up against a tree nearby. Grayson stumbled over until he was close enough to be sure of what he was seeing: it was the body of Tina Wilson.

He fell to the ground next to her and broke down in tears. He gasped but no words would come out. He couldn't bring himself to touch her. There was so much trauma to her body. She was covered in so much blood. Her chest was splayed open, and her ribs were broken. Her heart had been ripped from her body. Inside her chest cavity, someone lit a single black candle, and the flame flickered deep down inside the pillar. The sight of it and the realization was too much for him. He tried to crawl away but fell as he vomited onto the forest floor. The retching hurt his chest, but he couldn't control it. When he finally finished, he fell to the ground and rolled over onto his side.

Grayson stared at her body, ragged and lifeless against the tree. Someone had carved a large pentagram above her head. This wasn't the work of a devil worshipper. This was done by the Devil himself. A hazy memory wafted into his brain just then. He remembered the doctor's face. Then like a flash, the memories came flooding back to him. He had to get back to town. He had to tell the chief before it was too late, but he couldn't move. He was too tired. He just needed a little rest.

The sun was directly overhead when it stirred Grayson awake. His eyes were still a little sensitive to the light, but the pounding in his head had subsided, and he was able to get himself to his feet. The pain in his ribs was still very much present, and he was certain he must have fractured one. He could see the tall smokestacks of the power plant nearby, giving him a bearing on where he was and which way to walk to get back into town.

"Grayson Ender!" a voice called out suddenly from somewhere behind a tree.

Grayson knew that voice. He felt a wave of relief. As if by divine intervention, the chief had found him.

"I'm over here, chief!" Grayson called back. "Please, help me!"

Grayson looked around but couldn't see the chief. He took a couple of steps forward and saw Chief Danbury had shielded himself behind a tree with a rifle in his hand.

"I need to know, son, do you have a weapon?" Chief Danbury shouted.

"No!" Grayson shouted back. He didn't understand.

Chief Danbury stepped out from behind the tree, his weapon trained on Grayson. When he got closer, he froze in shock at the sight before him. He ripped off his sunglasses.

"Sweet Jesus," he whispered.

Grayson saw him looking at Tina's body.

"Sheriff...I... I…" Grayson sputtered.

Chief Danbury pointed his weapon back at Grayson as he marched forward. "Grayson Ender, you are under arrest for the murder of Tina Wilson. Turn around, son. Let's not make this harder than it needs to be."

"I need help," Grayson pleaded. "I'm injured."

Chief Danbury hesitated for a moment as he assessed Grayson's condition. He reluctantly lowered his weapon but put Grayson in handcuffs before trying to help him.

"Listen, chief, please, I'm gonna go with you, okay? But I'm telling you I did not do this. Please, you have to believe me. I know how it looks—"

"Let's just get you on down to the station. You can explain it there. And get cleaned up. Jesus Christ," muttered the chief. "Can you walk?"

"Yeah. I think I have a broken rib, though," Grayson said.

"Let's go then," the chief demanded.

Chief Danbury marched Grayson down the hill toward a dirt road. Grayson recognized that road. His eyes followed the road until it terminated at a wooden fence with a red stop sign nailed to it.

"Sheriff! There's a mine up there, past that fence!" Grayson exclaimed. "Wait, please! Hold on. That's where Tina was being held captive. I swear! Up there!"

The chief stopped and gripped Grayson's shoulder.

"Another one of your visions?" he asked gruffly.

"Yes."

"Now I just found you ten feet from the body of Tina Wilson and covered in her blood. You give me one good goddamn reason why I should listen to a word you have to say," Chief Danbury shouted.

"Please, chief, call Roxanne. She'll tell you. I was on the phone with her last night after I had my vision and...and," Grayson struggled to catch his breath. "The doctor. He, uh, Doc Weaver. He killed Tina. I can prove it. Please, Chief Danbury. I'm telling you the truth."

"You're trying to tell me that the doc did that to Tina? And is trying to pin it on you? I just wanna make sure I heard you right," the chief replied.

Grayson let out a frustrated groan. "Yes! Please. I can show you where she was."

"And you said you told Roxanne that the doc did this?"

"Yes. I told her everything about the vision, that the doctor abducted her. All of it," Grayson knew he was lying to the chief, but he needed Danbury to believe him so he could prove his own innocence.

He looked Grayson dead in the eyes, then glanced over at the road and back at Grayson.

"Alright, Mr. Ender. Up there, past that fence?" he asked.

Grayson nodded.

"Lead the way. But don't get cute," the chief warned.

"No, sir, I won't. I just want you to see. She was there, I know it."

Grayson led the chief back up the hill and beyond the fence, across a small clearing until they came upon the mine shaft. It was exactly as he had seen it in his vision from the Beast. When they arrived at the entrance, he noticed that the lock was missing.

"There was a padlock here," Grayson said.

"There should've been. This mine is dangerous. It's been off limits for more than a decade," said the chief.

"We have to go in," Grayson urged.

"It's not safe to go in."

"Sheriff, please. You...and I both need proof that I didn't do this. There's...proof in there," Grayson wheezed.

Chief Danbury shrugged and swung the large metal gate open with a sigh. "Watch your step."

Grayson led them into the tunnel. The familiar smell of the mud and moist cave walls sent goosebumps rippling across his body. "It's like I said, chief, the dripping water, the muddy cave floor."

"That describes about a hundred caves around here, Mr. Ender," the chief retorted. "There's footprints though. Look there, in the mud."

There were boot prints with a distinctive heel and toe pattern in the mud, like cowboy boots. Grayson placed his foot next to the prints, which were several sizes smaller than the muddy impressions.

"Well I'll be damned," Chief Danbury whispered.

When they reached the point where it was becoming difficult to see, Chief Danbury pulled out his flashlight and clicked on it. Grayson knew they were close now. He led them a few paces further into the shaft and then came to a sudden halt.

"Here," Grayson said. "Look down."

At their feet was a large disturbance in the mud, as if someone had been lying there and moving around. Grayson knew exactly who and what had created that impression in the mud.

"This is where he kept her, chief. Until he did that to her. Look there. See that little plastic thing? It's a cap for the needle of a syringe. I'm telling you, Doc Weaver's the one who did that to her. He drugged her with something."

"Now look, those footprints prove someone was in this mine. It doesn't prove that you didn't kill Tina Wilson, or that the doc did. Doc Weaver's been a pillar in this community for longer than you've been alive," the chief pointed out.

Grayson sighed in frustration. "Sheriff, I'm telling you the truth! The doctor held me captive, too. He drugged me and must have dumped me off next to the body to make it look like I was her killer." As he traced the events of the evening backward, Grayson suddenly remembered the car that pushed him off the road. "And, oh God. My Jeep. Sheriff. I had my vision last night and I was headed here, to this mine, and I was on the road and a car ran me off into the ravine. I rolled my Jeep and—"

"Okay, whoa, whoa, slow down. I know you got run off the road, alright. We found your Jeep. You were on the phone with Roxanne when it happened. She already told me all that. When we got to your Jeep, you were gone," the chief explained. "So how did you go from rollin' your Jeep down a ravine to waking up covered in Tina Wilson's blood next to her body?"

Grayson shook his head. “I don’t know. I remember going off the road and the next thing I knew I was in the Doc’s office, I think. It was dark. But I remember the wallpaper. It had flowers. And there was a light over my head, like, like an exam light kinda thing. And then…” Grayson began to recall the details of his conversation with the doctor. He took a step backward from the chief and glared at him. “And then he started asking me about the visions I had. Visions that only two people in this whole town know about. You and Roxanne. Why’d you tell him, chief?”

Chief Danbury extended one hand out to tell him to be calm, though Grayson saw him place his other on his handgun. “Now hold on a minute. Yes, that’s true. I did tell him, but not for whatever reason you’re thinking,” he cautioned. “I told him about your visions because I wanted a medical opinion about them before I took your story to the mayor. I admit the Doc’s a friend of mine, so I just asked, okay? I didn’t know he would do this.”

Chief Danbury took his hand off his gun and held them both up in peace.

“I don’t know who to fucking trust, chief,” Grayson whispered, tears welling in his eyes.

“I know. I know. Look, I believe you, okay? As a show of good faith, I’m gonna take those handcuffs off of you, alright?”

For a moment Grayson didn’t know whether to believe the chief or not. He’d have to turn his back to the chief and he’d be completely defenseless. Then again, if the chief were going to kill him, he could have already done it. Cautiously, he turned around.

“Thank you for trusting me,” Chief Danbury said. He reached over with his key and removed the handcuffs.

"I don't have any more proof than what I've already given you, chief," Grayson pleaded. "I didn't do this. I would never."

Chief Danbury nodded. "I believe you. But if you're right about Doc, that's gonna cause a whole lotta problems for the town. Look, come down to the station with me and get cleaned up. You'll be safe there. I'll get the coroner up here to handle Tina Wilson."

***

Back at the station, Grayson changed into a jumpsuit and turned his bloody clothes over to Officer Stanley, who bagged them for evidence. It was kind of the chief, Grayson thought, that he made sure no one in town saw him, especially in his current state. Even rumors that he was involved in the death of a student would be the end of his teaching career.

Deputy Thorne had been at the station when they arrived and helped to patch Grayson up and tend to some of his wounds, including what she suspected was a fractured rib. Deputy Thorne couldn't do much more than wrap his chest and give him a cold compress, but it was the best he was going to get, considering the town doctor was a homicidal maniac.

In the long couple of hours that Grayson sat alone in his cell, all he could do was mull over the details of his accident and kidnapping as he waited for Chief Danbury to return with Doc Weaver in handcuffs. He wanted so badly to call Roxanne and let her know that he was okay, but he'd lost his cell phone and didn't know her number. Maybe the chief had already told her that he was safe. Thank God she'd been on the line with him when the accident happened, he thought. It was lucky, too, that the chief had been the first to find him this morning. Grayson wondered how the chief could have known that he was there on that hill, and worried that maybe someone who lived nearby had seen him there, bloody and unconscious, and called it in.

Grayson stood up to ask Officer Stanley for a phone book to try to find the number to Roxanne's bar but was interrupted by a commotion at the back door to the station. Chief Danbury and Deputy Thorne came marching through with Doc Weaver in handcuffs.

"I didn't do it, you sons uh bitches. I'm telling you I didn't do it. I'm gonna sue you! Both of ya!" Doc Weaver raged.

Deputy Thorne opened the door to one of two holding cells. Chief Danbury pushed him in and slammed the door shut.

"You're gonna regret this!" Doc Weaver cried.

"Shut the fuck up and sit down! I will fuckin' Taser your fat, child-murdering ass if you don't sit down and be quiet!" Chief Danbury screamed, turning bright red.

The doctor went immediately silent and sat down.

Deputy Thorne brought a plastic bag to Grayson. Inside were his keys, phone, and wallet. She opened the cell door and motioned for Grayson to come out, and she handed him the bag. As she did, the deputy's cell phone rang, and she stepped away to answer the call. Chief Danbury walked over toward Grayson.

"We found these in the doctor's office hidden under some folders in his desk. That's proof enough for us," he proclaimed.

Grayson couldn't believe it.

"So that's it? I'm cleared? Free to go?" he asked.

"You're free to go," Chief Danbury acknowledged. "But as a matter of policy, I gotta ask that you stick around town until everything is totally cleared up and the doctor has signed a confession."

"I understand," Grayson nodded.

"I hope there's no hard feelings," Chief Danbury said, extending his hand as an olive branch.

Grayson shook it. "No, no hard feelings. I understand how it looked. I'd have done the same thing in your shoes. Honestly, I'm just glad to be free. And glad that *he's* where he belongs."

"You got very lucky, Mr. Ender," Chief Danbury said solemnly. "This could have ended real badly for you in a lot of ways. You owe Roxanne a lotta gratitude. If she hadn't already corroborated your story before I found you, I might not have believed you, and you wouldn't be walkin' out of here a free man."

Deputy Thorne returned with a serious expression on her face. She sighed and shook her head.

"That was John Arthur. Jimmy Wilson's at the church causing a ruckus. Asked us to come down," she said.

Chief Danbury shook his head. "Alright. Why don't you go on ahead. I'll meet you there in a bit," he directed. He turned to Officer Stanley. "Stanley, I want you to take Mr. Ender here back to his place."

Stanley groaned softly as he swung his feet off the desk and stood up. "You got it, chief."

Chief Danbury turned back to Grayson. "I want you to go inside, lock the door, and don't answer it. Not for anyone. I got a bad feeling about what's going on at the church. I know you're injured and we'll get you over to County Medical as soon as this is done."

"I could call Roxanne and have her take me? As long as I'm alright to leave Breakvale?" Grayson suggested.

The chief paused and exchanged glances with Deputy Thorne, who simply shrugged. "Yeah, alright. That's fine," he nodded. “There and back, though, till this is all cleared up. Do not go anywhere else, and you stay with Roxanne.”

“I understand.”

Deputy Thorne put her sunglasses on and gently clasped Grayson’s shoulder. “You did good. Now go get some rest,” she said with a flickering smile.

“Let’s go, kid,” Officer Stanley called from the back door, waving him on.

Grayson took one long, final look at the monster sitting in its cage, then turned and walked out the station doors as a vindicated man.

When they had rounded the corner and were out of sight, Chief Danbury stepped over to peer outside. He closed the blinds and locked the front doors. The heavy clacking of his boots on the tile floor echoed in the empty station as the chief walked over to where Doc Weaver sat in his cell. The doctor cackled obscenely.

“That was a good performance there, Roland. The boy don’t suspect a thing,” Doc Weaver grinned. “Now, let me outta here.”

Chief Danbury just blinked and shook his head. “Can’t do that, Doc,” he stated. “You took one outta turn, and then you got sloppy with it. We can’t afford sloppy, Doc. Whatever drug you gave the boy didn’t take. He still remembered every bit of what you said. Now I gotta clean up your mess.”

Fear flickered for a moment in the doctor’s eyes. “You can’t be serious. Look, let me out of here. I’ll slip out the back, go kill the little queer in his sleep before he can tell anyone, and then I’ll disappear and lay low for a while until it’s safe to come back.”

Chief Danbury stared at the doctor for a hard minute, then reached down for his keys. The doctor let out a nervous laugh as Chief Danbury unlocked his cell and swung the door open. He extended his arm in invitation for the doctor to exit the cell. As the doctor walked past him, Chief Danbury reached up quickly, grabbed Doc Weaver by the head, and then snapped his neck in one swift motion. The doctor's body slumped to the floor.

"Sorry 'bout that old pal. But you broke the rules. We can't allow that," he admonished, shaking his head at the doctor's lifeless body.

The chief entered the cell, stripped the sheet from the bed, and began to fashion it into a makeshift noose, which he suspended from the top bars of the cell. He dragged the body far enough into the cell to close the door, then took out his phone and dialed a number.

"It's done. Get down here and help me hoist this fat son of a bitch up," he demanded.

13

Officer Stanley dropped Grayson off at home. As soon as he had locked himself safely inside, he scooped the phone from his pocket to call Roxanne. She picked up immediately.

"Oh thank God. Grayson, you're alive. I've been worried out of my fucking mind," Roxanne answered, trying to steady the quiver in her voice.

"Hi. I'm so sorry. I wanted to call you sooner, but I didn't have my phone. I'm at home, but I need to go to County Medical. Can you take me?"

"I'm on my way."

Barely ten minutes passed before Grayson heard a knock at the door. He glanced out the peephole, then opened the door. Roxanne sprang through the doorway to hug him, and he grimaced as she squeezed him tightly. She backed off as he drew a deep breath from the pain.

"Oh, oh my God. I'm sorry. Are you okay?"

"Pretty sure I have a fractured rib," he breathed. He smiled at Roxanne and held back as his eyes grew dewy.

They embraced for a short while, then Roxanne took a step back and closed the door.

"You really scared the hell out of me," she told him. "Being on the phone with you and hearing the sound of you crashing was the most terrifying thing I've ever experienced. I didn't know what to do. I just stood there screaming and crying in the kitchen.

Keith didn’t know what to do either, poor guy. By the time I got the words out, he already had the chief on the line.”

“Yeah, I know, I’m sorry. That must’ve been really hard on you,” Grayson said softly. He hugged her again. “Rox, you saved my life. The chief said that if it hadn't been for you, he probably wouldn't have believed me. He was ready to shoot me on sight.”

Roxanne took Grayson’s face between her hands. “Hey, first of all, you have nothing to be sorry for. It wasn’t your fault. And I'm glad he didn’t,” she laughed, trying to break the tension of the moment. “The chief and I go way back, as you can imagine. I'm just glad it made a difference.”

“Well it did,” Grayson sighed. He paused a moment. “Rox, it was Doc Weaver. He’s the one that killed Tina Wilson. He’s the one that ran me off the road, I’m sure of it. After the crash, I woke up and I was in his office and he had me strapped down and drugged me, I think. It’s all kinda fuzzy still.”

“He did what? Doc Weaver?” Roxanne gasped.

“It’s a lot,” Grayson sighed.

Roxanne grabbed her car keys from her pocket. “Come on, you can tell me about it on the way to the hospital.”

Grayson shook his head. “No, no I don’t want to go yet. Come sit with me. I gotta make sense of this first.”

They sat down on the couch and Grayson recounted the events as he remembered them for Roxanne. When he finished, Roxanne struggled for words to say.

“So now I don’t know what’s gonna happen,” Grayson said, bridging the silence. “Breakvale doesn’t have like a judge or court or anything right?”

Roxanne shook her head. “No, the doc’ll probably get handed over to the county to stand trial. That’s gonna be a fucking mess, though," she predicted, pressing her face into her palms.

"A trial like that's gonna get attention from the media. He'll say that the Beast of Breakvale made him do it. Then all of a sudden Breakvale will be in the spotlight. And people died the last time that happened," Grayson recalled. "But surely no one here is going to talk to investigators. Not when they know it could put them at risk."

"Well, I dunno. People outside are gonna hear his defense and think he's a lunatic and that'll be the end of it. No one actually gives a shit about this town. It'll be gone and forgotten," Roxanne assured.

"Yeah, I suppose. Once a jury sees what I saw, he's toast. You're right, they'll just think he's a lunatic. But *we* know for fact that there is a creature out there. It just makes me worry that this will happen again," Grayson stressed.

Roxanne's phone began to vibrate suddenly.

"It's Keith," she said, holding up a finger to indicate she'd only be a moment. "Yeah, what's goin' on Keith?"

As Roxanne listened to Keith, Grayson watched her face contort into a confused and concerned expression.

"Uh huh. Got it. Look, close the bar and lock it down," Roxanne instructed. Her wide eyes met Grayson's for a moment in disbelief as she listened. "No, no. You don't have to stay there. The bar will be fine...yeah...alright. Well, if you want. You know what to do if there's trouble...alright. I'm gonna go check it out. I'll be back soon."

Roxanne hung up the phone.

"What the hell is going on?"

Roxanne stood up and pulled her keys from her pocket again. "Jimmy Wilson saw his daughter's body and lost it, and somehow he found out about Doc Weaver and now there's a whole angry mob at the church."

"Fuck. When I left the station, Deputy Thorne got a call from John Arthur about a disturbance there," Grayson said. He pushed himself off the couch and up onto his feet. "What's going on at the bar?"

"Apparently there's talk about a lynch mob forming. Some of the folks at the bar got calls. Keith's worried about a riot. A riot. In Breakvale, of all places!" Roxanne said incredulously. "He's gonna lock up and stick around in case anyone tries to break in."

"No one's gonna be that stupid, surely," Grayson scoffed.

"They better not. But I've never seen this town up in arms about anything like this before. This one's got 'em rattled. Who knows what they'll do," countered Roxanne. "I'm gonna go down to the church and check it out. Are you okay here for a bit till I get back?"

"No way. I'm going with you," Grayson said as he reached for his coat.

"Oh no you're not. You have been through enough for one day. And you've got a fractured rib," Roxanne scolded.

"Either I ride with you or I walk there," Grayson shrugged. "And I'd really rather not have to walk. You can take me to County Medical after."

Roxanne rolled her eyes. "Alright, then. Fine. Let's go see about this."

Grayson and Roxanne walked to her SUV and she helped him up into the passenger seat. The rush of adrenaline he felt at the thought of what they might encounter at the church helped to blunt the otherwise sharp pain in his rib cage. Main Street looked conspicuously empty as they proceeded north toward the church.

All of the lights at Roxanne's bar had been turned off and the open sign flipped to closed. Several other shops along the street appeared to have done the same.

They rolled up to the gravel lane that led to the church. There were dozens of cars filling the small parking lot, and many more parked haphazardly on the grass around it. Grayson could see a huge crowd of people standing around the front of the church.

"It's like the candlelight vigil. Everyone's here," Grayson said lowly.

"More," Roxanne corrected. "I don't like this. This feels...bad."

They parked well off to the side at the end of the lane and meandered their way through the maze of vehicles toward the church. Even from a distance, they could hear people in the crowd shouting and chanting. The sun had slipped well below the mountains by this time, and they cast their long shadows over the valley floor. As Grayson and Roxanne neared the crowd, they saw several people holding candles, others with flashlights shining up at the steps of the church, and even a few waving lit tiki torches that flickered and fumed in the twilight. Grayson could see John Arthur standing near the doors of the church. Ross stood beside him, stalwart as he ever was, but glancing nervously around the crowd. Chief Danbury and Deputy Thorne both had their cars parked off to the side of the church and stood imposingly flanked on either side of Mayor Wallace, who seemed to have just taken the stage and was preparing to address the angry crowd in front of him. Grayson and Roxanne silently took their spots at the back of the crowd to listen. Mayor Wallace raised his hands in a bid to simmer the rumbling.

"Please, everyone. Please, can I have your attention?" Mayor Wallace struggled. "Friends, please. I can't..."

The mayor's voice drowned in the sea of voices until they couldn't hear him at the back. Finally, Chief Danbury cocked his shotgun and discharged it into the sky. The crowd fell mostly silent.

"Thank you. I appreciate you all coming here tonight to express your anger and your shock about Jimmy Wilson's daughter, Tina," Mayor Wallace began. "I feel it's important, as the man you chose to lead this town, to tell you the facts surrounding this horrible, horrible tragedy."

"Why'd he do it, Adam?" a woman shouted from somewhere in the crowd.

Mayor Wallace held out his hand. "Please, I know you all must have dozens of questions. Let me tell you the facts as we know them first, and then we'll address questions," he said. He cleared his throat nervously. "Today, around one o'clock in the afternoon, on an anonymous tip, Chief Danbury and Deputy Thorne arrested Doctor Weaver in his office in connection with the murder of Tina Wilson."

The crowd erupted in a cacophony of angry voices, prompting the chief to fire off a second shot to silence them. The mayor continued.

"Please, I know that you are angry. The doctor, he violated our trust, a sacred trust, that we all share in. Breakvale is the best place to live in this whole world, and that's because we trust each other. In Breakvale, Truth is Life. That's our way. Now, the doctor, he broke that trust. And he's tried to make it look like this was the work of the Beast. But folks, I assure you that this was not the work of the Beast. The Beast has already claimed two beautiful, bright souls—"

"How do you know for sure? If he killed this girl, how do we know he didn't kill the other two kids before?" a husky voice interjected.

Mayor Wallace turned to Chief Danbury. "Sheriff, you wanna answer that one?"

The chief took a step forward. "Deputy Thorne and I are one hundred percent certain that the injury patterns found on Andrew McIntosh and Alexis Carter are consistent with those found on other victims associated with the Beast of Breakvale. However, the injuries Tina Wilson sustained are not consistent with those injury patterns."

"Based on the evidence presented to me by the chief," Mayor Wallace began slowly, glancing reassuringly from Chief Danbury back to the crowd. "I am absolutely certain that Doctor Weaver committed this crime alone and with the intention of blaming it on the Beast. Now, we all know in order to preserve our idyllic way of life, every so often we have to make a sacrifice. This year, that price was paid by two wonderful, beautiful, brave children. And what the doctor did...well that was a spit in the face to their memory. It wasn't right, and I'm telling you that Doc Weaver will be brought to justice."

"So what, he goes to jail? Where he gets cable and three meals a day and gets to keep living while little Tina's in the ground?" a woman cried out. "Where's the justice in that?"

"Yeah!" a few people shouted in unison.

"I understand that you're all very angry. I'm angry as well. But Doctor Weaver is safely behind bars where he can't hurt any more of our children. And he will be punished," Mayor Wallace stressed.

“Damn right he will,” hollered a gruff voice from somewhere near the back. “He took one of our own. He broke the trust. I say we give him our own justice!”

“Doctor Weaver will stand trial for his crime,” Chief Danbury yelled back.

A man suddenly pushed his way to the front, dragging another man by the arm behind him. They faced the crowd.

“Y’all know this is Jimmy Wilson. Tina’s daddy,” the first man began. He clapped a silent and somber Jimmy Wilson on the back as he spoke. “Jimmy’s a good friend uh mine. I knew him and watched him give everything he had to raise Tina. He ain’t got nothin’ left now. Apparently we ain’t got just one monster here. We got two, ’cept this is one monster we can deal with. Are y’all just gonna let ’em take Doc Weaver up to some jail where he gets to keep on livin’, or are we gonna take care of this one ourselves?”

Chief Danbury swooped in on the man to force him off the church steps, but the spark had already been ignited. As the chief attempted to wrestle the man down, several other people started waving their candles and tiki torches and shouting. A chant broke out.

“Hang him high!”

“Hang him high!”

“Hang him high!”

Mayor Wallace lost all control of the crowd. Several people rushed the steps of the church and pulled Chief Danbury off of the man he had attempted to silence. The man sprang back up and grabbed Jimmy Wilson and dragged him back into the crowd.

“He’s at the station!” the man shouted. “Everyone to the station! Hang ’em high!”

Roxanne grabbed Grayson by the hand and pulled him away from the crowd. "Come on, we gotta go. Now."

All at once, the crowd broke, and people flooded toward their cars. Engines revved, and horns honked in a choir of mechanical insanity as trucks and cars tore across the churchyard, each trying to be the pace car in a race for vengeance.

Grayson barely had time to get himself buckled before Roxanne threw her SUV into gear and sped across the church grounds, driving away from the line of vehicles turning right off the gravel road toward town. Instead, she drove down a small hill, through the ditch, and turned left onto the road.

"It'll take forever for that procession to make it into town. We'll skirt the edge of town and pop out over by the station," Roxanne explained.

"Who was that man? The one that just incited a fucking lynch mob?" Grayson asked.

Roxanne sighed in frustration. "His name's Arnie Morgan. He's a mean son of a bitch. Used to come into the bar all the time until I finally had to ban him for life for trying to stab someone with a broken beer bottle. As far as I know now he just spends all his time drinking and beating on his wife."

"Do you really think they'll let the doctor get lynched?" Grayson asked gravely.

"Gonna be honest here, Grayson. I've never seen anything like this. I don't know what's gonna happen."

Much of the mob made it to the police station before Roxanne and Grayson arrived. There were vehicles parked in the middle of the streets on both sides of the station, forcing them to park a block down and walk to the station.

As they rounded the corner, Grayson saw Chief Danbury's squad car parked on the sidewalk in front of the station to barricade the door. The chief, Deputy Thorne, and Officer Stanley stood in front of the entrance to the station with their guns pointed at the mob to hold them at bay. Mayor Wallace stood on top of the chief's car and appeared to be in a shouting match with Arnie Morgan, who this time stood elevated above the crowd in the back of a truck bed as the mob around them continued to chant.

"Let us in, Sheriff!" Arnie shouted. "You caught the guy. You done your job. Alls you gotta do is look the other way while we do the rest."

"This isn't justice, Arnie. This isn't the way. The doctor should be put to death for what he did, I agree. But that's not for us to decide," Mayor Wallace shouted back.

"Lettin' him live is as good as lettin' him go free, Mr. Mayor," Arnie said. "He don't deserve it."

As they argued, Jimmy Wilson climbed up into the bed of the truck carrying a tiki torch in one hand and shotgun in the other. He waved the torch in the air.

"I got somethin' to say!" he yelled.

It was the first time Jimmy Wilson had said anything at all. The crowd took notice of him and fell into a hushed silence, eager to hear the judgment of the grieving father.

"Y'all know I'm hard-workin', honest-livin', God-fearin' man. I believe in the law and I believe in what's right and what's wrong. Now we all know this ain't the right way..." he began slowly, his voice quivering until it finally broke. "But this man. This monster. He tore my little girl's...he ripped it...her heart...he tore it right out her chest. My precious baby girl. I see it when I close my eyes—"

Jimmy Wilson dropped the torch and the shotgun as he fell to his knees in the bed of the truck and wept.

Arnie Morgan spun around, a frenzied look in his eyes.

"Hang 'em high!" he cried.

The crowd erupted in screams and chanting as Arnie jumped down from the bed of the truck and started pushing the squad car in an attempt to turn it over. Mayor Wallace jumped down as several others joined in to help rock the car, forcing Chief Danbury and Deputy Thorne to both fire a warning shot in the air.

They backed off, but not before a small brick went suddenly whizzing by and smashed into one of the large station windows. The window didn't break but gripped the brick as it cracked and protruded through the glass panel. A second brick was thrown, then a third, until the window finally shattered. Soon people in the mob were throwing anything they could grab and aimed for anything in front of them. Adjacent shop windows were shattered in the chaos, while someone a little way up the street set fire to small tree planted along the sidewalk. The chanting continued to grow louder still.

Mayor Wallace and Chief Danbury exchanged some inaudible words, then Mayor Wallace climbed back up on the squad car. He waved his hands in a bid to get everyone's attention.

"Alright. Alright!" he shouted. "This destruction has to stop. We'll open the station doors. Arnie, since you're the ringleader in all this, you'll accompany the chief inside to get Doc Weaver. Once he's outside the station, you all can do whatever you want with him."

For a brief moment, no one said a word.

Arnie slapped his knee. "Well hot damn! That's what I'm talkin' about Mr. Mayor. Let's do it!"

The chanting resumed as Arnie rounded the police car and entered the station with Chief Danbury. The crowd pushed closer toward the station, forcing the mayor and all the officers into it. A couple of minutes passed, and then Arnie emerged from the station. Several people at the front of the mob exchanged confused glances.

"He's already dead!" Arnie shouted. "The motherfucker hung himself in his cell!

People began to mutter and grumble until someone from the middle of the pack shouted, "Hang him anyway!" and the crowd erupted again into frenzied madness. Several people rushed into the police station with Arnie, only to return moments later dragging the body of Doctor Weaver by the sheet tied around his neck.

They dragged Doc Weaver's body down the sidewalk toward the corner streetlamp, and people in the crowd kicked his body and spat on it as it passed them. Someone from the crowd produced an actual noose rope and passed it overhead down the crowd until it made its way into the hands of the men dragging the doctor toward the light pole. They put the noose around his neck and cinched it tight.

"Strip him naked!" a voice called out.

The men complied and ripped his clothes off, leaving him in nothing but his white briefs. Then they tossed the rope around the crook in the light pole and pulled in tandem to hoist his limp and lifeless body up off the ground. The crowd continued to chant, growing more fervent with every pull of the rope.

"Hang him high!"

"Hang him high!"

"Hang him high!"

When his body reached its maximum height and the rope was tied off to ensure his body wouldn't fall, the crowd erupted in cheers. Sensing the turned tide, Mayor Wallace pushed his way through the crowd and stood under Doc Weaver's swaying corpse.

"Let this be a lesson! To anyone who would break our sacred trust. To anyone who would try to use the Beast to commit such a heinous act again. This will be your punishment," he shouted to raucous cheers and applause.

Then as quickly as it had all begun, the crowd dispersed almost immediately, scattering back to their vehicles or slinking off down side streets. A few people remained behind to ensure that the body wouldn't be taken down immediately, and Mayor Wallace assured them that he would leave it up for an appropriate amount of time.

Grayson and Roxanne stood rooted in their spots, transfixed by the horror they were witnessing. When it was no longer safe to lurk in the shadows, they moved silently back to Roxanne's SUV. Neither knew what to say at first, until at last Roxanne buckled herself up and burst into tears. Grayson reached over and held her hand.

"All my life, Grayson. In all my life, I've never seen something like that," she choked through tears.

The only thing Grayson could muster was a heavy sigh as he squeezed her hand tighter.

Roxanne wiped the tears from her eyes, pulled a pack of cigarettes from her center console, and lit one with a trembling hand. She started the car and rolled the window down.

"I'm sorry. I know you quit. You don't mind, do you?" she asked earnestly, before breaking into absurd laughter.

The break in her tension caught Grayson by surprise, and he laughed as well. "No. God no. Please."

"We should leave. Let's get you to the hospital," she said suddenly, finding a reason to pull herself together.

Roxanne shifted the vehicle into gear and drove slowly, burning her cigarette down to the butt as she navigated a couple of back streets before connecting to the main road out of Breakvale.

***

Grayson was discharged and allowed to return home from the hospital after a couple of days, much faster than he had projected to Principal Daggett when he called to inform him about the accident. He had indeed suffered a small fracture to one of his ribs, but other than a few bruises, he came out of the entire incident relatively unscathed. Deputy Thorne warned him that his Jeep was totaled in the accident, but Grayson didn't care all that much; he was happy to just be alive and to have escaped Doc Weaver. The trauma of being run off the road, drugged, and framed for murder, however, left him unable to sleep for more than a few hours at a time. He was afraid to close his eyes, because each time he did, all he could see was Tina's desecrated body propped up against the tree. His doctor prescribed him medication to help him sleep, but Grayson had no intention of taking it. He'd had enough visions and disturbing images seared into his brain to haunt him for the rest of his life. Eventually, he would be able to sleep again, but for now, he was content with just being perpetually exhausted.

Roxanne had made it a point to come pick Grayson up from the hospital and bring him home, and she met him with a smile as the nurse rolled him out the doors of the hospital in a wheelchair. Grayson stood up from his wheelchair as she moved to hug him. They embraced for a moment until he winced in pain.

"Careful of the rib," he grimaced.

"Oh my God, I forgot! I'm so sorry!" she exclaimed.

"It's okay. I'm glad to see you. I'm ready to go home."

Roxanne helped Grayson into the passenger side of her SUV, and they took off down the road. Roxanne turned and flashed Grayson a weary smile.

"You look better," she observed.

"I feel like shit. I can't sleep. I'm afraid to sleep, really," he confessed.

Roxanne pursed her lips. "Can't say I blame you. After everything."

"Is his body still hanging there?" Grayson asked.

"Yeah, it's still there," Roxanne confirmed. "I passed it on the way out of town to come get you. The chief wanted to take it down, but Mayor Wallace is making good on his promise to keep it up there. He really wants to send a message, I guess."

"Jesus," said Grayson. He paused for a moment. "You know, I thought a lot about the other night while I was actively not sleeping. I didn't realize it then with everything going on, but I'm pretty sure I saw some of my students in that mob."

"Probably. And you know what, it's the damnedest thing. Three nights ago, the whole town seemed like it lost its collective mind, and now no one wants to talk about it. People walk down the street and see his body hanging there and they just avert their eyes. Acting like they didn't have a part in it."

"Is no one concerned about the kids?" Grayson replied. "Like, is no one concerned about the long-term psychological damage these kids are going to suffer from seeing a dead man hanging from a streetlamp?"

It took Roxanne several seconds to consider her reply. Finally, she just gave a resigned sigh.

"I hate to say it, but is it really any worse than watching their friends go missing and turn up dead? Or spending their entire childhood living in fear that one day they could just get taken by the Beast?" she countered.

"I mean, well, yeah, obviously that's traumatic. Like, you grew up in Breakvale. And you turned out to be well-adjusted. But you never had to see anything like this, right? I mean..."

"Grayson, hun, I was a drug addict. I didn't turn out fine, believe me. I had to get fine. This place...it fucks with you in ways you don't even realize. And, yeah, I never had to see a body hanging in the street. Hell, I never even saw a kid go missing. The Beast never attacked a kid the whole time I was growing up."

"So what changed?"

"I honestly don't know. You get so used to it that you sorta stop paying attention to it. I mean, look at you. When you first moved here you were terrified. I'm not even sure why you stuck around. And now look at you. Coming back from the hospital after chasing down a real-life monster like some kind of movie hero."

Grayson laughed. "It is pretty fucked up, I guess. I dunno. I didn't go chasing after Tina to be a hero. It just feels like no one in Breakvale gives a shit about these kids. Well, almost no one. You care. Dale seems to genuinely care. It's just, like, how are people okay with this?"

"Complacency is a dangerous mindset. So is security. Everyone in Breakvale buys into the perfect little town bullshit. Like it's—"

"Mayberry," they said simultaneously.

"Yeah, I know. I've said that, too. Only no one in Mayberry ever lynched a dead man and left his corpse swinging over Main Street."

The pair fell silent for several minutes listening to Roxanne's Nora Jones CD play softly from the speakers.

"I didn't take you for a Nora Jones fan," Grayson chuckled, pointing to the radio.

"My regular life is stressful enough already. I like my music to be an escape. I don't need amped up, I need chilled the fuck out," she defended.

"That's fair," Grayson said, easing his head back against the headrest and closing his eyes.

They listened to several songs together quietly. This was the most relaxed he had felt in days.

"You know who seemed extra concerned about your well-being?" Roxanne began slyly. "Ross McCrory."

Grayson's eyes shot open. "Oh?"

"Yeah. He's been in the bar every day since your accident asking me how you're doing."

"That's kind of him," Grayson said coolly.

"Yeah, it really is. Especially considering I've only ever seen him in the bar maybe twice since I've owned it."

"He's a really sweet guy."

"He sure is," Roxanne said slowly. She paused to throw Grayson a wicked little smile. "So, are you two dating yet?"

Grayson whipped his head around and struggled for an answer. "I didn't know you knew I'm gay?"

"Oh come on, Grayson. Give me some credit. Some of us have seen the world outside of Breakvale. I knew you were gay the day I met you. And don't worry, this is all between you and me. I know what some of the parents would say if they found out."

"Yeah," Grayson sighed.

"So, you don't have to tell me if you don't want to, but have you guys, you know?"

"No," Grayson laughed. "Ross is…complicated."

"That's an understatement. Him being gay can't be that easy for him. Has he told you about his family?"

"No. Actually he's never brought them up."

"He's had a rough life, poor guy. Been through the wringer a couple times. I don't know much more than the town gossip, so probably better if he tells you. But yeah. He's a really sweet guy. Cute, too."

"He is very cute," Grayson grinned.

"Like I knew about you, I've known that boy was gay since he was a kid. I remember he used to come into the diner with his grandparents when he was maybe five or six. I was like, fifteen or so, helping bus tables for my dad. Ross was so particular about his blonde hair being brushed to the side just the right way and he'd get so mad when my dad would come along and ruffle it. Oh, he hated it, but he was always too polite to say anything. But you could see it all over his face."

"That's adorable. I'll have to ask him about it."

"I remember once," Roxanne began, her face growing more solemn. "This one time, there was a girl, about Ross's age, in the diner playing with some dolls at a table. One of the waitress's little girls had to stay home for some reason, and her mom brought her to work. The girl was playing with these dolls, and Ross came in with his grandparents. While they were busy talking to some folks they knew, Ross saw the girl playing with the dolls and got excited and ran over and asked to play with her.

And they did for several minutes, until his grandpa noticed and marched over and yanked him up out of his seat and yelled at him for playing with girl toys. Said dolls weren't for boys. You could practically see Ross's little heart break. He just wanted to play."

"That's awful!" Grayson scowled. "And no one said anything?"

"Come on, you know how it is. No one goes sticking their nose into something like that. It was family business. And this was, gosh, almost twenty years ago now. Things were different then."

"I guess so," Grayson mumbled.

"Again, not really my story to tell, but it also I think explains why he took a deep dive into religion. It sort of shielded him from anyone suspecting he might be gay."

"Well, he's not alone there. That happens to a lot of people," Grayson commented.

"Anyway, to circle back to the first thing, I think you two would be cute together," Roxanne smiled.

"Yeah. We've spent a few nights together just hanging out and talking. I don't know that he's really ready to date yet or anything. He's really trying to figure stuff out. You know, balancing his faith with his feelings. It's hard. And I don't want to push him."

"That's good of you," Roxanne encouraged. "Just keep that up. He'll come round. He's going to be excited to see you. I left him at the bar this morning to come pick you up. Ten bucks says he's still in that same bar stool when I get back."

At noon they crested the hill overlooking Breakvale and descended into the valley. They pulled up to The Sparrows, and Roxanne helped Grayson get inside and onto the couch. "If you need anything, you call me," she said. "And I'll be back later tonight with food for you."

"Grayson nodded. "You're the best. Thank you."

Roxanne flipped the lock on his doorknob and closed it tight behind her. Grayson sat there quietly on the couch, looking around and remembering himself waking up on the living room floor after his vision. He took a deep breath and felt the pain of it in his ribs. Lucky, he thought, that it was only a fractured rib. Still too afraid to sleep even though he was exhausted, Grayson reached for the television remote and prepared himself to finish the season of *Criminal Minds* he had been watching.

14

In spite of himself, Grayson did manage to take a brief cat nap, and he did it without having any nightmares, which was an immense relief upon waking up. Seven o'clock came around quickly, and as if in answer to the prayers of his rumbling stomach, there was a knock at the door.

"Roxanne, you angel," he muttered to himself, standing up and walking over to open the door.

To Grayson's surprise, Ross stood outside his door, clutching a couple of Styrofoam to-go boxes. He smiled and waved Ross inside.

"Sorry to drop in on you. Roxanne said she was busy at the bar and asked me to come bring you some food," Ross explained.

"Of course she was busy," Grayson smirked, shaking his head. "Thank you for bringing me food."

Ross walked through the living room and set the containers down on the table. "I brought extra for me in case you felt like company. I know I hate to eat alone sometimes. I mean, if you want? I don't have to stay if you don't want."

"Sit down, Ross," Grayson directed, trying not to laugh too hard. "I'd love it if you'd have dinner with me."

Grayson took a seat next to him at the table and opened up the container in front of him. He knew it was pot roast before he even opened the lid. It smelled exquisite. Ross handed him a plastic fork and they sat quietly together while they ate.

“So...on the drive back from the hospital, Roxanne and I were talking. She said you'd come into the bar a few times to check up on me,” Grayson told him. “That's very sweet.”

Ross blushed. “Oh, well, yeah, I mean. Car accidents are never good. And it sounded like you had a bad one. I was worried about you.”

Grayson smiled warmly at Ross.

“She also said that your family history is a little...complicated?” Grayson said gently. Ross’s eyes narrowed for a moment as he chewed his food, and though Ross turned his face away, Grayson could see his crestfallen expression. “You don’t have to talk about it if you don’t want to. Roxanne didn’t give me any specifics. She just said it wasn’t her story to tell, and I was curious.”

“No, it’s fine. It’s okay. If you didn’t hear it from me, you’d eventually hear it from someone around town,” Ross said, putting his fork down. “Both of my parents died when I was little. My mom was taken by the Beast when I was five. They found her body in the river a couple days later.”

“Ross, I’m so sorry,” Grayson reached out and put his hand on Ross’s knee in an attempt to comfort him.

“Well...after that my dad was so just...heartbroken, I guess. He went out to the barn and shot himself in the head. Grandad said he just didn’t know how to go on without her.”

This time Grayson said nothing but squeezed Ross’s knee a little tighter.

“I didn’t know it happened,” he continued. “Daddy waited until I was asleep in bed. He called my grandparents and told them to come over and get me in the middle of the night and then went out and, well, yeah. All I knew was granny waking me up and telling me that I had to come to their house. I could tell she had been crying, but she just always had this big smile that could make you feel easy. She helped me get some of my toys and some clothes and we packed 'em in my school bag. I didn't know what my daddy'd done until a couple days later. The school counselor told me, of all people. They never were very good at talking about feelings, my grandparents. I guess they just didn't know how to tell me."

"My God," Grayson whispered, leaning back in his chair.

They were silent for a moment.

"Eventually my grandad got sick. He had lung cancer real bad. I was maybe fifteen or so. And then he died and it was just my granny and me for a few years. She got to where she couldn't work on account of her bad knees and her arthritis, so I worked a lot to support us both and pay the bills. But she always made sure we were in church, every Sunday. And folks around town were real kind to us and would bring us food and stuff. And then I graduated high school and I knew I couldn't leave, even though I had the grades to go to college and stuff, and I wanted to leave real badly. But I couldn't. Well, then that summer, granny had a stroke and I was havin' to take care of her and work and stuff and I knew I really couldn't leave then."

"Putting her in a nursing home or something wasn't an option?" Grayson asked, then backtracked. "Sorry, I didn't mean for that to sound insensitive. I just meant, like, there wasn't a higher level of care available for her?"

"No. Couldn't afford it. Plus, there's not any place like that for miles and miles. And granny didn't want to leave her house. She was real stubborn about it," a smile broke across Ross's face. "She always said that was her house, she lived there all her life and she was gonna die there. And that's exactly what happened a few months later. But Pastor Arthur was so good to us and helped us. The church took up collections for us and stuff. And when granny died, I was eighteen and without any family. The church became my family. Which is how I ended up doing what I do now."

"Wow. That's, uh...gosh. I'm sorry, Ross. That's tough. I can't imagine what that must have been like."

"It's okay. It's been enough time now that it doesn't hurt so much to talk about it, you know? I mean, it was traumatic, but I guess it could'a been much worse. I'm just glad I had the time with them that I did."

"Sure," Grayson affirmed.

"Yeah, so, uh, I guess on the subject of traumatic things, how are you feeling, by the way?" Ross asked, changing the topic. "Roxanne told me you have a fractured rib?"

"Yeah. Other than that and some bumps and bruises, I'm okay…it could've been much worse," Grayson said with a chuckle. "How, uh, how much did Roxanne tell you about what happened to me?"

Ross looked at Grayson for a moment with sorrowful eyes. "At first just that you rolled your Jeep. But then today she told me everything that actually happened...Grayson, I am so, so sorry."

He could see the tears building up in Ross's eyes. He reached out and put his hand on Ross's hand.

"It's okay. I'm okay," Grayson eased. He paused for a moment, trying to decide his next words very carefully. "Look, Ross. I'm gonna say something, and I want to get it all out before you say anything, okay?"

"Sure," Ross nodded.

"I had a very near-death experience. The shit that I saw...it, uh, it's kind of fucked me up. Like, I don't know if I'll ever get the image of that girl's body out of my mind. This whole town...while I was in the hospital I thought really, really hard about just packing everything up and moving back to Charleston. Just fucking running away and never looking back. But running away won't stop the nightmares. And it won't protect the kids here. And it would mean having to leave you behind. And I... I just can't do that. Do you get what I mean?"

Ross waited to see if Grayson had anything more to say, then nodded. "Yeah, I understand. I get it. You don't want to abandon your students."

"Well, yes. But also...okay, look, I'm trying really hard not to freak you out because that's not what I'm going for here. But, like, I could have died. And it made me realize that I think I like you. A lot. And I know that this is all very new to you, and you're very nervous about stuff, and I want you to know that I absolutely respect all of that and I don't want to push you—"

Ross leaned over across the table and kissed Grayson on the lips. Grayson sat back in stunned surprise.

"Uh, huh. Yeah. That's it. Pretty much," Grayson fumbled, lost for words.

"My turn to tell you something," Ross said. "When I heard you had been in an accident, there was some part of me that was so terrified, like, more scared than I'd ever been for someone else. And then I heard you were okay and in the hospital, and I thought about you all the dang time. I just couldn't shake the image of you layin' there in that bed all alone with no friends or family and stuff. I wanted to come visit you so badly, but I didn't know if you would want me to be there while you were hurt. So I just kept comin' into the bar to check on you."

"Yeah, Roxanne said you were in the bar a lot asking how I was doing," Grayson chuckled.

"Well yeah, I didn't have your phone number and I didn't want to ask Roxanne for it because I didn't want her gettin' suspicious—"

"Oh, Roxanne totally knows, by the way. About you and me and what we've got going on," Grayson told him.

"How does she know?" Ross asked nervously. "She's not gonna tell anyone, right?"

"No, no don't worry. She really likes you. She would never," Grayson reassured. "She caught me off guard in the car this morning. Said she knew I was gay the first day we met. And she said she's known about you since you were, like, six. Anyway, you were saying?"

"Oh. Wow. Uh yeah, that makes me a little nervous, but if you trust her, then I guess it's alright," Ross responded. "But what I was sayin' is that I realized maybe what I was feeling about you was more than just as a friend, you know what I mean? And it's all kinds of scary and kind of exciting, and I'm still not sure how I feel about certain stuff. But I think I like you, too, Grayson, and I just hope you'll continue to be kind and patient with me while I figure everything out."

"I'm in no hurry. Take all the time you need. Just consider maybe staying the night more often? I like your company. And if anyone asks, tell them you're doing the Lord's work helping a sick man get better," Grayson joked.

"Hey, you know that's not a bad idea," Ross laughed.

They finished dinner with a more jovial conversation. For the first time, Grayson felt that they were able to talk more openly about mutual interests, as if the wall of formality between them had finally been torn down. The difference in Ross's body language was also noticeable; they had elected to migrate to the couch to watch television, and Ross cuddled up next to him without being prompted or meekly asking for permission. Every once in a while, Ross would move in such a way that Grayson felt a twinge of pain in his rib cage, but he didn't have the heart to say anything; Ross was far too apologetic for minor accidents or inconveniences, and though a part of Grayson found it sweet, he didn't want Ross to feel bad, especially in this moment.

Ross elected not to stay the night and left in the early hours of the morning after helping Grayson get into bed. As Grayson closed his eyes, he actually felt sleepy. Then images of Tina Wilson flashed like a photo reel projected against the inside of his eyelids. He took a slow, deep breath and tried to push them from his mind. Grayson grabbed a pillow and held it tight against him, focusing intensely on the feeling of Ross next to him on the couch. While it didn't completely erase Tina Wilson from his mind, it did help Grayson eventually fade into sleep.

He awoke the next morning to a missed call and a voicemail from Principal Daggett. Though he was still groggy, Grayson listened to the message intently, desperately hoping for anything that wasn't more bad news. To his relief, Dale simply wanted to drop by to check in on him. Perhaps it would do him some good to see the school and maybe a few smiling students, Grayson thought, and he phoned Ross to ask for a ride to the school.

Ross arrived twenty minutes later and helped Grayson to get himself ready, then drove him to the school. As they drove down Main Street, they passed the corner where Doc Weaver's body still hung from the streetlight. Ross made a grossed-out noise as they passed.

"I wish they would just take that body down and lay him to rest already. I know he did horrible things to you and to that girl, but it gives me the *willies*. I don't even like goin' past it now if I can help it," he said.

"I know. Looks like the birds have started to pick at it. I hate that the kids gotta look at it. I know that parents here want their kids to understand the Breakvale way of life, or whatever, but goddamn," Grayson muttered.

Ross shot him a dirty look.

"Sorry, I'll try to stop using that word," Grayson said guiltily. "But you know what I mean?"

They arrived at the school a short while later. Ross parked out front of the high school portion of the school building and turned the radio down. Grayson looked over at him and put a hand on his shoulder.

"Thank you for bringing me here," he said.

"Just doing the Lord's work, right? Ross laughed.

"Yes, exactly," Grayson smirked. He unbuckled himself and opened the door. "I should hopefully only be, like, twenty or thirty minutes. I won't keep you waiting too long."

"Take your time. I have nowhere to be," Ross affirmed, waving his hands.

Grayson slipped inside just as the lunch bell rang. He walked into the office and was greeted gleefully by Linda.

"Oh, Mr. Ender, I'm so glad to see you up and about! I heard all about what happened with your car accident. Such a terrible thing, but lucky you made it out okay. They really should do something about that road. So dangerous at night without any kinda guard rails up there, but the county won't do anything about it."

"Yeah, it's definitely dangerous up there," Grayson barely managed to say.

"Well maybe now they'll wanna do something about it. But anyway, hun, what are you doin' here? We weren't expectin' you back for a little while yet?"

"I got a message from Dale this morning wanting to check in on me. I thought I'd just come down here and see how my kids are doing," Grayson replied.

"Oh, well, Principal Daggett should be in his office, or maybe in the conference room. Why don't you go on back and say hello? I'm sure he'll be happy to see you," Linda smiled and sat back down. "It's good to see you, hun."

Grayson walked to the back of the office. He could see Principal Daggett sitting at his desk reading a piece of paper. He rapped gently at the door. Principal Daggett looked up but didn't smile as we waved Grayson into his office.

"Mind closin' that door behind ya?" he asked.

Grayson did as requested before taking a seat in front of his desk. It looked as though Principal Daggett had been crying.

"How ya' doin' there, Iron Man?" Principal Daggett said, attempting to make a light-hearted joke. "Rolled a Jeep down a cliff and barely a scratch on ya."

"A little more than a scratch, but it definitely could have been worse," Grayson replied.

"Oh yeah, yeah of course...say, I'm glad you're here, Grayson. Now this is probably gonna sound a little strange, but I've been thinkin' about some stuff, and you know, it's real hard sometimes to talk about things like this," Principal Daggett said, pausing occasionally to find the right words. "I've just got some stuff on my mind and, well frankly, I don't really know who to talk to about it, except I know you care a lot about these kids and you see things just a little different from other folks around here. We've had some good talks before, ya know?"

"Sure, Dale, I understand. What's on your mind?" Grayson asked gently, though he was privately taken aback at Dale's sudden investment of trust in him. He had no idea that Dale felt that close to him.

"Well, the thing is...it's my boy, ya see. He's real bent outta shape over Tina. I think I told you they were good friends, yeah?"

Grayson nodded encouragingly.

Dale drew a deep breath. "He's takin' her death real hard. Especially how she died, ya know? Well anyway, he comes to me last night and he's cryin' and he says 'dad, I got somethin' to tell you.'" he paused, growing misty-eyed. "And he tells me...he tells me they'd been seein' each other in secret. They'd been carryin' on in secret for a couple months now, but they didn't want her daddy findin' out. He said he'd planned on tellin' me but didn't know how so he wrote this letter and was gonna give it to me. They planned on movin' in together and startin' a life on their own. Even talked about startin' a family."

Principal Daggett handed him the letter. Grayson quickly skimmed the note, then handed it back with a concerned expression. "Dale, is your son alright? Did—"

"No, no, he didn't do nothin' stupid. He's just heartbroken. All he's done is sit at home and cry. Barely eats. Helen, my wife, she's worried sick over him, of course. And I am, too. Twenty years workin' with kids, a whole lifetime growing up here with people goin' missing and all that. The Beast. I thought I was pretty good at handling it all, and keepin' an objective distance, ya know? And now, now it's so close to home. Now it's my own boy. And it's like I ain't never lived a day in Breakvale. I don't know how to help him. I don't know how to help my family."

Principal Daggett wiped the tears from his eyes and put the letter away in his desk drawer.

"I'm so sorry, Dale. I can't imagine what you all must be going through right now. What your son must be feeling," Grayson consoled. He wanted so badly to tell Principal Daggett the truth about what really happened to him, about how he woke to find Tina's ravaged body propped up against that tree, but it wouldn't help things now. There was nothing either of them could do to change what had happened. Instead, Grayson leaned in and spoke softly. "Do you want me to talk to him? I'm not a counselor or anything, but I know what it's like to feel like a sudden victim in this town. Seeing Alexis and Drew was...well, there aren't really words to describe how it felt. Sometimes kids don't want to talk to their parents, you know?"

"That's mighty kind of you, Grayson. But it's my responsibility to see to him and help him get better. To be real honest, I'm not sure why I felt I had to talk to you about this. I know you're tryin' to get better and here I am layin' more problems on you."

"I don't mind, Dale. I want to help, if I can."

Principal Daggett sat pensively in his red leather desk chair for several seconds, staring intensely at his desk. "Do you...have you ever found yourself so deep in somethin' that you're not quite sure how to get out of it?" he asked quietly.

"Sure. I've felt like that before," Grayson nodded.

"You shall not bow yourself down to them, nor serve them. For I the Lord your God am a jealous God, visiting the iniquity of the fathers upon the sons to the third and fourth generation of those who hate Me," Principal Daggett whispered to himself, stirring himself again to tears. He looked up at Grayson. "What have I done?"

Grayson had no idea what to say. He'd never heard Principal Daggett utter anything that sounded like scripture before.

Though he knew it was biblical, it also reminded Grayson of a line from *The Merchant of Venice*. "The sins of the father are to be laid upon his children," Grayson replied.

This caught Principal Daggett's attention, and his eyes flicked upward from his desk to meet Grayson's.

"What's that now?"

"It's a line from Shakespeare,' Grayson explained. "It's all a bit complicated if you're not familiar with it. But in *The Merchant of Venice*, there are these two characters, Jessica and Lorenzo, whose parents hate each other. One is Christian and one is Jewish, you see. And neither believe their children belong together, but in the end Jessica and Lorenzo are able to work past this difference. While they bore the sins of their fathers, they also offer a kind of...hope. A hope that maybe our children will find a way to break the cycle."

"I'm not sure I follow, Grayson," Principal Daggett replied, shaking his head.

"Breakvale is simultaneously the easiest and the hardest place to grow up. You've had to stand by and watch while the Beast took people away because you didn't know what to do. I don't know what to do either. But maybe, somehow, your son and the other kids in Breakvale won't have to. Maybe they will be the ones who finally put a stop to it," Grayson suggested thoughtfully. "And as for God, I'm not sure what He might think, but I am sure that you're a good father, Dale. It's obvious you care very deeply for your son. You'll find a way to make things right, I'm sure of it."

The lunch bell rang out, giving Grayson the prompt he needed to excuse himself. He felt strongly for Dale Daggett, but didn't see how he could be of any further help.

"Ah!" Grayson exclaimed. "I told my ride I'd only be twenty minutes. They're waiting outside for me."

Principal Daggett wiped his face with his sleeve and stood up, reaching over his desk to shake Grayson's hand. "Right, yeah, 'course. I appreciate you comin' down here and lettin' me make a little fool of myself, Mr. Ender. It's nice havin' someone I can talk to."

Grayson stood and shook his hand firmly. "Any time, Dale. Just call me if there's anything I can ever do."

"I appreciate that. Truth is Life, Grayson," Principal Daggett said, his lips pursed in a sorrowful expression.

Grayson nodded gently, then spun around and made a hasty retreat from the office and out the door. When he got to Ross's car, he hopped in as fast as his ribs would let him and he slammed the door closed.

"I just had the weirdest conversation I've ever had with anyone in this whole fucking town," Grayson said slowly. "Let's get out of here please."

Ross just gave him a puzzled look but put the car in drive and headed for Main Street.

"Daggett's son apparently had a secret relationship with Tina Wilson, and they were planning on moving in together," Grayson revealed.

"What?"

"His son wrote him a letter and all this. Apparently, he's not doing very well. He's having a hard time with Tina being gone. And, you know, with everything that happened."

"Sure, sure. That's understandable," Ross mumbled.

"And Dale blames himself. He quoted some scripture, I think. Something about the sins of the father following the kid for three or four generations—"

"That's in Exodus, Numbers, and Deuteronomy," Ross informed. "There's a few verses about it."

"Right. Well, then we started talking about Shakespeare because that phrase comes up. Sins of the father..." Grayson trailed off, suddenly remembering the mysterious note that Emily Hunt left behind. So much had happened that Grayson had completely forgotten about her disappearance, about the bullet hole in his bedroom.

"What about the sins of the father?" Ross asked, prompting Grayson out of his thoughts.

"Oh, that was it. I dunno, it was all just really strange. I hope he'll be okay," he said finally.

"I'm sure he will. We can say a prayer for him and his family later if you want?" Ross offered, throwing him a hopeful sideways glance.

For maybe the first time since he was a child, Grayson didn't recoil at the thought of saying a real prayer. He actually felt a little surprised at himself.

"Yeah, maybe we should," Grayson nodded. "What could it hurt, right?"

Ross simply smiled, secretly happy that Grayson was willing to share in this part of his life with him, even if it was only in this small way.

15

In the three weeks since their impromptu dinner date and sudden heart-to-heart, Grayson's relationship with Ross had developed rather rapidly. Ross had visited his home almost every night since, even sneaking in late on a Sunday night after church. He had grown comfortable enough to stay the night and even slept next to Grayson in bed, though he was always adamant about waking up and leaving before anyone might notice. Ross still wasn't ready to engage in any kind of sexual activity, though he had proven to be an adept kisser, and for right now Grayson was content with that. He had barely thought about Seth at all during this time. He still loved Seth, but he no longer wasted his time daydreaming about trying to rekindle that old flame. Six months ago, he would have given anything for it, but now, with Ross beside him in his bed, Seth didn't feel so coveted.

Like the last few nights, he and Grayson sat together on the couch, snuggled up under a blanket, watching TV to relax. As they continued their binge of *Star Trek: The Next Generation*, there was a sudden and urgent knock at the door. Grayson and Ross looked at each other, both wondering who could possibly be at his door at nine in the evening.

"Were you expecting anyone?" Ross asked nervously, casting the blanket off of them.

"No."

Grayson stood up from the couch and crept over to the door to look out the peephole. It was Chief Danbury.

"It's the chief," Grayson whispered.

Ross leapt up from the couch and quickly put on his pants before Grayson opened the door. The chief looked up at Grayson standing in the doorway in just his boxers and a t-shirt, then looked over at Ross, who was red in the face but pretended to be on his phone. He cleared his throat.

"Evening. Sorry to interrupt your boys's—"

"Bible study," Grayson interjected.

"Right," the chief said skeptically. "Mr. Ender, I'm gonna need you to get yourself together and come with me."

Grayson was taken aback. "What's going on, chief?"

He looked over at Ross and made a face at Grayson to suggest that he couldn't say it out loud. Grayson stepped outside and pulled the door closed behind him.

"A boy's been abducted. We think it was the Beast."

"What?" Grayson said incredulously. "When?"

"Sometime in the early hours this morning. Just disappeared right out of his bed."

"Who is it this time?"

Chief Danbury hesitated for a moment. "It was Samuel Daggett. Dale Daggett's boy."

Grayson's heart sank. "Oh my God. I... I haven't had any visions. I had no idea. We're sure it's the Beast? This kid didn't just take off with friends or something in the middle of the night? He's a teenager, after all."

"We can't say for sure. But his sheets were found all slashed up and his room was messed up pretty bad. Can't be good, whatever happened," the chief said.

"What do you need me for?" Grayson asked.

"Well, given everything that happened between you and the doc, I thought it might be best if you came down to the station with me and just stayed there for a while until we got this cleared up."

"Are you arresting me, chief?"

"No, no, nothing like that. If you're at the station, then we can say for certain that you're not involved in any way. I'm just trying to look out for you," the chief explained.

Grayson didn't like the idea at all. He considered Dale to be a good friend, and if his son was missing, he wanted to be out there looking for him. But Grayson got the sense that Chief Danbury wasn't going to take no for an answer.

"Alright. Give me a minute to put on pants and get my phone and stuff. I'll be right back," Grayson said.

"Sure, sure. Just, uh, I think it would be best if Mr. McCrory there didn't know anything about this. For your security and his. Yeah?" said the chief.

"Absolutely. I'm just gonna tell him you need me to fill out some paperwork last minute about my car accident or something," Grayson said.

Grayson stepped back inside and closed the front door behind him. He immediately rushed over to Ross and discreetly beckoned him to follow him into his bedroom. As he put on his pants, he motioned for Ross to come closer.

"Something bad is happening. Dale Daggett's son is missing. The chief wants me to come down to the station," Grayson whispered. "I need you to get your stuff and leave with me. Wait until we're out of the parking lot, then go down to Roxanne's and find her. Tell her the chief is taking me to the station."

"Wait, why is he taking you to the station?" Ross asked with a puzzled expression.

"He says it's so they can make sure I can't be implicated in this kid's disappearance. But something feels off. Tell Roxanne, but don't tell anyone else," said Grayson. "Come on, we gotta go."

Grayson put on shoes and scooped up his phone from the couch as they proceeded out the front door together.

Ross nodded politely at the chief before turning around suddenly. "Be sure you read the verses I suggested from Ephesians so we can start our discussion there next time," he said smiling.

"Will do," Grayson said with a hammy salute.

When Ross rounded the corner out of sight, the chief turned to Grayson.

"Bible study, huh?" he said. "Guess I didn't take you for the kind."

Grayson just shrugged. "Shall we go then?"

The chief led Grayson around the corner to the parking lot where his squad car was parked. Grayson stood at the rear door waiting for the chief to open it. Instead, he opened the front passenger seat.

"Come on now, you're not under arrest. You can ride up front," the chief said with a small chuckle.

Grayson took the front seat and buckled himself in as Chief Danbury climbed in and started the engine. He turned left out of the parking lot and headed toward the main drag.

They rode in silence for the duration of the drive. Grayson thought about Dale and his missing son. For the first time, he hoped that he would receive a vision in time to save his son.

They didn't slow down as they approached the turn for the police station, and Grayson pointed out the window toward it, thinking the chief must be lost in thought.

"We missed the turn there, Sheriff," he said.

"We got a little stop to make first," Chief Danbury said.

Grayson suddenly felt uneasy, but tried not to let it show. As they kept driving north through town, Grayson began to grow more nervous. Suddenly, Deputy Thorne's voice came through on the radio.

"Sheriff, we got a report of shots fired at the Daggett residence. Looks like you're in the area. Can you go check it out? I'm ten minutes away. Over."

Chief Danbury slammed his hands against the steering wheel. "Goddammit Dale!" he shouted.

"Do you copy, chief? Over."

Danbury reached up and held down his button to respond. "Yeah, I copy. I'm on my way. ETA ninety seconds. Over."

He flipped on his siren and instructed Grayson to hold on as he made a sharp U-turn. They arrived at the Daggett residence in less than a minute. Chief Danbury slammed the gear shift into park and unbuckled himself.

He turned to Grayson. "Stay in the car. Do not get out. Do you understand?" he said severely. Grayson nodded.

Chief Danbury got out of the car and drew his firearm as he slipped across the yard and kicked the front door in. Grayson rolled down the window, cupping his ear to listen for anything he might hear. Right away he heard a gunshot and a woman screaming inside the house. *Fuck this*, he thought, and unbuckled himself.

Grayson moved surreptitiously up to the front door and peeked around the door frame into the house. He could hear Dale yelling but couldn't see them. He moved around the house toward the side yard, ducking under the bay window that looked out onto the front yard, until he came upon the kitchen window.

It had been shattered. Grayson popped his head up quickly to look through the broken window. Dale Daggett stood against the sink with a gun pointed at someone. His wife was off to his left. *He must be pointing it at the chief*, Grayson thought.

"Please Dale! Just put the gun down!" Grayson heard the wife scream.

"Shut up, Helen! Just shut your fucking mouth and be quiet!" Dale screamed.

"Come on, Dale. This doesn't have to be this way," Chief Danbury urged.

"You shut the fuck up, too! Don't tell me how it has to be. What about my boy, huh? What about my Sammy!"

"Dale, we all knew there would have to be sacrifices," the chief urged.

"He was supposed to be safe! Families were supposed to be off-limits! Why is it me, Roland? Why is it my boy? He never did nothin' wrong!" Daggett yelled, trying to choke back his tears.

"You cracked, Dale!" the chief shouted back. "You showed weakness. You didn't think we noticed, but we did. The whole council saw it. You started to doubt our mission."

"Fuck the mission. I'm so tired of it! All we've done is watch our kids die. I can't live with the guilt anymore," Daggett cried. "Why's it gotta be the kids? Why can't it be me? Take me!"

"You know that's not how it works, Dale. They have to be unwilling. You're willing. Taking you wouldn't work," the chief said, bringing his voice down to normal volume.

"Why'd they take my boy, Roland?" Daggett cried.

The room was silent for a moment. Finally, the chief spoke out calmly. "Dale. You know how this has to end now. You know what Elder Arthur's gonna say. You've betrayed us. Your heart isn't pure anymore. There's nothing you can do for your boy. He's already been chosen. You should be honored that he'll be the final sacrifice. It's his soul that will usher in a new—"

A gunshot echoed from inside the kitchen. Grayson covered his mouth to muffle his scream. He heard something heavy hit the wooden floor, and the woman inside gasped before breaking into hysterical wailing.

"Helen, I am so sorry. I am so, so sorry," Dale sobbed. "I couldn't protect our boy, and I couldn't protect you. But it's okay. We're all gonna be together again."

Grayson stood underneath the window struggling to catch his breath as his heart beat more rapidly than he'd ever felt it beat before. He closed his eyes when he heard the woman begin to whimper.

"I love you," he heard Dale say softly.

There was another gunshot. This time the woman didn't scream. He heard Dale weeping. Grayson mustered the will to turn around and look up through the window. Dale Daggett was kneeling over his wife's body. He had his back to the window, unaware that Grayson was watching as he put the gun to his head and pulled the trigger. The sound of the gunshot reverberated through Grayson's body, and he closed his eyes tight to shut out the scene in front of him, but it was too late. Grayson sank to his knees. For a moment he couldn't think or feel anything.

Get it together, he told himself.

He focused on a few quick breaths to psych himself up, then stood up and sprinted around to the front door and pushed it open.

Grayson ran into the kitchen. Chief Danbury was lying dead on the floor in a pool of his own blood, a bullet wound in his chest. Dale Daggett was slumped over his wife's body, both with gunshot wounds to the head. Grayson felt ridiculous at that moment, but somehow the sight of these three bodies didn't faze him. Nothing compared to seeing Tina Wilson's mutilated body in the woods. He stood there for a moment, trying to make sense of what to do next when suddenly, a nagging feeling overtook him. He ran through the house until he found what he was looking for.

Grayson flipped on the bedroom light. It was unmistakably a teenage boy's bedroom. But it wasn't in disarray at all. The sheets weren't ripped, nothing was overturned. There was no indication that a struggle of any kind had taken place. In his heart, he already knew, but this confirmed his suspicion that the chief had lied to him. Had it not been for Dale Daggett, Grayson wondered where the chief would have taken him. He shook the thought from his mind. He dashed outside, leaving the bodies for someone else to take care of. Roxanne's was several blocks away, but he had the adrenaline to sprint there, fractured rib and all. He didn't have a choice.

As he hit the front door, he stopped suddenly. Several of the neighbors stood outside their homes or gawked out their windows at the chaos that had unfolded in their neighbor's house. They all stared at Grayson.

"What are you all staring for? Someone call for help!" Grayson shouted.

No one moved. Then, one by one, they closed their curtains or slinked back into their homes and extinguished their porch lights. No one was going to help.

He tried to get his bearings to make a run for the bar, until it occurred to him that he didn't need to run. He dashed across the yard and hopped into the chief's car.

Grayson peeled out of the gravel driveway, spraying rocks as he turned out onto the road. He had to get to Roxanne. Something was going to happen to Samuel Daggett, and it was going to happen soon. If they stood any chance of finding him, they'd have to do it on their own, without any visions. It's a small town. He had to be somewhere.

Grayson thought back on everything he heard, trying to remember as much as possible. Then it struck him, something he didn't catch before. Chief Danbury said the name Arthur. Elder Arthur. That could only be one person. He slammed his foot into the gas pedal.

Grayson reached Roxanne's bar in record time. He parked the chief's car behind the building and made a mad dash for the door. He wrenched it open and ran in, startling the few patrons remaining in the bar. Ross sat at the bar talking to Roxanne, and they both snapped their attention to the commotion.

"I'm gettin' real tired of that look on your face every time you walk into this bar," Roxanne said, running to hug him. "What the hell is going on now?"

"We gotta go to the back," he whispered.

She led him past the bar, and Grayson motioned at Ross to follow them. When they got to the back office, Grayson whipped around.

"Ross told me about Daggett's kid. Did you have a vision?" Roxanne asked.

"No. I have no idea where he is, but I have a hunch. But look, you gotta know some stuff first," Grayson said. He took a deep breath to steady himself. "The chief is dead. I was in the car with him and we were supposed to go to the station but we passed it and I had no idea where he was taking me, and then there was this call about gunshots at Dale's house so we went there and he told me to stay in the car, but I heard screaming and a gunshot so I got out and snuck around to the window and listened to what was going on and then they said a bunch of stuff that I don't understand and then Daggett shot the chief and then his wife and then killed himself."

"Oh my good Lord," Ross whispered.

"And then I stole the chief's car to come here," Grayson added, staring wide-eyed at both of them.

"Jesus, Grayson," Roxanne said. "What the *fuck* is going on with this town? Wait, what did you hear them say?"

"Dale was upset about something. About all the kids that had died. And then he was hysterical about his son going missing. He kept asking, 'why does it have to be my son?' and said something about how family was supposed to be off-limits. And then the chief, uh, he...he said something about a mission and Dale failing them because his heart wasn't pure anymore and that sacrifices had to be made."

"Who? Who did he fail? Who is them?" Roxanne urged.

"I don't know. But he said something about how he knows what Elder Arthur would say he had to do," Grayson turned to look at Ross. "Ross, I'm so sorry. I know this is going to be hard to hear, but I think maybe somehow John Arthur might be involved."

Ross shook his head. "No, no that's impossible. He would never be mixed up in something like this. He's the one keeping people safe."

"I'm just telling you what I heard. He said, 'Elder Arthur.' Is there anyone else in this town he might be referring to?" Grayson asked. They both thought carefully for a moment, then eventually shook their heads. "Okay then. Ross. Where does he live?"

Ross stood there with tears in his eyes. "You really think he's involved?"

Roxanne put her hand on his shoulder. "There's only one way to know for sure. We must find him. If he's not involved, then he could be in danger. But we need to know."

"I can take you to his house," Ross said finally.

Roxanne charged out of the office into the dining room.

"Hey everybody!" she shouted, commanding their attention. "I'm so sorry but there's been an emergency and I need to close up right now. Donald, I see you're still eating. I'll get you a box. Your meal's on me. Everyone's drinks are on me. Kay, will you get Donald a box? And then help Keith break down and clean up? I'll pay you out for the rest of the night."

"Sure thing, hun," Kay said, nonchalantly smacking her gum as she dipped behind the bar and marched a to-go box over to the one poor man still eating food.

A few people wished Roxanne well as they exited, others just got up and left. Grayson and Ross waited until the last patron walked out the door. Kay and Keith came out from the kitchen, standing anxiously at the bar as Roxanne locked the doors.

"Everything alright, hun?" Kay asked.

Roxanne hesitated to tell them the truth of what was happening. "Kay, Keith, we're gonna go after someone," she said. "The real someone that's been hunting our kids. I need you both to not say a word about this to anyone until I get back."

"Wait, wait, shouldn't you call the chief?" said Keith.

"Chief Danbury's dead," Grayson said dryly.

Roxanne jumped in before they could ask more questions. "I need you both to just pretend like everything is normal. Be cool. Remember, not a word to anyone. I promise when this is all done, we'll explain everything."

"You got it, boss," Keith said, hoisting his spatula in a salute.

Kay gave Grayson and Roxanne a suspicious, side-eyed look. "Y'all be careful alright. We'll clean up and stay a while here 'case you need anything."

They slipped back into the kitchen, where Grayson was sure they would spend the rest of the night speculating about what was going on.

"I'm sorry you had to close down," Grayson said.

"They'll be back. I'm the only bar in town. But we're gonna owe those two a beer and an explanation later," she said coolly. She walked behind the bar and reached underneath for something, then pulled out a shotgun and offered it to Grayson. "Do you know how to shoot?"

Grayson looked at her with surprise.

"What? You think I'd operate a bar in this town and not own a gun?" she responded.

"Not sure a gun is very effective against a supernatural monster," Grayson replied.

"It's not the Beast starting drunken bar fights."

"Yeah, uh, right. I haven't shot a gun since I was twelve," Grayson admitted.

"Great, so the gun stays with me then," Roxanne smirked, though Grayson could tell she wasn't joking. Roxanne shoved some extra ammunition in her pockets. "Come on, let's go guys."

She led them out back to her SUV. Grayson jumped into the passenger seat while Ross took the back seat and buckled himself into the middle. She whipped around.

"Where am I going?"

"South on Main Street until you hit the last left turn before the road to the out of town," Ross instructed.

Roxanne threw the vehicle into reverse, backed hastily out, and launched onto Main Street. In minutes, Roxanne turned left, sailing past the row of houses that skirted the edge of town. Ross guided her east out of town until they came to a three-way intersection with a gravel road.

"Here, turn here," Ross pointed. "That road ends at his house up the hill."

The SUV kicked up dust and rocks as it tore across the gravel road. All the lights in the house were off, and they were nearly right up on it in the darkness before it came into view. Roxanne parked the car.

"Remember, we don't know what's really going on, so be cool," Roxanne instructed.

They stepped out of the car and stalked quietly up to the front porch. Roxanne held the gun low, concealing it behind Grayson, but ready to draw it quickly. They exchanged assured glances, and then Grayson knocked on the pastor's door. They waited for a moment. There was no answer, and no lights were switched on in the house.

"Maybe he's not home?" Ross suggested.

"Where would he be at this time of night, though?" Roxanne questioned.

Grayson knocked again, louder this time. No one came to the door. He turned to Roxanne.

"What do we do now?" he asked.

"Maybe we should just kick the door in?" she suggested.

"What! No, don't do that. Come on," said Ross. "Wait, hold on."

Ross fumbled with his keys in the darkness for a moment before finally holding up a singular key.

"Here, I have a key. He gave it to me for emergencies."

"Ross. Why didn't you say that in the first place?" Grayson moaned.

"Because it's for *emergencies*. If we go inside and he's asleep upstairs in his bed and he comes down to find three people breaking into his house, he's gonna be so mad," Ross defended.

"Yeah well, he could be hurt or dead in there for all we know. I think under the circumstances he'll forgive you if everything is fine," Grayson countered.

"Alright, alright. Here," Ross stepped up between them and unlocked the door. "There. Just, let's be quiet."

The wooden door creaked as they pushed it gently open and walked inside. The living room was pitch black as they pressed slowly forward into the center of the room, listening quietly for any sound or hint of movement. Suddenly the light from the ceiling fan flipped on, dazzling their eyes in the process. Roxanne jumped and gave an audible gasp at the sudden illumination.

"Sorry," Ross said from behind them. They spun around to find his hand on the light switch. "We already broke in. At least this way he'll see it's us if he's home."

Ross closed the door behind him, and they proceeded to search the house. "He's probably asleep upstairs," Ross whispered, pointing toward the staircase.

He led them upstairs toward the bedroom, their footsteps causing each board to groan under their weight. It was dark upstairs, with light from the living room below barely filtering up to the second floor. Ross inched closer to the bedroom door, which was slightly ajar. Fully expecting Pastor Arthur to be asleep in his bed, Ross attempted to call out to him.

"Pastor Arthur?" he whispered. "John? It's me, Ross. Are you in there? Are you awake?"

Roxanne pushed past Ross and swung the door wide, flipping on the bedroom light. The room was empty.

"He's not here," she said, abandoning her hushed tone. "Let's search the rest of the house."

"If he's not here, then we absolutely have to find him," Grayson said. He turned to Ross. "Can you call him?"

"I would, but John doesn't believe in carrying or using a cell phone. He says being in constant contact with people would take away from his time with God," Ross informed.

"Of course," Roxanne scoffed. She turned to Ross. "I'm sorry, I know he is your friend and mentor. This can't be easy. We just need to find him so we can figure out what the fuck is going on."

"It's okay, I know. I want answers too," said Ross.

They checked the remaining rooms upstairs before Roxanne went barrel-first back down the staircase and into the living room, with Grayson and Ross close behind her.

"Is there a shed or a barn or anything else on the property?" Grayson asked.

"No, just the house. I'm pretty sure. I don't know of anything else unless it's beyond the clearing and in the woods behind the house," Ross replied. "I've never heard him mention anything though."

They crossed the living room and into the kitchen, flipping lights on as they explored.

"Are all the rooms in the house this...sparse?" Grayson observed, standing in the large wooden door frame between the two rooms. "There's hardly any furniture. Or any kind of decorations. No character."

"John's pretty simple," Ross acknowledged. "He doesn't believe in having more than the basic necessities. Everything else is 'frivolity' or 'excess' and can lead to 'covetous and morally decadent behavior' as he likes to say. He doesn't hold it against other people, but he says he thinks it's his duty to lead by example."

"Looks like he does a fine job of that," Roxanne cracked.

Grayson stopped in the kitchen next to Ross as Roxanne stepped out the back door and into a small sunroom off the kitchen to look around.

"Looks like nothing but a bunch of plants back here," she called out from around the corner.

Grayson gawked at the old mid-century-styled wallpaper plastered around the room. It was an unsavory mixture of pea green, golden yellow, and brown, and the whole room looked like something from a fifties issue of Good Housekeeping.

"Is that a pantry?" Grayson asked, nodding toward a small door against the far wall.

"No, I'm pretty sure that leads down to the basement," Ross speculated. "John never goes down there, though, because of the mold or something."

Grayson stepped over to the door and turned the handle. It was locked. He took a deep breath and stepped backward.

"Rox!" Grayson called out. "We've got a locked door here to a basement that no one's allowed to go into."

Roxanne flew around the corner and into the kitchen. "You're fucking kidding me. Is there a key somewhere? Check on top of the door frame."

"Nope, nothing," Grayson said, reaching up to feel along the top of the frame. "Ross, do you have a key to this door? Or know where one is?"

"No, he never gave me one," Ross said, shaking his head.

"You two stand back," Roxanne commanded, waving them away.

They each stepped backward and out of her way as Roxanne pointed the shotgun just to the right of the door handle and pulled the trigger. The gun blasted a sizable hole in the door and its frame, sending splinters of wood flying in every direction. The door swung open. Roxanne pulled a long string that popped an old, incandescent bulb to life.

"Let's go check out the creepy basement," she said.

They hit the bottom of the staircase and searched around for another light source, as the light from the old bulb at the top of the stairs barely reached the bottom steps. The basement smelled earthen and damp, like wet clay. As they felt around in the darkness, Grayson got the impression that it wasn't a very big room, and he gasped after bumping into something that rattled like a plastic sheet. He jumped backward but then reached out to feel something hard underneath the plastic.

Roxanne bumped into something hanging from the rafters and screamed, shouting several colorful profanities. She felt around with her free hand until she grabbed onto Grayson's arm.

"Will someone please find a fucking light?" she shouted.

"Oh, dammit, hold on. Should've thought of this before," Grayson said as he pulled out his cell phone and clicked on the flashlight. He cast the light toward the thing hanging from the rafters. "What is that?"

At last, Ross made an excited sound. There was an audible crackle and buzz as the basement's fluorescent lighting scattered the darkness. Grayson was correct, it was a very small room. The object hanging from the rafters appeared to be something in a zippered bag. Grayson cautiously unzipped the front and held his light up to it. It looked like something white and dingy and covered with lace. Right away Roxanne recognized it.

"It's a fucking wedding dress!" she seethed. "Fuck."

Grayson put his phone away and started to look around the room more carefully. What little furniture or forgotten objects were stored down here were all covered by sheets of heavy, opaque plastic, ostensibly to ward off dust and water. They flipped back some of the plastic sheets to peer underneath but didn't see anything of particular concern or interest, just an old couch, a chest of drawers, and an old end table with what looked like an antique Victrola with the letters M.A. engraved on a small, affixed brass plaque. The far wall was mostly empty except for some pipes and a storage shelf filled with dusty knickknacks. Odd that everything was stacked neatly against the walls of the room instead of being haphazardly placed in the middle, Grayson thought.

Roxanne and Grayson poked through the contents on the shelf. He didn't see anything unusual or out of the ordinary—old tools, spare nuts and bolts, empty tin cans, and glass bottles. Suddenly Roxanne tapped him on the shoulder.

"Hey, take your flashlight out again," she said quietly. "Shine it on the floor there."

Grayson pulled out his phone and clicked on the light, which he pointed down on the concrete floor.

"Good eye," he said. "How'd you see it?"

"I didn't. I felt it under my foot," Roxanne replied.

Ross stepped up from behind them. "What did you find?"

"Grooves in the concrete. A false wall," Grayson muttered.

"Ross, come over here and give him a hand," Roxanne instructed. She took a step back to trade places with Ross, then pumped the shotgun and held it out straight at the ready.

"I swear to God, Grayson, if there's a fucking body behind this door, I'm gonna kill you," Roxanne said.

Grayson and Ross both grabbed onto the left side of the shelving unit and pulled hard. At first, it didn't budge. On their second attempt, the seal broke loose, and the door started to swing open on its sagging hinges as it scraped against the floor.

16

They stepped into the room. No one said a word as they attempted to process what they saw in front of them. The room was brightly lit by the fluorescent lights overhead, and this room was clean and sterile, standing in stark contrast to the musty, conjoined basement. The white tiled floor was scrubbed clean. In the far-left corner stood a large cage made from sturdy iron bars that were bolted at all points to the floor, the corner walls, and the ceiling. It looked like the jail cells at the police station. Bolted to the wall to the left of the cage was a set of ankle and wrist shackles with metal cuffs. There was a metal table just to the right of the center of the room, with worn leather straps meant to restrain the arms and legs. A camera was mounted on a tripod facing the table and the shackle wall. Behind the camera hung several implements of cruelty. At the far end of the room, Grayson could see a large wash basin with a metal counter, above which hung a rack full of more sharp blades and brutal implements. Though it wasn't the same room, Grayson went cold as memories of his captivity in the doctor's office came flooding back.

"It's a fucking torture chamber," Roxanne whispered breathlessly. "Guys, do not touch anything."

They proceeded further into the room. Ross clung to Grayson's arm as he dragged him toward the back left corner of the room to inspect the cage. Unable to look at the gruesome things around her, Roxanne turned and kept the shotgun trained on the door.

“Grayson. There’s another door. Over here in the corner,” she whispered.

“Hold on. There’s something in this cage,” Grayson whispered back.

He got up closer and noticed the door was slightly ajar. He pulled the door open and stepped inside the cage. Reaching down, Grayson picked up two torn articles of clothing. He took a deep breath to steady his trembling hand.

“It’s a shirt and underwear,” Grayson said. “Rox, these look like a boy’s clothes.”

Roxanne looked over her shoulder. “Grayson, I said don’t touch anything. Come on.”

Grayson dropped the torn clothing and turned back around. A sudden spark of rage ignited inside him. He hoped, prayed, that he wasn’t right. He circled around to the video camera pointed at the wall and opened its small LCD wing. He pressed the power button and held his breath as the lens shuttered and the screen lit up.

“Grayson, seriously,” Roxanne pleaded. “I don’t think we should be messing around with this stuff.”

He pressed the camera's review button to review the last recorded videos and images. Two thumbnails appeared: one showing a still image of a man chained to the wall and another of the same man on the table.

“I have to know, Roxanne. I have to know for sure,” Grayson said. He shivered as he stood there. He started to press play but turned to Ross. “Close your eyes. Please. Close your eyes.”

Grayson hit play on the first video. He could tell by the man’s appearance that he was young. He squeezed his eyes shut tight, unable to look for a moment at the boy on the screen. This had to be Samuel Daggett—he knew it in his gut that this was Dale's missing son. Grayson opened his eyes. For several seconds nothing happened except for Samuel stirring occasionally. He looked like he'd been drugged. He could barely hold his head up and was leaning with most of his weight against the wall. Then suddenly, a man walked into the frame. He was wearing a set of full-body surgical scrubs and a mask over his face. Initially, Grayson couldn't recognize him. Then he spoke.

"I need you to know, Samuel, that I take no great pleasure in this. But it is my duty to ensure that as a vessel, you're properly prepared," the voice said.

Ross began to shake and squeeze Grayson's arm tighter. He recognized the voice, too. It was John Arthur. Grayson skipped ahead, trying not to let more of the audio play. He watched through brief flashes of images as Arthur flogged and bloodied the boy's body. As he let off the fast-forward button to stop the video, a brief and searing scream echoed in the chamber from the boy on the recording.

"Jesus, Grayson, enough! I think we know exactly what happened. I don't need to hear any more," Roxanne yelled.

Grayson clicked on the other thumbnail. This time Samuel was lying naked on the surgical table, completely restrained and bloodied. Arthur walked in front of the camera and picked up something from a tray nearby, then circled around and stood over Samuel's head. He held up a long, sharp needle. Samuel cried and begged for release, even as Arthur told him not to. Ross tightened his grip on Grayson's arm. Arthur took the needle and inserted it into the boy's right ear, rupturing his eardrum as he screamed out. Grayson stood there, paralyzed by the horror playing out on the screen. Suddenly Roxanne slammed the wing shut.

"Enough!" Roxanne shouted. "Grayson? Listen to me. We need to leave this place. Now."

Grayson snapped back to his senses. He shook his head.

"No, no we can't leave yet. I need to see what's in that other room, Rox."

He wrenched himself free of Ross's grip and brushed past Roxanne toward the door in the corner. He reached down and turned the handle. This one wasn't locked.

This room was smaller, maybe a third of the size, and dark, except for the glow of two computer monitors on a desk shoved up against the wall at the far end of the room. Grayson instinctively reached up for a light switch and found one along the wall.

Roxanne followed in behind him. "Goddammit, Grayson! Are you listening to—"

She froze when she entered the room.

In addition to the computer at the desk, there was an old analog TV with a DVD/VCR player resting on top of it. Along the right wall were three bookshelves stacked with VHS tapes and DVD cases. Grayson walked into the room, almost automatically, like he was outside his body and something else goaded him onward to look at the tapes on the shelves. But he was in full control. It was an emptiness inside him that prodded him forward, a desperate need for answers. There was nothing on those shelves that could shock him anymore. He scanned the DVD cases, tilting his head sideways to better read the handwritten labels on the spine.

"They recorded them, Rox. Every single one of them," Grayson whispered. There were many names he didn't recognize with past dates on the labels. Then he saw a name he *did* recognize. The label read “E. Hunt — Summer Solstice”. Grayson pulled the DVD case from the shelf and opened it. Inside was a picture of the woman he’d seen before in his visions. It was Emily Hunt. Her eyes were stitched shut. Grayson put the DVD back. Next to it were more names he recognized: “A. Carter — Autumnal Equinox” and then “M. Seevers — Winter Solstice”. He didn’t need to look at those to know who they were or what he’d find in them.

“Hey, hey, Roxanne! Samuel may still be alive!” Grayson shouted. “Look. Look at these.”

Roxanne moved away from guarding the door to look at what Grayson had found.

“What is it? How can you be sure?” she asked.

“Look at these labels. These are videos of everyone that’s gone missing over the last year. Emily, Alexis, Mikey. Well, almost everyone. It looks like there isn't a video of Drew here,” Grayson replied.

“We found Drew two days before Alexis. Maybe they didn't need Drew,” Roxanne suggested.

Grayson shook his head. The thought of Drew being killed just to get to Alexis made him sick. He was nothing more than collateral damage to these perpetrators.

“Look, all these videos happen to coincide with an equinox or a solstice,” Grayson pointed out.

“So what, it’s some kind of ritual sacrifice or devil worship or something?” Roxanne speculated.

“I don’t know. Maybe. Maybe not. But Samuel doesn’t have a video yet. The vernal equinox is tomorrow. As in, like, an hour from now. It’s nearly midnight. If they are trying to time up the murders with the equinox, that means they'll do it sometime in the next twenty-four hours."

"It's as logical as anything else," Roxanne responded. "But look, Tina's not here. She's not here at all. All of these are in order. She should be the last one here, but she isn't."

Grayson hadn't noticed, but Roxanne was right. "I don't know," he said. "Maybe there was something different about Tina. Wait, the computer!"

Grayson and Roxanne both moved swiftly toward the computer on the desk. Grayson wiggled the mouse and the screensaver shifted to a generic blue desktop with nothing except a row of folders with labels similar to DVDs and VHS tapes on the shelves.

"It's not protected by a password," Roxanne said in astonishment.

"Arthur probably never expected anyone else to be down here without him."

"It doesn't look like Tina is on here either, Grayson," Roxanne said as she scanned the screen.

"No. But Mikey is. So are all the others. Plus some names I don't recognize."

"I do. Those are all people who were attacked and killed by the Beast in the last four years. Look, there's all the ones from this year plus six more. One or two a year over the last four years. I told you that there was more than normal this year," Roxanne said.

"I have to open at least one of these folders. You'd better look away if you don't want to see. I need to know, Rox."

Roxanne looked at him sternly, her eyes begging him not to open the folder, but Grayson didn't waver. She just sighed.

"Alright. Do it."

Grayson opened the folder labeled “M. Seevers”. Inside the folder was an assortment of pictures and videos. He opened one video and played it. Roxanne had to look away immediately, but Grayson’s gaze was transfixed as he watched John Arthur, Chief Danbury, Dale Daggett, and someone else he couldn't identify holding Mikey down, trying to restrain him from thrashing as the doctor stitched his lips shut. He was conscious for almost the entire procedure until he appeared to finally pass out from the pain. The screaming was intolerable. Grayson paused the video.

“You can open your eyes. I’m not going to play any more of the video,” Grayson told Roxanne. “But Rox, look. That’s Arthur, the chief, the doctor, and Dale. All together there.”

“You were right, Grayson. I... I don’t even know what to say. Except that this is the proof we needed. That these sick, twisted fucks have been behind all this,” Roxanne raged. “But why?”

Grayson closed out the video and they scrolled down through the pictures. Some appeared to be still frames from the videos, while others look like they were taken by a different camera. The images were graphic and violent and told Grayson a complete story of the abuse this man suffered at the hands of these monsters: disfigurement, torture, rape, and eventually, mercifully, death. There were pictures of the body posed ceremoniously on a table, a stone table, taken in a different location. Grayson closed Mikey’s folder. He couldn’t bear to look at the folder for Alexis and instead opened Emily’s. Its contents were all exactly like the contents of Mikey’s folder.

Suddenly, Grayson heard Ross burst into tears and collapse onto the floor behind him, snapping him out of his fixation on the computer screen. Roxanne and Grayson both ran over and knelt beside him. Ross held a tape in his hand as he cradled himself and rocked back and forth.

"Ross, what is it? What's going on?" Roxanne urged.

Grayson saw part of the label on the VHS tape in his hand and had to use both of his own hands to pry Ross's fingers loose. He flipped the VHS tape around to read the label— "G. McCrory".

Ross was barely intelligible as he tried to speak. "That's my mom," he managed to finally say between gasping breaths. "That's my mom. That's my mom."

He continued to rock back and forth, wailing and sputtering hysterically, repeating that same phrase until he simply couldn't speak anymore and gasped for air. Roxanne and Grayson both held him tightly as he shook. Over his shoulder, Roxanne glared at Grayson.

"We need to leave now," she said severely through clenched teeth.

"I know, I know. But Roxanne, all the answers are right here. Everything we've been searching for. It's *right here*," Grayson stressed. "What if he comes back and sees someone's been in here and destroys all the evidence?"

"Then we have to find John Arthur before he comes back! You said it yourself he could still have that boy alive out there somewhere. But we can't save him if we don't leave. We'll call the county chief's office when this is all done and tell them what we found."

Grayson nodded.

Roxanne looked down at Ross.

"Hey, Ross. Ross, honey? Listen, you gotta pull yourself together so we can get out of here, okay? Can you stand up?"

Ross didn't say anything but moved to get up on his feet, and Grayson and Roxanne both helped him to stand up. Grayson put Ross's arm around his shoulder and helped guide him out of the room. He could feel Ross's entire body trembling and had to use considerable effort to steady their pace. The pain in his ribs hurt like hell from supporting his weight, but he knew it was nothing compared to how Ross felt at that moment. Roxanne grabbed her shotgun off the floor and led the way out of the house.

When they got out the front door and into the cool night air, Ross took a deep breath and screamed in anger before beginning to sob again. The violence of the outburst made him throw his weight against Grayson, who buckled from the sudden shift and the pain it caused in his side, and they both fell to the ground. Roxanne spun around and helped to sit Ross up straight before taking him by the shoulders and shaking him.

"Ross McCrory, you listen to me right now," she snapped. "I know that what you just saw is really painful and really traumatic and you have every right to grieve and be sad and be angry. But right now, I need you to button up and get it together."

Ross snapped out of his hysterics almost immediately and stared blankly at her. For a moment, Grayson was unsure of how Ross was going to react. Then Ross nodded his head.

"You're right. You're right. I'm sorry. I'm sorry."

"You have nothing to be sorry for," Roxanne said more softly. "That was a lot for all of us to take in just now. Your world especially just got rocked pretty hard. And when this is over, we'll all go to therapy and unpack this shit together, okay? But right now, there's a young boy out there who may still be alive, and he needs all three of us working together to save him. Can you do this?"

Ross continued to nod vigorously. "Yes, yes, I can do this. I'm sorry. I'll button up."

"Good. Let's get you up and dust you off," Roxanne said, helping him to his feet once more.

Grayson stepped up to Ross and put his arms around him in a tight embrace. He leaned in to whisper in Ross's ear.

"I'm sorry about your mom. I promise you, we're gonna get the men responsible for this, and we're going to get justice for your mom. I promise you, Ross. I promise you."

Ross put his arms around Grayson and held him for a moment, then leaned back.

"I know we will," Ross sniffled. He wiped the tears from his eyes. "Come on, let's go save that boy."

Grayson heard a shriek come from somewhere behind them. He knew that shriek. Grayson spun around and stepped in front of Ross and Roxanne as the Beast hurtled across the lawn directly at them from the tree line, growing more massive in size as it approached. Roxanne pumped her shotgun before taking aim and fired on the Beast. The buckshot from the shell scattered and pierced the Beast in a dozen places, passing straight through its ethereal form.

The Beast soared up higher into the air, its shrill screech cutting through the otherwise soundless night air. It spun in the air and swooped down at them a second time. Roxanne aimed and fired again, but the Beast deftly swirled out of range and barreled down on them until it reached out with two massive tendrils and swatted Roxanne and Ross to the ground. It landed in front of Grayson and wrapped itself around him until he was completely enveloped. He felt his limbs go ice cold as he struggled to break free from its grasp. For a moment there was nothing but intense darkness, until its ruby eyes glimmered faintly in the void. Distant at first, they twisted in a kaleidoscope of red hues, growing larger as they spiraled toward him. Grayson's eyes rolled back into his head as the Beast's crimson eyes merged with his and he slipped out of consciousness.

Grayson opened his eyes as he floated across the church grounds toward the church. He was hovering several feet above the lawn. He could see two figures carrying something large below him. The half-moon above struggled to break through the cloud cover, and the figures wore dark, hooded cloaks. He couldn't see their faces. Grayson drifted gently closer to them, careful to avoid their detection. It appeared to be some kind of wooden box with symbols carved across the top. He didn't recognize them. He tried to push himself closer, but instead felt himself dive headlong into the ground beneath him, passing through the rock and soil, until he emerged in a tunnel below.

The tunnel was bathed in an amber glow from a series of industrial bulbs strung along the top and anchored into the arched rock ceiling. They looked like old mining lights. There were symbols carved into the rock walls, but Grayson drifted too hastily down the tunnel to study them. The tunnel seemed to terminate at a dead end, until he got close enough to see the stairs that led deeper below. As he approached the stairs, one of the hooded figures came up from the shadows, brandishing some sort of carved effigy in his right hand. He waved it around wildly.

"Away!" the figure commanded.

Grayson shrieked in anger. He felt as though something was tugging him backward, like a marionette puppet, back down the tunnel, up through the rocks and soil, until he emerged above the church lawn.

Grayson's eyes rolled out from the back of his head, paralyzed as the kaleidoscope of ruby light spun in reverse and faded back into the void. All at once he felt the Beast release his body from its grasp and he collapsed into the grass. The Beast propelled itself silently upward and zipped across the sky until it seemed to blink out of existence.

Roxanne and Ross both sprang up and ran immediately over to him.

"Grayson! Are you okay?" Roxanne asked frantically.

She took his face in her hands and seemed to be checking his eyes. Grayson reached up and put his hands on hers.

"Yes, yes, I'm fine," he said.

"What did the Beast do to you?" Ross asked, standing somewhere behind Roxanne.

"I don't...I... nothing, uh, it...it didn't do anything to me," he stammered. "I think maybe it was trying to show me...like it was trying to help."

"Help how? What did it show you?" Roxanne asked, helping Grayson to his feet.

"It showed me the church, and then two people carrying some kind of wooden box, like a casket, kinda. And then there was a tunnel underground and then someone came up from some stairs and waved something at me and I went flying back out of the tunnel and then I was back here."

"It showed you another vision," Roxanne replied.

"I feel like it was trying to show me where Samuel is. Every time I get a vision, either in a dream or from contact with the Beast, it's always about a victim. That has to be it," Grayson stepped around Roxanne and clutched Ross's shoulders. "Is there any kind of tunnel or basement under the church? Anything you can think of?"

"No... not that I know about," Ross said, wide-eyed and fearful at Grayson's vigorous grip.

"There were lights, like, old lights in a mine hanging from the ceiling. Is there a mine or something near the church?" Grayson pressed.

"No, no there's nothing like that," Ross winced.

"Think, Ross! Think! There has to be something around there," he shouted, shaking him.

"Stop shaking me!" Ross yelled.

Roxanne stepped over and grabbed Grayson's arm.

"Grayson, stop. There aren't any mines or caves near the church, Grayson. I'm sure of it, too," she said.

Grayson relaxed his grip and let go.

"I'm sorry, Ross."

"Please don't ever do that again," Ross replied.

Grayson paced a few feet away and screamed out his frustration. He turned back around.

"Come on, we have to get to the church," said Grayson, marching toward the SUV.

"Wait, wait, wait," Roxanne urged. "I know I just gave a big speech about going to save this kid, but if we're about to run into some underground tunnel chasing a murderous cult, maybe backup isn't a bad idea."

"Who are we going to get in time? Even if we called the cops now it would take the county chief's deputies thirty minutes or better to get here. We don't have time to wait around."

"Well we don't have time to rush into getting ourselves killed either," Roxanne rebutted. "I know Danbury was involved in all this, but what about Deputy Thorne? Do you trust her?"

Grayson hesitated for a minute. "I didn't see her in any of the pictures or videos we found. Yeah, I guess I trust her. Officer Stanley, too. I didn't see him either."

"Then we need to find them," Roxanne said.

"She's gotta be at Dale's house, right?" Ross said suddenly. "If I were the deputy and found out my boss had been murdered, that's where I'd be. At the crime scene."

Grayson and Roxanne exchanged nods.

"Officer Stanley's probably there, too."

"Take me back to my car," Ross said. "I can go find Deputy Thorne while you guys go to the church and—"

Roxanne shook her head before Ross had even finished. "No, absolutely not. We have to stay together."

"The fastest route from here to the church takes us right back by the bar anyway. I can find her and bring her to the church. You just have to tell me where the tunnel is when you find it," Ross said firmly.

"He's right, Rox. It's already nearly midnight. We can do this faster if we split up."

Roxanne shook her head but relented. "Alright. For the record, I don't like it. But if you're sure?"

"I'm sure. I'm no good with a gun, and I don't have the weird visions like Grayson. But people in town trust me. If I say I need help, they'll come," Ross reasoned. "I'll find them and bring them to you as fast as I can."

"Okay. Now can we get moving?" Grayson stressed, motioning them toward the car.

They loaded into the SUV and rushed back into Breakvale. In the parking lot outside the bar, Ross bid them both good luck and leaped out of Roxanne's SUV. Grayson hastily unbuckled himself and threw his door open.

"Ross!"

Ross turned around as Grayson rushed up on him, taking him around the waist and kissing him there in the dimly lit parking lot.

"Look we can figure this out later, but I could be dead before this is done. I love you. Please be safe," Grayson said.

This time Ross kissed him. "We'll be back to falling asleep together on your couch before you know it. Now go!"

Grayson turned and ran back to the SUV. As they pulled out of the parking lot, he watched Ross get into his car and follow behind them until they reached the intersection and turned in opposite directions. He drew and released a deep breath.

"Don't worry, you'll see him again," Roxanne assured.

"I know."

"Not to kill whatever romantic moment you're having in your head, but I need you to open up the glovebox and get the gun that's in there."

"Jesus, Rox! You have a gun in your car, too?"

"Old paranoias die hard," she said casually.

Grayson reached into the glove box and pulled out a polished-looking revolver in a holster. He unbuckled the top strap of the holster and pulled out the gun.

"Careful," she cautioned. "The safety's on, but it *is* loaded. This one should be pretty straightforward. Just point the gun and pull the trigger."

"Right. I can do that."

"Good. Look, Grayson, you had me concerned for a minute down there in that basement. You got really weird and obsessive over the shit we found, like you dissociated for a while. I know you need answers, but if shit gets real down in that tunnel, you gotta be focused. Do you trust me?"

"Of course."

"Then if I say we need to go, we need to go. If we're outnumbered, it's better to fall back and wait for backup than to rush in and try to save the kid by force."

"No, you're right. I'm sorry I didn't listen to you before. I don't know what came over me," Grayson said guiltily.

"We're nearly there. Are you ready?"

Roxanne reached out and took Grayson's hand, squeezing it firmly. As the steeple of the church came into view over the hill, Grayson's stomach twisted in a knot. He squeezed Roxanne's hand tighter.

17

As they approached the church, Roxanne switched the headlights off and navigated the rest of the way by the scant moonlight. She parked the SUV near the edge of the church parking lot and then climbed out quietly. Roxanne took a moment to reload her shotgun and showed Grayson how to disengage the safety on the revolver. They looked at each other for a moment.

"Ready?"

"I'm ready."

Just as they had done at John Arthur's house, Grayson and Roxanne moved stealthily up to the church doors, careful to watch for any signs of movement inside the building. All the lights in the building were off. Grayson attempted to gently push the doors open.

"They're locked," he whispered.

"These doors are too big to kick in. There's gotta be another door somewhere around the building. Come on," Roxanne whispered back.

As they stalked around the side of the church, Grayson peered into the windows, but there wasn't a single light on anywhere inside. They reached a small side door around the back. Grayson turned the handle, but it was also locked. Roxanne pursed her lips, then threw her weight into the door and smashed it open, splintering the door frame in the process. Grayson stood back, thoroughly impressed, though not surprised.

They walked through the church barrel-first but didn't see anything suspicious. They moved carefully and quietly down a dark hallway, clearing the few small rooms on either side. They emerged from a door into the main sanctuary, just behind and to the right of the pulpit. Roxanne inspected the two small rooms on either side of the main entrance as Grayson stood in the center of the aisle, listening quietly for any other sounds or movement.

"There's no one here," Grayson said finally.

"I was looking for some kind of trap door, or door to a basement or something. I didn't see anything like that," Roxanne sighed. "Did you?"

Grayson shook his head. "No."

"We're missing something," Roxanne said, continuing to look around.

"He's here somewhere, I'm sure of it."

They retraced their steps through the church, double-checking that they hadn't missed anything, then exited out the back door they smashed in. Grayson sat down on the small stone steps in front of the door and hung his head, trying to recall any small detail or feeling from his vision that he might have neglected.

"Grayson…" Roxanne whispered suddenly, tapping him on the shoulder. "What about there?"

Grayson looked up to find Roxanne pointing at the old well house.

"The well house?" Grayson shrugged. "Yeah, fuck it. It's worth a look."

As they approached the well house, Grayson felt an uneasiness in the pit of his stomach. This felt familiar. They reached the door to find it unlocked. Grayson opened it slowly as Roxanne took aim over his shoulder in case anyone decided to spring out at them. No one sprang out at them, but they stood for a moment in awe of what they found on the other side of the door: a set of steep earthen steps leading underground.

"Is it really that easy?" Roxanne whispered.

"Maybe Arthur was expecting company, or they forgot to lock it behind them?" Grayson suggested.

He pulled out his phone and sent Ross a message instructing him to come to the well house, then they carefully descended the steps, trying to make as little noise as possible so as not to give away their approach. Grayson could see a faint yellow light coming from a tunnel at the end of the stairs. When they reached the landing and Grayson took in the full view of the tunnel, he was certain.

"This is it. There's another set of steps at the end of this tunnel. That's where he'll be," Grayson whispered.

About halfway down the tunnel, the walls became smooth and polished, and Grayson and Roxanne were puzzled by a strange set of reliefs that lined the walls on either side of the tunnel. They paused only briefly to investigate the drawings and symbols on the walls more closely.

"What are these?" Roxanne asked quietly.

Grayson didn't recognize anything on the walls. His eyes scanned the glyphs, trying to discern some kind of story or pattern, but he couldn't make heads or tails of it.

"I don't know," Grayson finally whispered back. "I don't recognize any of these symbols."

They pressed on, gawking at the images carved into the smoothed rock face while trying not to take their eyes off the dim path ahead of them. Roxanne stopped abruptly.

"Do you hear that?" she whispered.

Grayson listened intently. The sound hadn't registered until Roxanne pointed it out. They heard the faint sound of someone whimpering as it carried up from somewhere below and echoed through the tunnel. The whimpering continued intermittently, growing louder as they reached the second set of stairs at the end of the tunnel. They peered down the stairs. A small amount of light filtered up from somewhere down below, helping to illuminate their descent.

They emerged from the shadows into a large, circular cathedral carved out of the natural rock. Massive stalactites bore down from the high cavern ceiling, occasionally meeting the imposing stalagmites along the cavern floor in an alternating pattern like the teeth of some ancient subterranean predator. The cavern floor was smooth like the polished stone walls of the tunnel. Just a few yards in front of them, Grayson saw the massive stone dais, encircled by tall, wrought-iron pillars bearing flickering candles that he'd seen previously in one of his visions. They found Samuel Daggett naked and restrained to the dais. He fought against the gag in his mouth trying to scream out a warning to them as Grayson and Roxanne rushed to free him. Grayson placed his revolver next to Samuel's leg, then set about trying to free his ankles, but struggled to loosen the leather straps.

They froze at the sound of a cocking gun. John Arthur stepped out from behind one of the stalagmites with his weapon aimed directly at them.

"Put your gun down, Roxanne, and step away from it," Arthur demanded calmly.

Grayson's revolver must have been hidden from Arthur's sight by Samuel's leg because John Arthur didn't direct him to do the same. Roxanne placed her shotgun on the ground and stepped away from it, putting distance between herself and

Grayson. She was trying to draw Arthur's attention away from him. He placed his hands conspicuously on the table, then gripped the handle of the revolver.

"We're here for Samuel. Let us take him, and this doesn't have to end badly for you," Grayson warned.

Arthur smirked. "Don't threaten me, Mr. Ender. It's pitiful coming from you. No, I don't believe either of you will be leaving here tonight."

John Arthur kept his gun fixed on Roxanne as he crossed over to a small pedestal several feet to his left. He picked up some kind of small, carved statue from the pedestal and held it up to them. Grayson recognized that statue. It was the same as the one that someone waved at him in his vision to drive him out of the tunnel.

"Do either of you know what this is?" Arthur inquired, waving the statue around.

"It's what you use to control the Beast," Grayson replied.

"Come here, now!" Arthur barked. "And remain still until you're released."

A singular moment passed, then the Beast materialized from out of the cavern wall behind him and drifted begrudgingly toward John Arthur's side where it came to a halt. The Beast hung there in the air, its opaque form swirling four feet above the ground. Grayson noticed that its powerful red eyes were absent from the hood of its face, almost as though it were looking down.

"Very good Mr. Ender," Arthur said wryly. "It's an effigy to which the Beast is bound, created by the original inhabitants of this land more than half a millennium ago. Made from the very rock of this cave that gave birth to this monstrosity. Unsurprising, though, that you would know what it is."

"Why is that, John?" Grayson said sharply.

"The Beast has seemed to take an unusual liking to you. I had no idea at first. That day at the diner, when I sent it to learn what secrets our new resident teacher harbored, I never would have imagined that it would choose you of all people. Hell, I didn't even know it could do that. Fifty years of sending it to spy on the people of this town and it never gave anyone visions. Imagine my surprise when the chief came to me with a story about you having some kind of strange connection with this creature."

"You had no idea the Beast was working against you. It was rebelling because it knew you were using it to keep people terrified," Grayson spat.

"I had no idea the creature was capable of such duplicity. Yes, I knew then that the Beast had found a way to work against me, even as I controlled it. But there was too much at stake to stop now. That's why I sent the doctor to frame you for murdering Tina Wilson."

"You sent the doctor to kill me."

"No...no, the doctor broke our cardinal rule by taking that girl when he wasn't supposed to," Arthur revealed. "It seemed tidy, though, to let him clean up his own mess by pinning it all on you. Unfortunately, I didn't count on Ms. Dawes being on the phone with you when the good doctor ran you off the road, or that she already had knowledge of the doctor's involvement in Tina's abduction."

Roxanne glanced back at Grayson and then at John Arthur. "I didn't know the doctor was involved until after they arrested him," she admitted.

A flicker of confusion betrayed Arthur's otherwise icy demeanor. The realization hit Grayson at once.

"Oh my God. That's why he didn't kill me that morning on the ridge," Grayson uttered. "The chief...he thought I told Roxanne that the doctor was in my vision. I lied to him because I wanted him to believe me."

"Yes, well, that little bluff saved your life. We had to bide our time until we could remove you once and for all. Ms. Dawes, however, made finding that moment exceedingly difficult," Arthur confessed.

"Because she knew everything I knew, but you couldn't send the Beast after her in public first to cover up her murder. She's protected because of the charm on her wrist," Grayson followed.

"Very good, Mr. Ender, you're more astute than I gave you credit for. An ancient ward for an ancient spirit," Arthur professed. "You became a threat to our way of life the day you confessed to having visions, Mr. Ender. Unfortunately, you have also been extraordinarily lucky. The chief was meant to kill you tonight to ensure that our final rite could be conducted without interference, but we see now how that worked out. I suppose it's as they say, if you want something done right…"

"Keep talking you sick son of bitch," Roxanne growled. "I want every reason to kill you myself right here."

John Arthur bellowed with laughter. "Truthfully, I take a rather perverse pleasure in telling you all this. You've both worked very hard to unravel the mystery. It seems only fair that you get to hear how miserably you've failed before you die."

"You use the Beast to learn everyone's secrets. Why?" Roxanne demanded.

"Secrets are currency, Ms. Dawes. The more you have, the more powerful you become."

"So you learn everyone's secrets to hold them over their head? To control them? You're the pastor. People in this town love you. They look up to you!" Grayson shouted.

Arthur began to pace as he talked. Grayson took his hand off the revolver to move without raising Arthur's suspicions.

"You mean people like Ross McCrory, that wilting homosexual that you've been courting? Come now, Mr. Ender. Surely you don't think that I believe all that religious swill I preach?" Arthur scoffed. "It's all about *control*. About keeping the population afraid and complicit."

"No, I don't think you believe it all. I saw what was in your basement. I've seen what you've done to the people you kidnapped. You and the chief, and Dale and the doctor," Grayson snarled with contempt.

"Went poking around where you shouldn't have and found my little playroom, did you?" Arthur sneered.

"We saw everything," Roxanne shouted. "All the tapes, all the sick, twisted stuff you've been doing, using Breakvale as your own perverted hunting ground for—"

"For half a century, Ms. Dawes. More than half a century. We've always had the Beast at our disposal, but no one ever thought of using it as a smokescreen to allow us to indulge our more...hedonistic pleasures."

"So all these deaths, all the suffering, it's all some kind of sadistic game to you?" Roxanne said scathingly.

"No, no you don't understand. Neither of you do. How could you? Those who we take, whose bodies we maim and destroy, are simply being primed for offering. The pleasures of the flesh we enjoy during this process are only a token reward, a novel and momentary delight, in the pursuit of something greater," Arthur spiritedly professed.

"And what is that?" Grayson scoffed.

"Immortality, Mr. Ender. Ever-lasting life on Earth, with the freedom to take and enjoy as we please."

"All you have to do is offer up human sacrifices to the devil," Grayson mocked.

"Something like that, yes," Arthur grinned, sending a disgusted shiver down Grayson's spine. He pointed at Grayson with one long, gnarled finger. "I've seen the thoughts buried deep in your mind, Mr. Ender. In another life, the Cult of Vale might have welcomed you. Regrettably, now I have to kill you both."

"Wait!" Grayson shouted. "Wait, hold on. I have one more question before I die."

Arthur hesitated for a moment but couldn't help indulging him. "Very well, Mr. Ender. One final question before I make you watch Ms. Dawes's execution."

"Why this boy? Why Samuel Daggett? His dad was a part of this...this Cult of Vale thing, right? Aren't family members supposed to be off-limits?"

"Where did you hear that?" Arthur asked calmly, though Grayson could see the question caused another momentary crack in his facade.

"I was with the chief when he went to Dale's house. Dale was hysterical and talked about wanting to quit before he shot the chief and then turned the gun on himself and his wife. Dale wanted to leave the Cult of Vale, didn't he?"

"A peculiar final question. But if it's the one you want," Arthur shrugged. He wandered slowly and deliberately toward Roxanne, who now stood on the opposite side of the dais from Grayson, waiting for her shot. "I couldn't permit Dale to leave. He knew too much. But his weakness was a liability. I knew that giving up his only son as an unwilling sacrifice would either galvanize his loyalty or break him. I was fine with either outcome."

"So you need an unwilling sacrifice to complete your ritual or whatever? You can take me. I'm unwilling. I don't want to die. Especially not by your hands," Grayson offered, taking a step forward toward the dais.

John Arthur wagged his finger. "That won't work, Mr. Ender. Just offering makes you too willing. And now you're out of questions."

John Arthur pulled back the hammer with his thumb and held the barrel of his gun to Roxanne's head. As soon as John Arthur turned his head to look down at Roxanne, Grayson lifted his gun hidden behind Samuel's leg. John Arthur caught the sudden movement from the corner of his eye, spun around, and aimed at Grayson. Seizing the momentary distraction, Roxanne tackled John Arthur to the ground as his gun went off. The bullet missed Grayson and shattered a stalactite above him, causing a piece of the rock to fall onto his head and knock him to the ground.

Roxanne's tackle jostled the effigy loose from John Arthur's hand. It hit the ground and rolled toward the dais as they struggled on the floor for control of his gun. Roxanne managed to grab him by the wrist and slammed his hand against the ground repeatedly until the gun came loose and bounced several feet away. John Arthur grabbed Roxanne by the hair and slugged her in the gut before kicking her off of him. Roxanne fell backward and tumbled a few feet away. John Arthur crawled over to his gun and picked it up, then staggered to his feet.

Roxanne rolled across the sanctum floor, scooped up her shotgun, and took aim as John Arthur turned around. He reacted quickly, pointing his pistol at her and squeezing the trigger. There was a loud, deafening bang that echoed through the sanctum as the firearms discharged simultaneously. Roxanne screamed out in pain. John Arthur took a step forward, then dropped his pistol. He fell to his knees, trying to speak through the blood gurgling up his throat and out of his mouth, spitting flecks of blood across the sanctum floor. John Arthur slumped sideways onto the ground.

The sound of the gunshots stirred Grayson. He rolled around and dizzily crawled across the sanctum floor, scrambling to get to Roxanne and screaming out her name.

"Fuck!" Roxanne screamed. "Goddammit that hurts! Motherfucker!"

Grayson pushed himself to his feet and shook off the dizziness. Roxanne was on her back, holding her left forearm.

"Oh my God. Roxanne. I thought he shot you," Grayson whispered, before breaking into inexplicable laughter. "Fuck, you're okay."

"I'm not okay! He did shoot me! He fucking shot me in the arm!" she yelled.

"But you're not dead! You're not dead," Grayson cried out, feeling an overwhelming mixture of fear and relief that left him unable to hold back his tears as he sobbed and laughed in equal measure.

Grayson walked over to Arthur's body, careful to avoid stepping in the blood that had pooled around him, and rolled him onto his back with his foot. His chest cavity was mangled from the shotgun blast. He stared into John Arthur's glassy, lifeless eyes for a moment, contemplating whether the Devil would welcome him with open arms.

Grayson felt a sudden and overwhelming rage at the sight of the old man's face, and he screamed in teary anguish as he stomped on the dead man's chest. He splattered his shoes and pants with blood, but he didn't care. The release felt exquisite.

"Grayson! Stop!" Roxanne shouted.

She got to her feet and managed to pull Grayson away from Arthur's body. Roxanne never let go, keeping a firm grip on his shoulder as she tried to soothe him. It took several deep breaths for Grayson to bring himself back down from the rage. At last, he turned to look at her.

"You good?" Roxanne whispered.

Grayson nodded slowly. "Yeah. Sorry. I'm good."

"Great. Remember when you promised that we'd leave if I said it's time to leave? I think it's time to leave," she urged.

"Yeah."

As he turned toward the dais, Grayson noticed the effigy on the floor. He ran over and picked it up. In all the chaos, he had forgotten that the Beast had been a silent, dispassionate observer of his slaver's showboating.

"Roxanne, I need your shotgun," Grayson yelled.

"What are you going to do?" Roxanne asked, handing him the gun.

"I'm going to set it free."

The Beast remained motionless as Grayson cautiously approached it. He set the effigy down on the ground away from it, took aim, and squeezed the trigger. The effigy shattered into a dozen pieces on impact.

The Beast roared to life. It swelled to a tremendous size as it shrieked louder than he'd ever heard it. Grayson watched its nebulous form twist backward on itself and contort, as if in either exuberant pleasure or extreme pain. Then it shot up through the cavern ceiling.

"I guess that's it?" Grayson said uncertainly.

As he took a step toward the dais to help Samuel, the Beast suddenly rose up out of the ground in front of Grayson, towering over him. Its red eyes flashed somewhere in the back of its depthless face. For the first time since their very initial encounter, the Beast of Breakvale spoke to him.

"*Wallace*," it hissed.

Grayson understood.

The Beast unleashed one long, final, ear-splitting shriek, then rocketed itself up through the cavern ceiling.

Grayson ran over to the dais and handed the shotgun back to Roxanne.

"I saw you nod at the Beast. Did it say something to you?" Roxanne asked.

"You didn't hear it? It said the mayor's name. That other man in the video I couldn't identify. I bet that was him."

"So we're not done yet," Roxanne sighed.

"Not until every one of them is hunted down. This ends tonight," Grayson vowed.

"First maybe we get the Daggett boy to safety, huh?" Roxanne pointed to the trembling kid on the dais.

Samuel Daggett had his eyes closed tight as they began to undo the buckles on his restraints. He must have felt the tension in his ankles release because his eyes shot open, and he began to sputter and cry.

"Thank you...thank you, thank you," he cried.

Roxanne held his face in her hand while Grayson freed him from the remaining restraints.

"Everything's going to be okay. You're safe," she smiled.

Samuel cried out and shook his head. "I can't hear you," he said. "I can't hear you."

“They punctured his eardrums, remember?” Grayson said. “I saw it happen on the video.”

Roxanne pursed her lips and kept smiling down at Samuel to let him know it would all be okay. Grayson undid the final restraint, and they helped Samuel sit up and get to his feet. Taking his arms around their shoulders, he and Roxanne helped the weakened, battered young man walk carefully up the stairs, down the long tunnel, and out of the nightmare.

18

Grayson could hear a police siren wailing in the distance as they reached the top of the stairs and pushed the well house door open. They continued to support Samuel on both their shoulders as they limped together across the field toward the parking lot. The red and blue flashing lights of Deputy Thorne's cruiser illuminated the trees as she sped into the church parking lot. Grayson flailed his left arm trying to get her attention. The car suddenly shifted direction and vaulted over the edge of the parking lot and into the grass as it raced toward them. Deputy Thorne came to a screeching halt about thirty feet in front of them and burst out of her car.

"Are you alright?" she hollered.

"He needs medical attention!" Grayson shouted back.

They reached the squad car and Deputy Thorne opened the back door so they could help Samuel into the back seat. He slumped over immediately but waved to indicate that he was alright. Ross jumped out of the passenger seat and ran around the nose of the car. He practically leaped at Grayson.

"Oh my God, you're okay. Thank God. Thank God," he cried. "I got the deputy but I didn't know what else to do so I just prayed to God that you'd be okay. That you'd both be okay. And you're okay. You're alive."

"Yeah, we're okay," Grayson smiled weakly at seeing Ross's face. "What the hell took you guys so long?"

"I got to Dale's house but the deputy wasn't there. It was just the coroner and Officer Stanley. He radioed for her and I just had to wait until she got there," Ross explained. "Every minute that went by I just kept having all these horrible images in my head about what was happening down in the tunnel. Then she got there and we came as quick as we could. I think we went over a hundred miles an hour. Yesterday that would've been the scariest thing to me. After all this, though..."

He released Grayson to hug Roxanne. She grimaced as he squeezed her injured arm. Ross let go and saw the blood on her arm, and the blood now smeared on his shirt.

"Roxanne, are you alright? What happened?" asked Ross.

"That fucker shot me," she grumbled. "Then I shot him."

"Is he...?"

"Oh yeah. Yeah, Ross. Arthur's dead," Grayson said softly, putting his hand on Ross's shoulder in consolation.

"Good. Well good," Ross nodded vigorously. "Lord forgive me. But he did some awful things. And he would have kept doin' them if you didn't stop him."

Deputy Thorne had popped her trunk and was digging around for something until she returned with a blanket and an emergency medical kit. She reached into the car and covered the boy up, then whipped around to the three of them standing there.

"Are either of you hurt?" Deputy Thorne asked, then took notice of Roxanne's arm. She opened the kit on the roof of the car and took out some swabs and bandages. "You're injured, Roxanne. Come here. I called for a bus, should be here any minute, but I can at least try to stop the bleeding."

Roxanne took a small flashlight that Deputy Thorne handed to her and held it on her left arm.

"Looks like the bullet just gashed your arm there. You got lucky, girl," Deputy Thorne told her. As she cleaned and dressed Roxanne's bullet wound, she looked between the three of them. "Now, one of you tell me what in the *hell* is going on."

"You want the long or short story?" Grayson quipped.

"I want the truth. I got a dead chief, a dead principal and his wife, and about a half dozen witnesses putting you at the scene of the crime. And then this guy shows up at the crime scene goin' on about John Arthur having a torture chamber in his basement and that he's got Daggett's boy and there's some kinda wacko cult that's gonna sacrifice the boy at midnight."

"Well, then you pretty much know the whole story, Lisa," Roxanne said defensively, sucking her breath in as the deputy pulled the bandage tight around her forearm.

"Where's John Arthur?" Deputy Thorne asked.

"He's dead, ma'am. Down there through that tunnel," Grayson informed, pointing toward the well house.

"Dead how?"

"I shot the fucker, Lisa," Roxanne said briskly. "He was gonna kill the boy and then he tried to kill me."

Just then the flashing lights of an approaching ambulance came into view and lit up the trees. Deputy Thorne waved the ambulance over and spoke to the paramedics as they unloaded a stretcher from the back. As they neared the squad car, Grayson tapped Samuel on the leg and pointed toward the ambulance. Samuel sat up and saw the men were coming. Grayson stepped in front of them to get their attention.

"His eardrums are ruptured. I don't think he can hear anything at all. Please be careful with him. He's been through hell," he told them.

The paramedics handled Samuel calmly and gently as they helped him ease down onto the gurney and loaded him into the back of the ambulance. Deputy Thorne had a few more private words with the driver, and then the ambulance flipped on its lights and blared the siren to rush Samuel off to County Medical.

Deputy Thorne walked back across the grass to her car and leaned against it with a heavy sigh.

"What a goddamn mess this night is. Alright, you two, is there anyone else dead down there? Or is it just him?"

"No, just Arthur," Grayson said, taking a step toward the deputy. "But we're not done yet. We need to get to the mayor. We're sure he's involved in this, too."

"And you know this how?"

Grayson took an uneasy breath. "Basically, John Arthur's been controlling the Beast, but we set it free. After we set the Beast free, it was able to talk to me kind of."

"You want me to go arrest the mayor because the Beast of Breakvale told you?" Deputy Thorne asked skeptically.

"Come on, Lisa. That's not the weirdest part about this whole thing and you know it. If it's proof you want, it's in Arthur's basement. But if Mayor Wallace finds out we know he's involved, he could disappear for good," Roxanne urged.

"Alright, but y'all better be right about this," Deputy Thorne warned. "If you're wrong, all our necks are on the line. I'll radio Stanley and have him meet me at the mayor's house to bring him in for questioning."

"With all due respect, Lisa, I've seen what these men are capable of doing. Right now, it's just you and one other officer. You need our help," Roxanne said.

Deputy Thorne's eyes narrowed as she shifted her glance between Grayson and Roxanne.

"Alright. But we do this by the book. We arrest him and bring him in for questioning. He can't confess if you shoot him dead like John Arthur. Understood?"

"Sure. We just want this to be over with. For good," Grayson said.

"Get in the car. I'll radio Stanley on the way."

Ross had been right about Deputy Thorne being unafraid of breaking a hundred miles per hour on the roads outside of town. There were no other cars on the road at this time of morning, even down Main Street. Deputy Thorne barely slowed down as they sailed through Breakvale toward the mayor's home. Grayson looked out the backseat window as the lights from the streetlamps whizzed by, trying to keep his breathing under control as he remembered the feeling of speeding along the outer road trying to outrun the car that forced him off the edge into the ravine.

Suddenly, Deputy Thorne slammed on the brakes, and Grayson lurched forward hard enough that the seat belt locked and took his breath away. The squad car's tires squealed and smoked as the brakes brought the car to a halt.

"Son of a fuck!" Roxanne screamed.

"What the hell is it doing?" Deputy Thorne shouted.

Grayson looked out the front window in time to see the Beast hurtling toward the car. In an impossibly quick moment, the Beast swooped up and over the top of the car as it came to a complete stop. From inside the vehicle they watched as the Beast wrapped itself around a power line and effortlessly ripped the wires down, plunging the entirety of Main Street into darkness. It shrieked incessantly as it soared from power line to power line, ripping each one down and extinguishing more of the lights around the city.

Deputy Thorne unbuckled and got out of the car.

"Stay put!" she barked.

She pulled her gun from her holster and trained it on the Beast as best she could, but the creature was too well-occluded by the starless sky. Deputy Thorne heard its cry from somewhere back down Main Street. She whipped around and pointed her gun down the street, waiting for the Beast to reappear. Grayson, Roxanne, and Ross each turned around in their seats to peer out the back window, looking down the long stretch of street for any movement.

The windows of the car began to vibrate, then rattle. It felt like the start of an earthquake. Even from inside the car, they could hear the Beast's screeching grow louder as it approached. Deputy Thorne fired several shots down the street into the darkness, but the shrieking grew louder still. Grayson watched shattered glass scatter like diamond dust as shop windows on either side of the street began exploding outward. The Beast had its long tendrils stretched out, spanning the width of the street, smashing through the windows as it careened toward the squad car. Deputy Thorne jumped back into the car and pressed the gas pedal to the floor. The tires squealed again as the engine revved and bucked them forward.

"Hang on!" she shouted.

At the very moment the Beast should have slammed into the rear of the car, it immediately righted itself and vaulted upward into the sky. The force of the sudden shift launched the car forward several feet, but they remained in motion.

"What the fuck was that!" Deputy Thorne shouted.

Grayson felt a pain in his wrist. He looked down to find Ross clenching his arm so hard his nails had begun to draw blood, though he was so focused on saying a prayer he didn't seem to notice the intensity of his grip. He put his hand over Ross's and gently tried to shake his grip loose.

"I've never seen it do anything like that," Roxanne said.

"No one's ever seen the Beast free before. We have no idea what it can do," Grayson replied.

Finally, Ross looked up and, realizing what he'd done, mouthed an apology to Grayson.

"I don't think I can take much more of this," Ross said breathlessly.

"If the Beast is capable of doing that, maybe keeping it controlled was the right idea," Deputy Thorne said.

"No. It's angry," Grayson realized. "I don't understand how, maybe because I'm still somehow linked with it, but I can feel it, like, seething. We have to get to the mayor, now."

They turned off the main drag onto a gravel road, going as fast as the tires could manage on the loose rocks until they arrived at the mayor's house, a two-story brick home with a long, paved driveway closed off by a security gate. When Deputy Thorne didn't slow down as they sped toward the gate, Grayson gripped Ross's hand.

"Hold on again!" Deputy Thorne shouted.

She adjusted the car for a straight impact, held the car steady, and smashed through the gate. It proved to be flimsier than any of them expected, and immediately gave way, sending pieces flying in every direction behind them. Deputy Thorne pulled up in front of the mayor's garage, blocking the door with the length of her car.

"If he didn't know we were coming, he will now," she said. "Grayson, you're coming in with me in case the Beast shows up. Roxanne, stay here in case he tries to slip out the back. Ross...say a prayer for us."

They sprang out of the vehicle. Grayson disengaged the safety on the revolver and followed Deputy Thorne as she kicked in the front door and checked that the coast was clear. Despite the blackout across town, the mayor's home seemed to still have power.

"Adam must have a backup generator," Deputy Thorne said. "Stay close to me."

Grayson followed Deputy Thorne through the living room, into the kitchen, and down a long hallway adorned with pictures of the mayor and his wife. There weren't any pictures of children. Knowing what he might have done to them, he hoped this man didn't have any children.

Deputy Thorne came to a sudden stop. "Do you hear that?" she whispered.

Grayson shook his head.

She pointed toward a door that was slightly ajar. "Fire," she mouthed, then indicated for Grayson to get ready.

Deputy Thorne pushed the door open. There was no one in the room. They swept in and looked around at what appeared to be the mayor's home office. Grayson went immediately to the fireplace. On the floor next to it was a box full of photos.

"Deputy Thorne, I think you need to see this," Grayson whispered.

She circled around the desk she'd been rifling through and looked down into the box in front of the fireplace. Grayson picked up a couple of pictures that showed Adam Wallace and John Arthur naked and engaged in the sexual assault of a young woman strapped down to a bed.

"Here's your proof," Grayson said bitterly. "He's trying to burn it."

"He's here somewhere," Deputy Thorne nodded. "He must've fled when he heard us kick the door in. Come on."

They left the office and followed the hall back into the living room. Just as Deputy Thorne signaled to move up the staircase, they heard a man scream from one of the rooms above. They charged up the staircase and through an open door at the end of the upstairs hallway.

The Beast hovered in the middle of the bedroom, towering menacingly over the mayor on the floor. Its tendrils bristled as it sensed Grayson and the deputy enter the room. Deputy Thorne fired off several rounds at it, causing the Beast to twist its body around and shriek at her as it whipped the pistol from her hand with one of its tendrils. Grayson dropped his gun immediately. The Beast stared at him with its piercing red eyes but snapped its attention back to Wallace as he scrambled backward on the floor toward the open balcony doors. Wallace managed to pull himself up by the balcony ledge as the Beast drifted toward him.

"Get away!" Wallace screamed. "I won't let you take me! I command you to go away!"

The Beast hissed as it lunged toward him. Grayson watched in agonized silence as Mayor Wallace threw himself off the balcony in a desperate attempt to escape. The Beast shrieked and sprang off the balcony after him. Grayson scrambled outside to the balcony in time to see the Beast catch Wallace falling in midair. It snagged him with several outstretched tendrils and carried him higher into the air. Like a man being drawn and quartered, the Beast used its tendrils to effortlessly rip Adam Wallace into a dozen pieces, scattering him in every direction like an exploding firework of sinew and blood.

The Beast wheeled around in the sky and locked its gleaming red eyes on Grayson standing there on the balcony. At that moment, Grayson felt a wave of serenity crash over him. The Beast of Breakvale cried out one final time, then darted toward the forest along the ridgeline and vanished into the night.

Grayson looked down at Roxanne and Ross below him, rooted there in shock and horror. Deputy Thorne came up behind him and pulled him away from the ledge. She led him back downstairs and out the door. Roxanne and Ross both rushed over to them, unable to say anything at all, but hugged them both.

"I called for the county police. They're on their way. And an ambulance," Roxanne informed them.

"Good. Yeah, good," Deputy Thorne said mindlessly.

They sat there on the front steps of the mayor's home in almost total silence until, at last, they heard the sirens and saw the lights of the ambulance and county police officers come up the road and pull into the driveway.

Deputy Thorne got up to meet with the arriving officers and explain the situation. Grayson didn't envy her having to explain how the town mayor ended up in a dozen pieces all over his front yard. The paramedics came over to the three of them and helped them over to the back of the ambulance to assess their trauma. Grayson sat in the back of the ambulance next to Ross as the paramedics worked on Roxanne's arm. For the first time all night, Grayson heard insects chirping and buzzing in the trees. Their rhythmic hum made him sleepy.

Ross leaned over and rested his head on Grayson's shoulder. "By the way," he whispered, taking Grayson by the hand. "I think I love you, too."

Grayson, Roxanne, and Ross waited together in the back of the ambulance, exhausted and propping each other up. Deputy Thorne finished her conversation with the other officers and crossed the lawn over to the ambulance. She stopped and spoke briefly with one of the paramedics, then rounded the back of the ambulance.

“They’re gonna take you on to the hospital. I’ll be up there to check in on all of you and give y’all a ride back after I finish up here,” Deputy Thorne said, gesturing toward the body parts scattered on the lawn.

“Thank you, Lisa,” Roxanne said. “For believing us.”

Deputy Thorne nodded and clicked her tongue. “Things are gonna be different now.”

The paramedics helped secure each of them for transport, then closed the doors and started up the ambulance. Grayson peered out the small window as they drove away, his mind drifting closer to sleep as the deputy and the mayor’s house disappeared behind a cluster of tall oak trees. For the first time in a long time, Grayson felt like he could rest.

As she watched the ambulance carry the trio away down the gravel road toward County Medical, Deputy Thorne pulled her phone from her pocket and placed a call. She stared vacantly into the darkness for several moments as the phone rang, until someone picked up the other end.

“Ed. Is it done?”

“Yes, ma’am. Burnin’ as we speak. Won’t be nothin’ of Arthur’s house left. Nothin’ to trace back, just like you instructed.”

“And his body?”

“Exactly where you said to put it.”

“Good. Gather our remaining brothers and sisters. We got a lot of work to do.”

The story continues...

Grayson, Ross, & Roxanne will return in

Breakvale: Cult of Vale

About the Author

Dustin Howard is a Poet Laureate Emeritus of Reno. He is the author of *Breakvale*, several collections of poetry, and an instructional book on poetry writing. He resides in Reno, Nevada, though his heart will always belong to the Ozarks. To learn more or purchase his books, please visit www.dthbooks.com.

www.ingramcontent.com/pod-product-compliance
Lightning Source LLC
Chambersburg PA
CBHW020336310726
48979CB00015B/2387/J

* 9 7 8 1 7 3 6 8 5 0 7 0 1 *